SAFETY VALVE

Books by David Chill

SAFETY VALVE

A Novel By

DAVID CHILL

Front cover art photography provided by John James Ahearn IV

Back cover art photography provided by Jennifer Nicolaisen

For Muriel

One

Cliff Roper was someone I hoped I would never see again. He had been arrested numerous times, he had an obnoxious personality, and he possessed a manner that could easily engender mistrust. But when Cliff Roper was suspected of trying to kill his business partner, the calculus changed. He arrived at my office with $10,000 in cash, along with a story that was compelling, even if he himself came to it without a moral or ethical compass.

"You gotta help me," he said.

"I don't gotta do anything," I countered, wondering why my command of the English language had suddenly disappeared.

"I'll pay you a month's wages."

"I charge a thousand dollars a day," I informed him, suddenly raising my daily rate to factor in any combat pay that might come along with this case. It also served to give him pause.

"You're kidding me."

"I don't kid about money."

"Crap," he said, as the wheels inside of his head seemed to turn furiously for a few moments. "Make it two weeks."

"I never accept a job just because of the money," I told him. "And I haven't even decided to accept you as a client yet."

"Oh, you're going to decide? Like hell you will. I'm the decider here, Burnside. The client gets to choose. I know that from personal experience."

He certainly had a lot of experience from which to draw. A small, wiry man with a deep tan and close-cropped silver hair, Cliff Roper was a very successful sports agent. He represented athletes in nearly every sport you could think of, and possibly a few you couldn't. He was well-dressed, sporting a gray blazer and slacks, and wore a white oxford cloth shirt with the first three buttons open.

Despite the debonair look, Cliff Roper was someone well acquainted with the inside of a jail cell. He had been detained numerous times for everything from embezzlement to manslaughter, although none of the charges ever turned into a conviction. He was tough, savvy, intense, and rich. And my one interaction with him last year was not pleasant. The thought of doing business with him made me more than a little apprehensive.

"If I recall, you threatened to have me killed last year," I said, leaning back in my chair and eyeing him across my desk.

"And if I recall," he countered evenly, "you threatened me with blackmail. Sounds like we're even."

"Even?"

"More or less. Look, why don't we just try and put all that history behind us. I need someone like you."

I took a deep breath and looked around at my sparsely furnished office. Business had been very slow lately. With an upcoming wedding to pay for, not to mention my monthly bills, I was getting more than a little concerned. When I launched my private investigations business over five years ago, I hoped I would never have to take a case strictly for financial reasons. There had to be something more.

"Why don't you start by telling me what brings you here," I said.

"Someone's trying to frame me," he declared.

"For what?"

"For what? For attempted murder is for what."

"Who'd you try to kill? Allegedly, of course," I asked.

"I didn't try to kill anyone. That's the point. Geez. Do I have to spell it out for you?"

"Yes. And start from the beginning. It'll make things easier. At least for me."

Cliff Roper took a deep, long sigh and glanced out my window for a moment. I doubt he saw anything more than a smoggy morning in April. The winter rains that moved through Southern California had ended a month ago. Without them, the air had begun to grow stale and gray again. Diffuse sunlight was starting to emerge from the thicket in the sky.

"I have this partner," Roper said. "Or former partner as of recently. Name's Gilbert Horne. We've been running a sports agency for a few years now. But I'm the only one bringing in new clients and he's the only one losing existing ones. It's not a good balance."

"So you split up."

"Yeah, yeah, we split up. Or more to the point, I told him to take a hike, because he wasn't holding up his end of the business. He didn't like that too much. He made some threats."

"What were the threats?"

"Ah, the usual. He'd sue me, bankrupt me, ruin me. Chop me into little pieces."

"I see. The usual."

"Right," he said. "I told him to get lost. I've been threatened by guys a lot tougher than him."

"Then what?'

"Then last week my office gets burglarized. Someone cracked the safe. I don't keep a lot there, but they took some cash, a few contracts. And they also took my Glock."

"Your gun?" I peered at him, assuming he was referring to a Glock semi-automatic pistol.

"Yeah, yeah, my gun. It was a Glock 34 if you want to get technical."

"You kept it in a safe."

"Look, I'm not Wyatt Earp. I don't walk around carrying a heater."

"And you think your partner took it."

"He's the only one who could have gotten the combination. Anyway, what happened next is where it gets weird."

"So *now* it's getting weird?" I asked, my eyebrows shooting up involuntarily. I was glad I didn't have anything else to do this morning. Cliff Roper had, if nothing else, high entertainment value.

"Yeah," he continued. "Someone took a couple of shots at Horne the other night. Outside his home. Didn't hit him but the bullets lodged into the outside wall of his house."

"And he thinks it was you."

"Who cares what he thinks. The important thing is the police think so. They got it in their heads that I'm trying to kill my ex-partner."

"Where does Horne live?"

"Lookout Mountain. Off of Laurel Canyon. Not far from where I live."

"Hollywood Hills," I said.

"Yeah. Close to my office. And I don't need to tell you this, but it's a rotten time for me to have a problem with the law. The NFL draft is next week. I have a lot on the line. Got a couple of college guys that could get picked early, but they're wavering now. Other agents are circling, trying to pull these guys away from me. There's big money on the table."

"Your partner sign any college players?"

Roper scoffed. "Just one. A running back out of some mid-major school, some Buttcrack State. Gil said he was clocked at a 4.25 in the 40."

"That's pretty darned fast. Starting to approach Olympic levels."

"It's bull. He was clocked on his pro day at his cow college. And that college has a track that slopes downward. Everyone in the business knows that players' times there are artificially fast. That is everyone who pays attention. My idiot ex-partner didn't know this. He even loaned the kid five large to get him to sign with our agency."

I shook my head. A loan of $5,000 is tantamount to a bribe. In the agent world though, that's sometimes the price of doing business.

Roper sensed my disapproval. "You want guys to sign with you? It's a difference maker."

I rubbed the bridge of my nose and tried to get his attention focused once more on the shooting. A few things didn't add up here. "So let's go back to the other day. The bullets they found were from a Glock."

"You're a genius. I just told you that, remember?"

"You file a police report on the burglary?" I asked.

"I don't do that sort of thing."

"Of course you don't," I said. "Because that would be a matter of public record. And it would alert your existing clients and maybe make them a little nervous about who's representing them."

Roper nodded slowly as he looked at me. "I knew you weren't stupid."

"And I know that too," I responded sharply. "The larger question is are *you* stupid?"

"Me?" he asked, the shocked look on his face appeared genuine. I didn't imagine Cliff Roper had ever doubted himself in his life. "How'd you wind up there?"

"Someone stole your pistol. They had plans for it. You don't report the theft. The gun gets used in a crime. The gun's fired at someone so it's attempted murder. They tie it back to you. In the eyes of the police, you're now a person of interest."

Roper slumped back in his chair. It was hardly a soft chair, but Roper wasn't a soft man. He took a deep breath and his mouth contorted into an ugly expression. He did not strike me as a man who liked to be toyed with, and I could only imagine the revenge he was conjuring up in his head.

"Okay," he said, finally. "You got me."

"Let me ask you this. Who filed the police report regarding the shooting?"

"Horne's wife. Said her husband was in hiding now. He knows someone wants him dead."

"Did she identify you?"

"I don't know what that crazy broad said. She's a gold digger. Anything that comes out of her mouth is designed to put money in her pocket or diamonds on her hands."

"And the police questioned you when?"

"Last night."

"You have an alibi for where you were?"

"Don't worry," he said, dismissing the concern with a wave of his hand. "I arranged for one."

"Wonderful," I said. Clients like Cliff Roper were a double-edged sword. They paid a lot of money, but were high maintenance and they were flexible with the truth. It was nothing more than a tactic to get them past obstacles. They were untrustworthy and secretive and they withheld certain facts and details which they didn't feel like sharing. But I was starting to find this case intriguing, even if the client himself would be a burden.

"Well then," I continued, "who do *you* think fired the shots at Horne?"

Roper emitted a laugh that had a sneer hanging from the end of it. "I can give you a laundry list."

"Fine. Anywhere you'd like to begin."

"Hey, for starters, there are a couple of clients who were pissed as hell at him. He messed up Oscar Romeo's endorsement deal with a shoe company. Horne didn't follow through on the details, didn't present the client in the proper light. Cost Oscar a cool $3 million, so he dumped our agency."

"Okay."

"Then there's Oscar's pal, Patrick Washington. The two have been friends forever. The Raiders sent Patrick a five-year renewal contract, fully guaranteed. It just had to be signed and faxed back by midnight at the end of March. Patrick signed it, but Horne, the dimwit, he couldn't figure out how to operate the fax machine, and his assistant wasn't working that night. The schmuck never thought of going to Staples? So Patrick has to go the free agent route so he drops us too. And his new agent still doesn't have a deal for him yet. Horne was asleep at the wheel. You can't operate like that in this business."

I had heard about both players. Romeo and Washington grew up here in Los Angeles, although both had played college football elsewhere. Southern California was rich with talented prospects. Along with Texas and Florida, it was prime recruiting ground for every college football coach in America. The high school stars were offered scholarships to colleges all over the country. They sometimes made it to the pro ranks, but many still returned to L.A. in the off-season. This was their home.

"Who else?"

"That's not enough for you to start with?"

"It is. I just like to be thorough."

Roper processed this for a minute. "There's Brendan Webster."

"The name sounds familiar."

"It should. He was a five-star recruit out of the O.C.. Played defensive tackle at Texas A&M for three years. Was all set to go pro after his junior year. Then he got his knee torn up in a bowl game. Never recovered. Works as a leg breaker now. How's that for karma?"

"Who does he work for?"

Roper hesitated. "Couple of former associates. Let's leave it at that."

"I take it Brendan didn't stay at A&M to get his degree."

"You kidding? He was a moron. Guy couldn't spell dog if you spotted him the 'd' and the 'o' for crissakes. We fed him the answers to the Wonderlic test and he still got most of the questions wrong."

The Wonderlic test measured cognitive abilities, and was designed to evaluate prospective employees before a firm hired them. It was also the standard exam given to college football players hoping to move on to the NFL, and served as a *de facto* I.Q. test for them. Interestingly, offensive lineman often scored highest on these exams. Brendan apparently wasn't one of these.

"Tough break for the kid," I said, "especially if football was all he could do. You know, that's how my football career as a safety ended. Knee injury. I was a four year starter at USC. Only difference was I ended up in law enforcement. Sounds like Brendan ended up on the other side of the fence."

Roper shrugged. "You're all part of the same sewer system. You just operate on different sides."

"Thanks. You have a nice way of putting things. Anyone else a possibility?"

"Look, Horne just got kicked out of his agency, he lost most of his clients and his other investments are tanking. The list can be as long as you want it to be. There's no shortage of people who might have wanted to take a pop at him."

"Investments?" I asked. "What investments are tanking?"

"Yeah, I forgot about that. He's part owner of a car dealership in Santa Monica. Luxury imports. Did well at first, but the recession took a lot of money off the table. Can't imagine things are going so great there."

"Guy sounds like he's got a lot of problems. Maybe contributed to his under-performing as an agent?"

"Yeah, sure, whatever. But I don't care about excuses. I got a business to run. I can't carry dead weight."

"Of course not," I said. "What about women?"

"What about them?"

"You said he was married. He have a girlfriend on the side?"

"Sure. Who doesn't?"

I rubbed the bridge of my nose once more. "Go on."

"So he had a few girlfriends on the side. I don't know them personally. But I also don't know why they would take a shot at him. His wife, maybe. But not them."

"Sometimes the girlfriend believes the guy will leave his wife."

"No," he said, feigning disbelief. "You think?"

I did my best to ignore his grating personality. It wasn't easy and I suspected part of that was because my own personality often grated on others. Getting a taste of your own medicine is often unpleasant. But this was just one of the factors causing internal conflict. Part of me wanted to throw him out of my office. Part of me needed the money. Part of me was very intrigued with this case. And a part of me was wondering if Cliff Roper really was uninvolved in this shooting.

"So you haven't brought up Horne's wife as a possibility," I pointed out. "When a violent act occurs, the spouse is normally the first suspect."

"April? I dunno. If she knew his financial situation was dire, then no. Why kill a drowning man? I don't know what motive she'd have. Besides, she was right next to him when the shot was fired."

"Okay," I said, trying to process all of this. "I think I have enough info to get started."

"Then we're done here."

I continued to think about the type of individual with whom I was about to become involved. The ethical side of me said to walk away from this case. The practical side of me said to take the money. The investigator in me was now actively curious, and that was what ultimately drew me in.

"Not quite," I said.

"Meaning?"

"I'll need a retainer before I start. I think two weeks should work."

His eyes narrowed. "Paying ten large up front is a lot of money."

"It is. But I'm good and I think you know that I'm good. I'll do everything I can to find out who did this," I said, hoping that the culprit wasn't Roper himself. "You'll get your money's worth. That's the one thing I can promise you."

"This your only case?"

"I may have one other," I said, thinking about a phone call that I needed to follow up on with the Differential Insurance Company. "But yours is the one that's most pressing, and yours will come first. I'll work on the other when time permits."

Roper looked out the window for a long moment before turning back to me and posing an odd question. "You were asking about his wife and girlfriends. How about you. Are you married?"

"Engaged," I said. "Wedding's in a month. Why?"

"You know a lot about me. I just want to know a little something about you. What's your fiancée's name?"

"Gail," I answered, holding back on providing her last name.

"Your first time at the plate?" he asked.

"That's right."

"I've struck out four times. Would've been five, but the first one got annulled. She was underage."

"I'm planning on mine lasting forever."

"Yeah," he said, opening up a briefcase filled with rolls of hundred dollar bills and dumping them on my desk. "That's what they all think."

"Yes, yes, it's a double edged sword," he smiled. "That's where you come in. Have a seat. Let me tell you about this case."

"I'm all ears," I said, pulling up a comfortable chair facing his desk. Unlike the spartan decor in my office, Harold's surroundings featured hardwood flooring, mini-blinds drawn halfway, and a beautiful oak desk. There was enough paperwork on his desktop to communicate he was a busy executive.

"Okay," he started. "Listen to this. A woman takes out a renter's policy a couple of months ago. Name's Noreen Giles. Moves into a bungalow, not too far from here, actually. One of those adobe-style places they used to build back in the 1920s."

"Those types of houses are nice if they're kept up."

"And it seems this one was. Just off of Cahuenga, near Melrose. So she has this renter's policy for a couple months. Then she goes and files a claim last week, saying she lost over $100,000 worth of valuables in a burglary. There's the usual electronics equipment, some artwork, and too much cash lying around. But most of the claim involves jewelry."

"Isn't there a limit on how much carriers will pay for jewelry losses?"

"Yes, and it's normally about a thousand dollars. Except when the insured takes out a floater for individual pieces that are very expensive."

"And Ms. Giles took out a floater."

"She took out quite a number of floaters. They were all appraised when the policy was written. Seemed legit at the time. I mean this is L.A., there are some people out there with a lot of dough."

"Sure. Any other red flags? Other than the claim is large and was filed right after the policy was issued?"

"Yeah," Harold said, wiping his face with a large hand. "She had receipts for everything. Mostly from Harry Kingston Jewelers."

I whistled softly. "Champagne tastes. And you don't think she's just well organized."

"That's a maybe yes and a maybe no. My gut says no."

"What does she do for a living?" I asked.

"Realtor. Same as her husband. Can't imagine they're prospering in this economy. They advertise themselves as Giles & Giles, a real estate partnership."

"Sounds romantic."

"Yeah. Hopefully when you and Gail get married you can separate business and pleasure, what with the two of you both having careers in law enforcement."

"That should be the least of our problems," I said. Gail Pepper and I had been together for almost four years. For much of it we were separated by distance while she was earning her law degree up at Berkeley. She finished last June and started working for the L.A. City Attorney's office at the beginning of this year.

"Hey, how's Gail holding up with everything? The women are the ones who do all the work when it comes to planning out weddings. Our job is to basically show up and say I do."

"She's fine. But I'm handling a few things," I said, suddenly struggling to remember what they were.

"Uh-huh. When I got married, all I really had to do was make certain I had the address for the church. That and write some checks. The big date's coming up for you, huh?"

"One month," I swallowed. "It's getting closer."

"I'm hearing something less than exuberance."

"Oh, it's nothing. Gail's great, I've got the perfect partner for me. It's just a big step. An adjustment."

"At your age, absolutely. but you'll adjust. This is going to be good for you," Harold said. "Once a guy gets past 40, it's tough to hook up with someone. You get set in your ways. And that's why you need a woman in your life. Creates a good balance."

"True," I said.

"How's Gail liking her new job?"

"Loves it so far. She's prosecuting a ring of people caught stealing letters out of mailboxes. They were mostly after the bill payments so they could wash the checks."

"Nice world we live in," he said dryly. "But we know that from our jobs."

"There are still a lot of good people around," I pointed out. "We just see too much of the underbelly."

"Well, I'm glad you finally found someone nice," he smiled.

"I was waiting for the right girl."

"And you got her. Don't mess it up."

I smiled. "I will do my utmost best."

"Hopefully, I'll see you before the wedding."

"Hopefully I'll get paid quickly by the Differential. Weddings today are expensive."

Harold smiled as I got up to leave. "I'm sure you'll finish up on Mr. and Mrs. Giles before then. But I know what you mean. Everything's expensive these days. Wait'll you have kids."

I smiled too, although a bit more apprehensively. "One step at a time, my friend. One step at a time."

*

The Hollywood Division of the LAPD was located about ten minutes away from Harold Stevens' office, a few blocks west of Vine and a block south of Sunset. The Division was in a nondescript red-brick building that was off the beaten path, enough so that tourists would never notice it, but still set in the heart of Hollywood. While this area had been seedy for many years, a redevelopment project was slowly starting to make progress. Some new office buildings had been constructed, and some nicer shops and restaurants were springing up. But a complete turnaround of the Hollywood district would take a while.

I stowed my .38 special in the middle compartment of my Pathfinder, not wanting to have it confiscated after walking through the metal detector. Walking purposefully down the hallway, I quickly found the office I was looking for. Rick Taggart was a former colleague, a detective I had known for years. But when I looked around, his chair was empty and his desktop was uncharacteristically tidy. Nearby sat a short, stocky, barrel-chested plainclothes officer. He had short dark hair and muscles that were bulging out of his short-sleeve shirt.

"Hi," I said, approaching him. "Would you happen to know if Detective Taggart is around?"

"He's on vacation. Gone to Maui, lucky stiff. Can I help you?"

"The name's Burnside," I said, handing him my card. "I was hoping to speak with him about a case I'm on."

"He'll be back next week. I'm Sean Mulligan. I got a few minutes," he said, and motioned for me to take a seat. "Your name sounds familiar."

"I get that a lot."

He peered at me. "You play football?"

"I did. Played at USC."

Mulligan smiled. "I remember now. I wish I could have played there. But USC didn't recruit me because I'm only 5-foot-9. Too short for a linebacker. At least in their book."

"Did you play somewhere else?"

"Fresno State. The highlight of my career was the night we beat SC in the Freedom Bowl. Walking off the field that night, it felt like I got vindicated."

"I remember. I was watching that game from the stands," I said, cringing at the bad memory. The game was held on a cold, rainy night down in Anaheim, and the Trojans didn't play well. It later came out that one of the ball boys hated USC and was keeping the football dry when Fresno State was on offense. When USC had the ball, he made sure it had been soaking in water and was difficult to throw properly.

"Bad night to be at that game," he sympathized. "You probably got drenched."

"It's never fun to play in a downpour, either. But I know that when you're winning, you don't notice it as much."

"Oh yeah," he smiled. "That's a fact."

I looked across at Sean. "Been with the department a while?"

"A good while," he laughed. "Spent four years in the army. Started here after my tour ended."

"Were you over in the sandbox?"

He nodded. "Yeah. Afghanistan mostly. Glad to be back. This job is easy by comparison. The land mines in this city are easier to spot."

"I can imagine. I spent 13 years on the job here. Worked out of the Broadway Division."

"Uniform?"

"Mostly. Spent the last few in plainclothes," I said.

"Why'd you leave?"

"Long story," I sighed.

"I've heard 'em all," he shrugged. "What's going on today?"

"Does the name Gilbert Horne ring a bell?"

Mulligan shook his head yes. "Sure," he said. "The other night over on Lookout Mountain. I assisted on that one." He turned to a computer and typed a few things. "Yeah, here it is. I remember. It was the wife, April Horne, who filed the complaint. Shots fired at a residence; we came away with two bullets lodged in the exterior of the house."

"Anything else?"

"What's your angle?"

"I have a client who's been tagged as a person of interest."

"Oh, yeah. The business partner. What's his name again?"

"Cliff Roper."

"Roper, right. The wife said the gunman was after her husband. But the husband wasn't around when we spoke to her. She said he feared for his life, so he went into hiding. Disappeared."

"She say where the husband was?"

"Nope," he said. "Guess they don't trust the police."

"How many shots were fired?"

"Complainant reported a series of shots, but we only found two bullets. Forensics went over them after they pulled them from the outside wall. They were 9mm; could have come from a Glock. The wife said her husband was having a dispute with his business partner. The business partner owns a Glock. Not hard to connect the dots."

"Were you the one who followed up with Roper?"

"No, the investigating officer is Jim Johnson. But I doubt he got anything, or else I would have heard. There are a lot of Glocks out there, we can't just pin this on the partner. Not with what we have so far. The odd thing was that Roper said his gun had just been stolen. Very convenient timing."

"I know. He said he didn't bother to file a report."

Mulligan shrugged again. "Business relationships go sour sometimes. I've seen more than a few of these. It's a variation on a domestic dispute."

"Is this Jim Johnson around?" I asked.

"No, he comes in later. I can let him know you were here." Mulligan pulled out a piece of paper and wrote down a phone number. "You can reach him on his cell if you want."

"Thanks," I said. "You've been very helpful. P.I.s don't always get a lot of cooperation from the department."

Mulligan smiled. "I played at Fresno State, but I've always been an SC fan at heart. Grew up in the O.C. The Trojans are big down in Orange County. I have to warn you about Johnson, though."

"Don't tell me."

"Yeah," he smiled. "Johnson hates USC. He's a UCLA guy. Bleeds blue and gold."

Three

I did a bit of research on my iPad and learned that Patrick Washington, one of Horne's former clients, lived a few blocks north of Sunset in Beverly Hills. For me, that was good news; it was on my way home.

Beverly Hills is one of the most famous communities in the world. Sitting between Bel-Air and Hollywood, it is an independent city. Its boundaries extend from what's considered a relatively low-rent district south of Olympic Boulevard, up through the foothills leading to Mulholland Drive, the highest point in Los Angeles. Of course, the so-called low rents were at a level the average Joe could never begin to afford.

Patrick Washington's home was on Roxbury Drive, in a beautiful section of this beautiful city, albeit not the pinnacle. The house was a large, stately, two-story structure, painted white with black trim, and surrounded by palm trees. The circular driveway had a number of expensive cars parked unevenly, and they included a Porsche, a Jaguar and a Lamborghini. I pulled my black Pathfinder next to them, suddenly wishing I had taken the time to have washed it this week.

I rang the doorbell, and after about 60 seconds the door opened and I found myself facing a very large human being. Patrick Washington was black, stood 6-foot-8 and had to weigh at least 325 pounds. Not that he was soft, mind you. He was very big and very solid.

"Help you?" he asked.

"Hi Patrick. Name's Burnside," I said, and flashed my gold P.I. badge, which really wasn't a badge so much as it was a fancy-looking plastic shield. I had designed it to impress people and throw them off guard. At first, it looked like I was with the police, which is enough to give even the toughest guy a moment of pause. By the time they learned I was no longer with the LAPD, I had commanded their attention, and they were less likely to slam the door in my face. Even if they did, I was often able to pry some information out of them first.

"What's up?" he asked cautiously.

"I'd like to talk to you for a minute. It's about the shooting that happened at Gilbert Horne's house."

"Oh yeah" he said. "I heard about that."

"May I come in?"

He opened the door and led me into a living room that had a long, gray leather couch and a number of recliners spaced around the room. An 80-inch 4K TV was mounted on the wall, and three or four game controllers were sitting on the couch. Some voices could be heard from another room. Patrick moved the controllers to a glass coffee table and motioned for me to sit down.

"So how can I help you?" he asked.

"I understand you were a client of Gilbert Horne's."

"Used to be. I fired his sorry ass a few weeks ago. That punk messed up my deal with the Raiders. He faxed my contract an hour late. Tried to blame it on everyone but him. Cost me millions. Because of him, I probably won't be able to play on the West Coast this year. We're looking at Green Bay or Cincinnati. I'm an L.A. guy, grew up in Gardena. But I'm gonna be freezing my nuts off because my stupid agent couldn't do his job right."

"You sound really ticked off."

"Uh-huh. This guy made a ton of money off me, and he couldn't do the most basic thing like fax a contract on time. And now, the best deal I can land gets me $1 million a year less, and no guaranteed money."

"That's a rotten deal."

"Tell me about it."

"You know any other players, clients who had a problem with him?"

"Yeah, there's a lot of them. He represented some basketball players too. Not A-listers, but guys that can play pro ball. He didn't negotiate their contracts right either. No guaranteed money and a couple are looking to play in Europe next season. Got them on the wrong NBA team, was a bad fit. They didn't play up to their potential."

"You can add me to that list," boomed a deep voice, and another large human being, although not as large as Patrick, strolled into the living room. "My deal with the Chargers earned me a lot less than guys who couldn't carry my jockstrap. Plus Horne screwed up my shoe deal."

Into the room walked a muscular, good-looking young man, solid and thick, and not an ounce of fat on him. He had the golden skin tone of someone who might have been from one of the Pacific Islands, but his face was unusual and it was hard to pinpoint his ethnicity.

"I'm Burnside," I said, holding out a hand, which he shook with the grip of someone used to lifting 300-pound weights every day.

"Oscar Romeo," he said.

"Sounds like you were both pretty ticked off at your agent."

"We were," Oscar responded. "But what's your interest here?"

"I'm just doing some background work on the shooting. Strictly routine."

"Okay," Oscar said. "So things were good in the beginning. Horne did some things right by us. Got us some good money."

"He also did some quirky things," said Patrick.

"That's right," Oscar laughed. "He once told us if anyone ever needed to pee in a cup, he could always get piss that was trustworthy."

Patrick laughed as well, but more caustically. "Yeah, players who were using figured they could count on him when they suspected a drug test was coming. These guys didn't know the league had changed the rules on drug tests. Made you take a leak right in front of them. Gil said he could always get things done. Usually the things that fell somewhere in the gray area."

I took this in, but felt the need to change the subject. "You guys play together growing up?"

"Yeah, started in Pop Warner. Then high school. Down in Gardena. Same class."

"Must have been a terrific team."

"CIF champs our senior year," Oscar said proudly.

"I'm sure that felt great," I said.

"You play football?"

"I did. Played at Culver City High. We made it to the CIF title game my senior year. I also played at USC. About a million years ago."

They glanced at each other and smiled. "Not our favorite opponent. We went to Oregon," Oscar said. "Had too many tough losses against SC. What position did you play?"

"Free safety."

"A safety?" he teased. "Oooh. You must have been pretty smart."

"Still am."

"Ha! Yeah, for me the physical part of the game comes easy. I play Mike linebacker. Learning to bark out the right defensive signals took awhile."

"It's tricky," I acknowledged. "The simpler the offense, the more complex the defense has to be."

Oscar agreed enthusiastically. "You got that right. Otherwise the quarterback can just pick you apart. Learned that from experience. Sounds like you know the game."

"Some things never leave you," I said, and decided to move the conversation along. "So tell me something," I asked. "How did guys like you ever get hooked up with this agent, Horne?"

"It was through Ted Wade," Oscar said. "Played with us at Oregon, came in the same year as us. Good guy. He said he had an uncle who was an attorney, represented a few MMA guys, Mixed Martial Arts. Now he was looking to represent football players. We met him, seemed sharp, seemed hungry. We went with our gut."

"It's tough out there," Patrick pointed out. "We had agents approaching us all the time. Trying to figure out who was real just wasn't easy. Figured we'd go with someone who had a connection with us."

"Ted Wade," I recalled. "He didn't play very long in the league, did he?"

"Nope," Patrick said. "For a QB to make it in pro football it takes more than just a live arm and a big body. He's gotta be mentally tough, be a leader. Ted was a smart guy, but he wasn't a hard worker. Coaches liked to say he looked like Tarzan, played like Jane. He partied a little too much."

"Senior year in college, we voted him team captain," Oscar said. "On the outside, everyone thought it was because he was a good leader. But within the team, we just wanted him to grow up. We figured making him captain might give him some responsibility."

"Did it work?" I asked.

"It helped," he acknowledged. "Our senior year was a good year, we won the conference and played in the Rose Bowl. And Ted, he was a first round draft pick, went to the Bills. Got some really good money at first, hung on for a couple of years. But the NFL is no nonsense. It's a grown man's business. You either make it your focus in life or you're out."

"Where does Ted live?"

"Down in P.V." he said. P.V. meant Palos Verdes, a beautiful, hilly peninsula in the South Bay that overlooked the ocean. Next to Beverly Hills, it was probably the most expensive area in L.A.

"Lot of local guys play up at Oregon now?" I asked.

"Yeah," Patrick said. "They recruit heavy down here. A lot more talent in So Cal than in Oregon. For me, I wanted to get out of the hood, get some separation. Playing up in Eugene was far enough away so we didn't have to be around certain guys. But close enough so we could get home easy enough. It's a lot closer than Alabama or Florida. Those were the main offers I was considering."

"Makes sense. Anything else you can tell me about Horne? Something that might help figure out why someone might want to shoot him? I know you guys were angry about what he did, but I can't imagine your taking that step."

Oscar looked at me. "I heard he had money problems. But Gil always had money problems. First contract I signed with him, we got my bonus check and he took me right down to the bank and opened accounts for both of us. I guess he needed the money."

I didn't bother to tell him that that's how this normally worked, the teams don't write separate checks to the agents. It's up to the agent to get his commission straight from the player. "What about his partner, Cliff Roper? You know him well?'

"Not really," Patrick said. "I've met him a few times. When we were over at their offices, Roper would sometimes barge in and interrupt our meetings. It seemed to get on Gil's nerves. But Gil was our agent so when I'd go up to the office I mostly met with him."

I remembered something. "Either of you know a guy named Brendan Webster?"

They looked at each other. "Sure," Oscar said. "Why?"

"Just wondering. His name came up."

There was an empty silence for a long minute. Finally Oscar spoke. "We played with him at a high school all-star game. Must of been a few years ago. He was at Texas A&M, but he kinda went downhill. Injuries and stuff."

"Still see him?"

"Yeah," Patrick said. "He hangs around. People use Brendan for security now. You would think big guys like us don't need it, and we pretty much don't. But when we're out in public, at a club or something, it helps to keep strangers at a distance. We're out to have a good time, not sign autographs and pose for pictures. It's easier to have security say no."

"Okay. Any other thoughts?"

Oscar thought for a moment. "You talk to Horne's wife?"

"Not yet," I asked. "Why?"

"Her head's a little messed up. Not to say she had anything to do with this. But they had problems. You know. Marriage and all that. She's a lot younger than him."

"Okay," I said. "Any idea where Horne might be now? I understand his wife said he was in hiding."

They both looked at each other and smiled. "He liked to hang out at this hotel in the Marina. The Seaside."

I made a mental note. "Anything else?"

"He owns a car dealership by the beach," Oscar said.

"That's where we both got our rides. Mine's the blue Lamborghini. If the dealership closes, I may be doing the upkeep myself."

"Know anything about cars?" I asked.

"Actually, yeah. Dad owned a repair shop in Torrance for years. I used to work there part-time during the summers. Once I got drafted into the NFL, I helped Dad retire."

"Nice," I commented. "But Horne must have been doing great at one point to be able to buy a dealership that sold cars like that."

Patrick laughed. "Yeah, but that's not how he got it."

"How'd he get it?"

"He won it."

"Won it?"

"Oh yeah," Oscar laughed. "In a poker game. Pretty high stakes, huh? But that was Horne, that was what we loved about him at first. Guy lives on the edge. I'll give him that. But he's dealing with a lot of adversity right now. They say adversity builds character, but in Gil's case, I'm not so sure."

"I'm not so sure of that either," I said. "For most people, going through adversity tends to reveal character rather than build it."

Four

Bay City Motor Cars was located on Lincoln Boulevard, about a half-mile from Pacific Coast Highway. The dealership was close to my apartment, making it a convenient last stop of the day. I parked my dusty Pathfinder a block away and walked over. A homeless man lay asleep in front of a shuttered florist, his leg strategically wrapped around a shopping cart overloaded with personal belongings. Most of them were stuffed in trash bags.

I walked through the lot purposefully, avoiding eye contact with a group of salespeople who stood milling around. Entering the palatial showroom, the air suddenly became more rarefied, and a cool quiet atmosphere draped the room. The floors featured a polished white marble and the high beamed ceiling stretched a good 40 feet in the air. I picked up a brochure which had photos of the latest featured models, along with a variety of metrics delineating how each vehicle was better than the one before. In the last section were photos and biographies of the employees. A brief note from the owners was on the back pages, thanking customers for their patronage. One of the owners was Duncan Whitestone. The other was Gilbert Horne.

"So which one would you like?" asked a handsome, middle-aged man wearing a gold v-neck sweater and a broad smile on his face.

I smiled back. "Can't decide. They're all spectacular."

"They are, aren't they?" he agreed, and extended his hand for a shake. His big palm was warm and soft and he held mine for just a split second too long. "I'm Jason Greene. What are you driving now?"

My mind raced. "I used to drive a Mercedes," I said, thinking back to that one instance, a few years ago, when I needed to drive an inebriated client back to his home.

"Oh, Mercedes builds wonderful machines," he gushed. "And they're actually a great value."

"Are they?"

"Oh my, yes," he gushed, beginning to build a head of steam. "They totally hold their worth over time. Doesn't matter when you're done with it, you can always sell a pre-owned Benz. People in this town simply love Mercedes. These vehicles can be 20 years old and someone always will want it. Driving a Mercedes makes a statement about you."

I shuddered to think what statement my Pathfinder made about me and decided to change the subject. "I'm actually here to see Gilbert Horne. Is he available?"

Jason Greene's smile disappeared quickly. "His office is just down the hall," he said, his voice suddenly losing its brimming enthusiasm. He pointed a finger toward a corner of the showroom. I glanced down the hall, but when I turned back to thank Mr. Greene, he was nowhere to be found.

I walked slowly down the corridor taking things in. The walls were lined with artwork. At the end of the hall was a vestibule with a handsome, well-groomed, middle-aged woman sitting at a desk. Though she was seated, I could tell she was tall, with a decidedly statuesque figure. A younger woman, tall and shapely herself, stood in front of her desk, chatting away with her. Two offices sat nearby, both with their doors closed.

"May I help you?" asked the woman seated at the desk, whose name plate read, "Betty Luttinger."

"Hello Betty," I said. "I'm looking for Mr. Horne."

She frowned. "Did you have an appointment?"

"I'm afraid not."

"Oh, Mr. Horne doesn't come in much. And when he does it's at very irregular times. He comes and goes," she said.

"How about Mr. Whitestone?"

"He's gone for the day, I'm sorry. May I ask what this is regarding?"

I handed her my card. "It's a personal matter. When do you think I can get on Mr. Whitestone's calendar?"

"Oh, he's usually here in the mornings. But he's very busy. Perhaps I can call you with some times? But it would help if I knew more about what this was regarding."

"To be honest, I'm looking for Mr. Horne and was hoping to get some insight as to where he might be. He hasn't been seen in a few days. Some people are worried. I was hoping Mr. Whitestone might shed some light."

"Gil is missing?" frowned the younger woman standing next to us. "Do you think something is wrong?"

"Hard to say," I answered. "That's why I'm here."

"I'll call you as soon as I can," Betty said, concerned. "This is very disturbing news."

I smiled at her. "Appreciate it."

"I'll walk you out," the young woman said. "My name is Christy. Christy Vale."

Christy was nicely dressed and nicely coiffed. She was both slender and buxom, and her thick, golden blonde hair cascaded down past her shoulders. Her eyes were large and green, and she had the kind of high cheekbones that enhanced an already pretty face. She wore a smartly tailored cream-colored business suit, but under it was a low-cut scarlet top that revealed plenty.

"How long have you worked here?" I asked.

"Oh, a few years. This place is like home. In fact, my husband works here too. We actually met at the dealership. He's the service manager."

"You work at the same place. Is it hard to separate your home life and your business life?"

"Oh, sometimes," she said with a sad smile. "We try not to let work interfere with our off-hours, but this place is such a big part of what we do. Why do you ask?"

"I'm getting married soon. My fiancée works in a similar field."

She smiled warily. "It does take some effort to separate work and play. Taking breaks from each other occasionally helps. But congratulations. Are you planning a big wedding?"

"Not really. Maybe 50 or 60 people. We're trying to keep it intimate."

"I think those are the best kind," she said, as we walked onto the lot. "We had over 300 guests at our wedding; it was crazy. Seemed like everyone from the dealership was invited. But we were lucky. The owners gave us a nice big bonus before the wedding, and that took care of most of the cost."

"That's great," I said. "If you can't be rich, have rich friends."

"Oh, isn't that the truth! Especially in this business, things are so up and down. Thankfully Isaac is on salary here. When I make a few sales it's great, but some months are better than others."

"I know that for a fact," I agreed. My business had more than its share of peaks and valleys.

"Listen," she said, lowering her voice. "Would you like to take one of these out for a spin? You never know when you might be in the market."

I walked over to a red Porsche 911 Targa and did a circuit around the vehicle. The Monroney sticker on the driver's window listed the price at over $100,000. "I don't know that this is a market I'll get to for quite some time," I said. If ever.

"Even still, you never know," she said. "I just need your driver's license to show the manager."

I looked back at the gleaming Porsche. "Sure," I said, wondering why she was bothering with this. Most salespeople qualified a buyer right away. Judging from my attire, which consisted of a casual shirt, tan dockers and a pair of Nikes, it was unlikely that I fit the profile of a prospective Porsche buyer.

Christy Vale glanced at my driver's license. "Oh, you live in Santa Monica, too. And north of Montana!" she gushed excitedly. "Impressive. When the real estate market comes back, you might very well be in the market for a car like this."

She skipped off to get the keys. I didn't bother to tell her that I had a rent-controlled apartment and my most expensive possession was an 8-year old SUV. The volatile swings of the L.A. real estate market left my finances completely unaffected. I walked around the blatantly expensive sports car three times, and it still didn't seem like anything I would ever buy. Even if I hit the lottery, I would probably just trade in my Pathfinder for a newer version of the same model. Maybe add leather seats.

Christy came back, climbed into the driver's seat, and motioned for me to get in. "I have to be the one to pull out of the lot. Something to do with our insurance."

Steering the vehicle slowly through a ridiculously expensive cascade of motor cars, she pulled into the street. Despite Lincoln Boulevard being crowded with cars, she expertly navigated the vehicle in and out of traffic. We sped north toward Montana Avenue, as she simultaneously engaged the clutch and shifted the transmission in a smooth and effortless manner.

"You drive like a pro," I commented.

"Oh, I'm good at working a stick," she smiled. "Lots of experience."

We reached San Vicente Boulevard, where she pulled over to the curb. "Look, I actually was hoping to talk with you in private," she confided.

"I'm hurt. I don't strike you as a Porsche buyer?"

Christy threw back her head in laughter. "No, not at all. Maybe if you had on gold chains, wore an $80 haircut and got your fingernails manicured."

"Obviously not me. So what's on your mind?"

"It's about Gil," she said, her smile slowly evaporating and a more somber expression taking hold. Looking at her more closely, I noticed a small scar over her left eye.

"Go on," I said.

"I'm really worried about him," she said, taking a deep breath. "Gil is a good friend and, you know, he's been very generous. Paying for our wedding was all Gil's idea; Duncan didn't want to give us any bonus at all. But Gil was the one who helped out a lot. He's been really good to us. We owe him so much."

"Does Gil have any problems you know about?"

Christy sighed. "He has more than his share. Seems to come with the territory of being rich. Gil is nice, but his life is so disorganized. He gets distracted easily. I heard he was having cash flow problems lately. And I'm sure that led to his marital problems."

"How long's he been married?"

"Oh, about four or five years. I'm not sure if this is his second marriage or third. Or maybe even fourth. He's such a flirt, it's no surprise he moves from girl to girl. But he picked a real bitch with this one. April is out for one thing. Money. And once the money spigot gets turned off, I'm sure she'll hook up with the next rich guy."

"Did you know someone fired a gunshot at Gil the other day?"

Christy's green eyes widened even more, and it was apparent she had not been aware. Her mouth became slightly agape but then closed quickly. "That's awful," she managed.

"Any thoughts on who might have been involved?"

She started to shake her head and then stopped. Looking down, she tried to focus her thoughts. I waited until she composed herself. "Gil owed people money. Some bad people. Really bad people. He was worried. He even got a hold of a pistol. For protection. Although I don't think he even knows how to use it properly. I'm more concerned he'd turn it on himself before he'd pull the trigger on someone else."

I made a mental note of this. "Any idea who he was involved with?" I asked.

She looked down and shook her head no, and I sensed she was shutting down. Time to move in and push some buttons.

"You seem to know a lot about Gil and his issues. That's unusual for an employee. If you know something and aren't telling, it could get him into more trouble. I'm trying to help here. Your silence might actually get him killed."

She gasped for a moment at the thought and then swallowed hard. "Some people came by a few days ago. A couple of goons. They marched into Gil's office and locked the door. Betty said she heard a scuffle but none of us could get in. We heard Gil keep saying, 'Okay, okay, you'll get it, you'll get it.' They kept demanding something called a vig or maybe it was vigorish. Then they walked out and

Gil was just white as a sheet. He wouldn't say what was going on. But he left the office right away and he hasn't been back since."

"A few days ago. That was when?"

"Thursday."

I tried to process what I had learned thus far. The gunshots were fired yesterday, on Sunday. Maybe the two incidents were related. Maybe not. Vig was a street term for the interest payment on a loan, so it sounded as if Gilbert Horne indeed had debts and his creditors wanted him to make good. Shooting him would not achieve that, but a close call might spur him to come up with the money quickly. Christy had an unusually close relationship with her boss. Maybe it was paternal. Maybe not. And hidden somewhere in this morass was Horne's relationship with his partner at the sports agency, my new well-heeled client, Cliff Roper.

"Was Gil a gambler?"

"Oh, you could say that," she said in a sing-song voice.

I took this in. "So where do you think he might be?"

"I don't know," she shrugged. "I doubt he's left town though."

"Why?"

"If he's going to find his way out of these problems, running away won't help. It never does. Your problems just follow you."

"Well said," I commented.

With that, Christy seemed to compose herself quickly, wiped her eyes, and grabbed the gear shift. In a moment, we were flying down San Vicente. After a few turns, we were back at the dealership. As I got out of the car, Christy thanked me and began to walk away.

"There's one last thing," I reminded her.

She turned and gave me a puzzled look.

"I need my driver's license back."

Five

My apartment was on 4th Street a few blocks from the bluffs overlooking Pacific Coast Highway. The building was indeed north of Montana, but just barely. Montana Avenue separated the quaint bungalows and apartment buildings to the south of it from the strikingly large McMansions and estates to the north. In fact, my apartment was actually right on Montana, albeit on the northwest corner of 4th Street. I hadn't bothered to clarify this factoid with Christy.

I walked into my apartment and immediately smelled something good. The scent of garlic wafted through the air and the lovely view of Gail Pepper, hunched over the kitchen counter hard at work dicing vegetables, suddenly came into focus.

"I love the smell of garlic in the evening. Smells like ... home."

She turned and smiled. "Nice, isn't it?"

I returned the smile, walked over and kissed her. "Very much so."

"Now aren't you in a good mood," she said, her radiant smile still shining. Gail's shiny chestnut brown hair was tied back and she wore a purple apron over her dress. Gail was the most beautiful woman I had ever gone out with, and I still had to pinch myself at the mere thought of us getting married. Somewhere along the line, I had gotten lucky and the gods had smiled on me.

"I've had an interesting day," I said, "and a lucrative one."

"That sounds wonderful. I look forward to hearing about it. That is, after you set the table for dinner."

I laughed, gave her another kiss and went about my assigned chore. Gail and I had become engaged six months ago, and we quickly moved in together. Or I should say, she moved into my apartment. It was not a huge amount of space, and in some ways the apartment was now rather cramped. But oddly, I didn't mind. I had spent many years alone, too many perhaps, and sharing my home with a lovely young woman was a welcomed change. At some point we would need to look for something bigger, as the need for our own personal space would become important. But for now, we were two cooing lovebirds, discovering more and more about each other. And liking what we were finding.

I opened a bottle of chardonnay and poured two glasses. A few minutes later we sat down to dinner. Chicken, mushroom risotto, grilled vegetables and rosemary bread. I was duly impressed.

"This looks amazing. Especially considering you worked at the office all day," I said, taking a bite and smiling in appreciation.

"Part of it is timing things right. Part of it is Trader Joe's. I can do a lot of things quickly. Risotto takes all day to cook properly. That one came frozen. Sorry."

"No need to apologize. It beats anything I ever put together as a bachelor."

"I'm not sure I want to hear about those details. But I do want to hear about your day. It's been a while since you described your work as lucrative. In fact, I'm not sure you ever have."

"I know. And I actually have two cases," I bragged.

"When it rains, it pours."

"Indeed. The first one is through my old pal, Harold Stevens. Standard fraud case. A woman claims she was burglarized and lost a lot of expensive jewelry. But she doesn't live in an affluent area, and there's no reason to believe she had that much ice on her. And everything seems too pat."

"Did she file a police report?" she asked.

"I'm sure she did. Had to for insurance purposes. Her name's Noreen Giles. Why?"

"I can take a look at her background, if that's all right with you."

"Fine by me," I said. "I never turn down free information."

"How about your other case? And I guess that's the lucrative one."

"Ah yes. Does the name Cliff Roper ring a bell?"

Gail frowned, and those beautiful pouty lips protruded out in thought. "It does. The name sounds familiar, but I can't place it."

"Cliff was the sports agent I encountered last year. He was the one trying to blackmail Marcellus Williams from USC into signing with his agency. You might remember

Marcellus. After the UCLA game, he gave us both big hugs. You especially."

Gail laughed and her dazzling smile was again on display. "Oh, I remember now. Yes, Marcellus was quite ... enthusiastic. You got Roper to back off. But wasn't Roper the one with the checkered past? Didn't he even change his name at one point?"

"He did indeed. When he operated up in Vegas he went by the name of Hal Delano. I guess after being arrested a dozen times, he decided his brand name needed freshening up."

"Charming," she said. "Are you going up against him one more time?"

"Actually, no. He's my new client."

Gail gave me a look. It bespoke both wonder and a puzzled sense of disappointment. For now, I chose to focus on wonder.

"It's not quite what it seems," I started.

"It never is in the beginning," she said, putting her fork down and lifting the wine glass. "Do tell."

"Cliff Roper insists he's the victim in this case. He split up with his partner in the sports agency. Then someone went and fired a couple of shots at the partner. Name's Gilbert Horne."

"And Roper is a suspect in the shooting."

"Person of interest," I corrected her.

"I see."

"The gun used in the shooting was a Glock pistol. Roper owned a Glock, but claimed it had been stolen recently in a burglary."

"Not surprised he has an excuse," she said, taking another sip of wine.

"True. But there seems to be a growing list of people who were angry at Horne. Former clients he didn't service properly, and some rather unsavory creditors who want to be paid. It appears Gilbert Horne liked to gamble."

"You come into contact with such lovely people."

"And you don't, Ms. Assistant City Attorney? If I recall, you're working on a case where people are stealing checks out of public mailboxes. We're not working with the most upstanding individuals."

"And I'm trying to put them away, *señor*. You're now trying to help one of them get off."

"Hmm," I said, taking another bite of risotto. "So how's your case going?"

Gail looked across the room. "We have a great case," she began. "And I think we'll get the perps to go for a plea bargain. They'll do jail time. But there have been three more complaints this weekend about mail stolen right out of the mailboxes. We don't know if they're part of this same ring, or if we have an epidemic on our hands."

"Best to not drop mail in the box the night before."

"True, but not always convenient. And one of the victims told us today that he dropped his letters in the box outside his local post office. Someone actually stole it right out of there. They smeared some glue onto a rubber hose and pulled the envelopes right up out of the mailbox."

"Some thieves have no shame."

"Or brains," she added. "In public places these days, there are video cameras everywhere."

I picked up the wine glass and pretended I was a connoisseur. I swirled the wine around and examined the way in which it draped the glass. I lowered my nose below the rim and took in the bouquet. I then took a sip of the chardonnay and let it linger on my palate. It had what experts called a buttery finish, meaning it tasted smooth rather than tart.

"Cliff Roper is not someone who is short on brain cells," I pointed out.

"Some crooks are more clever than others," Gail responded.

"You know he's never actually been convicted of a crime."

"You've certainly had a change of heart about this guy," she said. "You're usually discerning about who your clients are."

"This case sounded interesting. I'm curious. I think there's more here than meets the eye. And oh yeah. There's one thing I should probably add here."

"What's that, Mr. Wine Expert?"

I smiled. "He's already paid me $10,000 in cash as a retainer."

Gail picked up her glass and took a sip, although she didn't bother with all the gesticulations. "It sounds like he's a little desperate."

"Could be," I agreed.

"It could mean he wants you to find a fall guy."

"That could be true too."

"And so what do you think after one day of investigating?"

"I think," I said with a smile, "That we have a nice, expensive wedding to pay for soon. The Miramar Hotel doesn't come cheap."

"Money shouldn't be the main reason you do things," she said.

"It's not. I'm actually intrigued by the case. But this is the world we live in. Money's not something I can just ignore."

*

The next morning started with another round of hazy sunshine. I knew it started that way because I was up at 5:30 a.m., with plenty of time to take in what one might liberally call a sunrise. I was up at 5:30 a.m. because my downstairs neighbor, Ms. Linzmeier, had started a new job which required her to be at work at 7:00 a.m. She liked to begin the day now by taking a long hot shower and singing every Beyonce song she knew. And she knew a lot of them.

Sitting at my desk, I combed through the Internet to see what I could learn about Gilbert Horne's online presence. After a half-hour of sifting through mostly innocuous information, I switched over to looking into Noreen Giles, the woman Harold Stevens suspected of engaging in insurance fraud. I noticed a number of name changes, although these could have simply been multiple marriages. Checking further into each name would take more time, so I made a mental note to return to this case in the next day or two.

I got up and made a pot of French roast coffee, and drank it slowly as I watched the black sky turn gray and hazy. I left the apartment at 7:30 a.m., just as Gail was stirring. She was unaffected by Ms. Linzmeier's schedule, blessed with the ability to sleep through almost any kind of noise. I kissed her goodbye, remembering to grab the Bay City Motor Cars brochure as I headed out into the gray day.

It was early enough that I could hop on the freeway without getting sandwiched in the mind-numbing morning rush hour that plagues Los Angeles. I drove a few blocks and turned down onto the California Incline, a steep service road which connects Santa Monica to the Pacific Coast Highway. The ocean looked dark and choppy, reflecting the gloomy marine layer overhead. PCH quickly led into the eastbound 10 Freeway and it was a pleasure to drive on a relatively empty road for a change. It took only a few minutes to reach La Brea, but another 25 minutes to navigate up through Crescent Heights and into Laurel Canyon.

In one sense, Laurel Canyon is an important north-south artery which connects the L.A. basin with the San Fernando Valley. In another, Laurel Canyon is a world unto itself. During the 1960s it attracted a counter-culture society, and numerous rock stars and entertainment industry folks migrated to it for the rustic style of living. Laurel Canyon allowed people to live in a seemingly rural area, yet be only a few minutes away from the conveniences of a bustling city. Over the years, the rustic feel gave way to a level of urban sprawl. There was still a country feel to the place, but with house after house built right next to one another, the ability to commune with nature became more difficult.

I turned left onto Lookout Mountain Avenue, and drove about a mile up the hill. The farther up I drove, the more the road narrowed. I passed a quaint row of rusty mailboxes, the kind with the little red flag you lifted when you needed the postman to pick up letters to be mailed. This was a throwback to another era. In most parts of L.A., those who still used these types of mailboxes made sure they came equipped with a lock on them. But this was part of the quirky charm of Laurel Canyon.

It was early enough so that most normal working folk would be up and about, but still likely to be at home. My guess was that April Horne would be home, though probably fast asleep. I parked in a driveway with a hand-carved sign that read, "The Hornes," posted nearby. Next to me sat a white Mercedes Roadster and a black Porsche Turbo Cabriolet. Leaning on the bell, I buzzed for a good five minutes before a drowsy looking woman in her late 20s opened the door and asked what the hell I thought I was doing.

"Good morning," I smiled.

"Look, whatever you're selling, we're not buying," she said, tightening the belt on her red robe. It didn't appear she was wearing much clothing underneath. It did appear she had more than ample cleavage to reveal.

I flashed my P.I. badge. "I'm not selling anything. I'm an investigator looking into the shooting the other day. Mind if I come in?"

The woman ran her fingers through her peroxide-infused blonde hair for a moment and blinked a few times. "I've already been through this with the detectives the other day."

"Just doing some follow up, ma'am," I said. "You're April Horne, right?"

"Uh ... yeah," she said, after a long moment's worth of thinking.

"Maybe we can talk inside?"

She stepped back, which was about as much of an invitation to enter as I would likely receive. "Give me a minute," she said, and pointed to a corridor. She turned and went in the opposite direction.

The interior hallway spilled into a living room that was awash in light. A large skylight in the ceiling, coupled with what seemed like a wall of glass windows, made it difficult to tell if you were inside or outside. The windows faced a back yard that consisted of mostly shrubs, trees and foliage. A small patio with a gas barbecue grill was nearby. I sat down on a bar stool next to a white countertop and waited for her to join me. After a few minutes, she returned in shorts and a tank top. Her hair was pulled back, and some quick makeup had been applied. She put some water in a mug and microwaved it, then slipped a Good Earth tea bag inside, dunking it half a dozen times. Sitting down, and without bothering to offer anything to me, she took a quick sip of her tea, winced at the heat, and gave me a blank look.

"So what do you want?" she asked in a monotone voice.

I refrained from making a smartass comment. No sense pushing her this early in the morning. "Has your husband been in contact with you since the shooting?"

"He's called me."

"Is he still in town?"

"I'd rather not say," she said.

"You know, we're just trying to learn who fired that gun the other night. Anything you can tell us is helpful."

She blew into the mug and took another sip. "Gil's in town. He's staying at a hotel but I can't tell you which one. In all honesty, I don't even know. He wouldn't tell me."

"Could it be the Seaside in Marina del Rey?"

She gave me a stunned look. "Why did you bring that up?"

"Let's just say I'm good at my job."

She stared at me blankly, in a way that said she didn't want to discuss this, and in a way that told me I had hit pay dirt. I tried another tack. "Don't you think that's strange that he wouldn't tell you where he's staying?"

"I think our whole marriage is a little strange," she said, a tinge of bitterness coating her voice.

"How's that?" I asked, trying to evoke her obvious need to vent.

"Look, we've been married six years," she said looking down into her teacup. "But his lifestyle has been pretty much the same as when he was single. He's always out hustling for new clients. Or whatever."

"That's the world of a sports agent," I pointed out. "Showing a player a good time is part of the deal. I'm sure you knew that going in."

"What I knew was that Gil was a fun guy. What I didn't know was that he had a gambling problem. And a womanizing problem."

I processed this piece of information. "The two sometimes go hand in hand."

"Yeah, and he also told me he had a fallout with his sleaze ball partner."

"You mean Cliff Roper."

She gave me another blank look. "Yeah. The two made a lot of money together. Gil brought in some big clients for a while. He had a cousin up at Oregon, this quarterback who was helping him sign a bunch of college players."

"And that pipeline was drying up."

"I guess. All I knew was that he was acting differently. And then we started getting some threatening phone calls."

"You think these calls were a precursor to the shooting?"

"I guess. Gil said he owed some money, gambling probably. He was talking about selling the car dealership. Ironic, I guess, since he won the damn thing in a card game."

"So I heard. Tell me about the womanizing."

"What's to tell?" she said in a dismissive voice. "He sometimes comes home and I know he's been with other women."

"How do you know?" I asked.

"I can smell it on him."

I leaned back and took a momentary break. There wasn't going to be a whole lot more I wanted to learn going down this path. But it was still bound to be a piece of the puzzle.

At this point I heard a rustling sound coming from another part of the house, a movement that seemed as if someone had just woken up. The faint noise of a door closing was audible. April Horne pretended not to hear it. I chose to not pretend.

"Is someone else in the house?"

She quickly said no. "It's our puppy, Chewy. She's probably gone out the doggy door. We don't walk her. She uses the backyard as her personal toilet."

There was something very pat and rehearsed about her response, something that told me she had thought about this scenario and had a ready answer. It was an answer that was clear and concise and made sense. It was most likely a lie, but pushing her would not change the story; it would only harden her position and shut her down.

"Is there anything else you can tell me about your husband? Anything that might help in getting to the bottom of this shooting?"

April sighed. "I don't know who did it. I'm just concerned that the shot came too close to hitting me."

"Maybe," I said, in as paternal a manner as I could, "that might have been the idea."

She stared at me in disbelief. "Huh?"

"If your husband owed people money," I said patiently, "then shooting him would not got them paid. Scaring him might. And scaring you might put even more pressure on him to come up with the money quicker."

She took this in. Another sip of tea and five seconds of deep thought. "I guess that makes sense. Although the way things have been going lately, seeing me in danger wouldn't motivate Gil one damn bit. As a couple, we're pretty much done."

I took this in. Over the years I had seen more than my share of bad marriages. From breaking up domestic disputes as a police officer to conducting private investigations on behalf of distraught spouses. I had learned more about the inner workings of bad marriages than anyone ever should. I stood up and handed her my card. "Give me a call if you think of anything else. Or if anything else happens around here."

Looking at the card for a long minute, she drew in a breath. She finally seemed to be waking up. "Hey, wait a minute. You're not with the police."

"I never said I was."

She slowly digested this. "A private investigator? Can I ask who you're working for?"

"You can ask. But I can't tell you. Sorry. Confidential."

"Great. Just great. For all I know you're working for the goons who took a shot at us."

"I'm not," I said, knowing she wouldn't be reassured at this point. "But I'm also trying to figure all this out. Just like you."

"Sure. Wonderful. I think you should leave now."

I rose and walked down the hallway, taking one last look out of the glass windows. The sun had started to peek through the clouds and it seemed like it might turn into a nice day. A small streak of sunlight reflected off the barbecue grill and I squinted to make out what looked like a small black cocker spaniel in the back yard. I watched it poke around before squatting to do its business. And then I saw a large, shirtless young man with short blond hair raise his arms skyward, stretching as if he had just woken up. He reached down to pet the dog, but the dog surprised him and jumped up to try and bite his hand. He jerked his hand away and gave the dog a dirty look before going back into the house.

Six

On the way back down from Laurel Canyon, I stopped off at La Brea Bakery and had coffee and a ginger scone. I sat on a surprisingly comfortable wooden bench outside the bakery, and watched the traffic flow past as I ate my breakfast. Enjoying it considerably, I went back in and bought a loaf of bread for tonight and some more scones for tomorrow morning: ginger, blueberry and currant.

I reached the Pathfinder, but just as I was about to climb in, my phone began to buzz. I looked at the caller ID and sighed. Cliff Roper wanted to talk.

"Hi there," I began.

"You find my ex-partner yet?"

"Hello to you, too."

"Yeah, yeah. Hello and how's the family. Where's Horne?"

"I don't know."

"Geez. What've you been doing the past 24 hours?!"

"You'll get a full report," I said evenly. Investigating for Cliff Roper paid generously, but the working conditions left something to be desired.

"Tell me you found out *something* at least," he said.

"I found out something."

"What?"

"Your partner's been staying in the Marina," I said, withholding the name of the actual hotel.

"What else?"

"He's owes money to people. And he's having trouble paying them."

"Uh-huh. Keep going."

"Horne's wife is having an affair."

There was silence on the other end of the line. I waited until it passed. It took Roper about three seconds to begin speaking again. "With who?"

"Didn't get a good look at him. Other than big, buff and he had a blond crew cut."

"Interesting. Okay. Anything else?"

"That's about it. A couple of his employees at the dealership are worried. They seemed to like him. Seemed genuinely concerned about him."

"Really. Well it's a lonely club they're in. That's all you got?"

"For now, yeah."

"Okay. At least you're doing something."

Yes, and at least I'm being paid nicely, I thought to myself. The client appreciation I was receiving could certainly stand an upgrade. "I'll call you when I have something more."

"No," he said before hanging up. "Call me when you have something I can use."

*

The freeway traffic had snarled, so it took 45 minutes to reach Marina del Rey. The Seaside Hotel was located across the street from a seemingly endless number of slips that housed hundreds of boats docked at the Marina. As is the case with most waterfront locales, Marina del Rey was upscale and encircled by expensive apartment buildings, condos and some luxury restaurants and hotels. The Seaside hotel was modest by comparison, but that just meant it was rather nice by practically any other standard. It had previously been part of a large hotel chain, but one day the chain's name was mysteriously taken off the building's outer signage, and it simply became The Seaside.

I wandered through the hotel's front lobby, which was quiet and peaceful. The early morning checkout rush had finished, breakfast had been served, and the employees were going through their mid-morning routines. The front desk associates were huddled over computer screens. Off to the side was a lounge area, where a pair of bartenders cleaned and arranged glassware. An attractive, young waitress straightened out some black Formica tables nearby and placed folded pink cloth napkins in the appropriate spots. I decided she would be my first interview, mostly because she was young. And younger people are often freer in sharing their comments and observations.

"Come here often?" I joked, as I took a seat at a table she was setting up.

She gave me a pretty smile and a flirtatious giggle. "Oh, now where did you come up with such an original pickup line?"

"I've been working on it all morning. Sounds like it could use some tweaking."

"No, the opening line's just the ice breaker. If a girl's interested, it almost doesn't matter what a guy says at first. As long as he says something."

"I'll remember that," I said, hoping my days as a bachelor would soon be ending forever. The waitress was very pretty, had a smooth complexion and was very well proportioned. She looked all of 21 years old. If that.

"What's your name?" I asked.

"Oh, I'm Gretchen."

"And I'll guess ... you've just turned 21."

She giggled again. "You're close. I'm 22. Say, can I get you an eye opener this morning? They make a mean Bloody Mary here."

"My eyes are already wide open," I laughed. "But I'll take one without the vodka. I think you call that a Virgin Mary."

"Indeed we do," she winked, and walked off to the bar. A few minutes later she came back with the large red drink, complete with a celery stalk rising dramatically out of the glass.

"Would you like to run a tab?" she asked.

I threw a ten on the table. "That's okay. I'm actually here on some business. Can you talk for a minute?"

"Sure," she said enthusiastically. "It beats setting up tables."

"I can imagine. How long have you worked here?"

"About a year. It's my day job. Pays the bills while I work on what I really want to do. I grew up in Nebraska. I'm just here trying to live the Hollywood dream."

"How's that working out?" I asked.

"Slow start. I'm making a few contacts. But things take time. I'm hoping mom and dad will finally accept this when I hit it big."

I didn't need to ask, but I did so anyway. She told me she was an aspiring actress who did some modeling on the side. When I was on the LAPD we used to refer to girls like these as AMWs, meaning Actress, Model, Whatever. The Whatever usually started off as a Waitress, but once in a while devolved into more sordid activities such as porn and prostitution. All too often, parents did not give their blessing to their daughters moving to California to take a shot at Hollywood stardom. So if the girls began to have money troubles, they often turned to other sources of income, and sometimes to the oldest profession. Not that that always happened, but it did so more often than one would think. I knew that better than almost anyone. My involvement with a girl like Gretchen had effectively cost me my job at the LAPD.

"I imagine your parents will be a lot more comfortable when you start to get some work in the industry."

"Oh, I'm sure they will be too," she smiled.

"So Gretchen, I'm looking for someone. I heard he comes here a lot." I pulled out the Bay City Motor Cars brochure and turned to the back page as I handed it to her. "Here's his picture. Name's Gilbert Horne."

She studied it for a second. "Oh sure. He was just in here last night. And well, the night before that too."

"He's a regular?"

"No, not exactly. He actually stays here sometimes. He said he was an agent, and I thought, oh wonderful, maybe

I'll get an in. Turns out he mostly works with athletes. I mean he told me he knew some producers, but I got the feeling he was just trying to impress me to get into my pants."

I smiled. Somewhat savvy for a 22-year-old. But this was L.A. You got savvy in a hurry or you went back home. "Was he by himself last night?"

"He came in alone, but you know, he left with someone. Are you a police officer?"

"No, not at all," I smiled. "I'm just doing a background check."

"Is he in some kind of trouble?"

"I don't think so. But that's why I'm looking into this. So from what you've described, he sounds pretty smooth."

Gretchen shrugged. "I guess, for an older guy. But the woman he met came right up to him, so it's not like he picked her up."

"This woman, what did she look like?"

"The usual. Blonde and pretty," she said, looking up at the ceiling as she spoke. Why people did that to help jog their memories was beyond me. Maybe they were hoping for some spiritual guidance.

"Is it typically a different girl each night?" I asked.

"Sometimes. But this one I've seen in here before," she said, looking down and skimming through the brochure. "Nice cars. I didn't know Mr. Horne was involved in a dealership."

"I think he's involved in a number of different businesses. Anything else you can tell me about him?"

"Hmmm. Not really. He's a good tipper. But other

than that, no. He's always been nice to me."

I said nothing and waited for her to continue. When you're quiet, people sometimes feel the need to say something and fill the void that silence brings.

"One other thing," she finally said, her brow furling into a frown. "And this happened last week. I didn't really think about it much at the time. But Mr. Horne was in here for a drink and another man approached him. Big guy. Thought he might have been a professional wrestler or something. Really strong looking, you know?"

I nodded in agreement, but again didn't say anything.

"Anyway, they talked for a few minutes and then Mr. Horne handed him an envelope. He told the big guy that was all he had. Then the big guy said his boss wasn't going to be happy about this."

"Anything else?"

"Not really. But Mr. Horne didn't look so good after that. He finished his drink quickly and then he left. Looked like he had a lot on his mind."

"Did Horne refer to this guy by name?"

She thought for a moment. "No. But they kept mentioning Texas A&M. Maybe he played ball there once."

*

The thin young man at the desk was smiley and pleasant. His white shirt and tie were covered by a snug gray vest. When he asked if I was checking in today, I told him no, but I was hoping to connect with a guest at the hotel.

"Their name, please?" he said in a high-pitched voice, looking down at a monitor underneath the chest-high counter.

"Gilbert Horne."

He typed a few things into the computer and then a few more things. He looked up at me. "What was that name again?"

I repressed my inner urges and smiled patiently. "Gilbert Horne."

He played around with the computer for another minute or two. "I'm sorry, but Mr. Horne checked out this morning."

"Ah," I said, and flashed my fake gold badge with my right hand. With my left hand I slipped a $50 bill across the counter. I imagined a client like Cliff Roper would understand the absence of certain receipts. "Any idea when he'll return?"

The young man discreetly slipped the bill into his pocket. "Mr. Horne doesn't have a specific date," he said. "But he's here a lot, so I imagine he'll be back soon."

"A regular?" I peered at him.

"I guess. He stays with us somewhat, uh, frequently. We have certain guests who come and go a lot. You know."

"Sure," I said, having a sneaking suspicion that certain rooms were available on an hourly basis. The fact that the big chain had disassociated its name from the hotel was now starting to make sense.

"Would it be too much trouble to give me a call when he returns?" I asked, handing him my business card.

"Oh. You're a P.I."

"I am."

"I thought you were a police ... oh, I guess it doesn't really matter. I thought maybe you were, you know, legit."

I smiled again. "I am legit. I'm just not with the LAPD anymore."

The young man looked around and lowered his voice. "I thought I might hook on as one of your confidential informants."

I considered this. "You still might. What's your name."

"Warren Tell."

"Okay, Warren. Let's keep this to ourselves. There may be opportunity to earn something down the road."

He gave me a long look and lowered his voice. "The pay here sucks. I'm good with helping you."

I gave him my final smile and walked out toward the parking lot. In many hotels that are located in upscale neighborhoods, valet parking is a given. At the Seaside, it's imaginary. At one point in time, this might have been a more opulent hotel. Times change. Nothing stays the same.

Seven

I ran a quick white pages search on my iPhone and found Ted Wade's address easily. Checking the traffic app, I smiled when I saw that the freeways were now wide open. Taking bites of a ham and cheddar sandwich I bought at the hotel's Grab n' Go kiosk, I drove out to my next unscheduled appointment. Once I reached the Harbor Freeway, it took me only 15 minutes to cruise down to San Pedro. But the drive through scenic Palos Verdes to the Wade residence took over half an hour.

Next to perhaps only Beverly Hills, the four communities perched on the Palos Verdes Peninsula had the highest priced homes in the L.A. area. Jutting out into the blue Pacific, P.V. offered spectacular views and even more spectacular homes. The area had a somewhat countrified feel to it, and at one point I passed a beautiful ranch with a series of stables. A couple of young women were riding a pair of golden palominos. A mile down the road, I slowed for a stop sign, only to encounter a group of half a dozen peacocks strolling across the road. One stopped in the middle and looked at me quizzically before turning and continuing his walk.

The Wade property was on an ocean-view street called Rocky Point Road. I pulled into the long driveway, which featured an enormous garage built to house five cars. The main residence was nearby. When I rang the doorbell, a tony looking woman in her 50s answered it. She was dressed casually with white slacks and a turquoise pullover.

"Hello," she said pleasantly.

"Hello to you," I said. "I'm looking for Ted Wade."

"Ted? He's not home right now. May I ask who you are?"

"My name's Burnside," I said, handing her my card. With some people I didn't get the feeling I'd need to obfuscate things with a fake badge.

"A detective?" she asked, her eyes widening. "Is Ted in some kind of trouble?"

"No," I said reassuringly. "I'm actually looking into an acquaintance of his."

"Oh, dear," she said and opened the door wider. "Why don't you come in."

I entered the spacious residence. The foyer was lined with a glossy tile floor, and a circular staircase was situated nearby. A huge crystal chandelier was hanging from the vaulted ceiling, a good 40 feet off the ground. We moved into what one might call a parlor area. There were two striped couches facing one another, a gorgeous mahogany table separating them, and a baby grand piano off to one side. Soft white carpeting lay underfoot. The window offered a panoramic view of the ocean. We sat down on one of the couches. It felt brand new.

"I'm Ellen. I'm Ted's mother."

"Nice to meet you."

"So what has he done this time?" she asked, in a resigned voice.

"This time?"

"Ted doesn't run with the finest crowd these days. I'm a little worried about him, considering the people with whom he associates."

"What I'm here for may or may not involve him," I started. "It's mostly background work."

"Background work?"

"There was a shooting in the Hollywood Hills a few days ago. No one was hurt, and I don't have any reason to believe Ted was involved. But he may have known people who were."

"A shooting? Dear God."

She sat down and took a breath. I sensed Ellen Wade was more than willing to talk, and possibly even looking for an excuse. "Has Ted's behavior changed lately?"

Ellen took a deep breath. "I don't know when it happened, but visits from the police are starting to become a regular event now. We've had to bail him out of jail half a dozen times. He leaves and doesn't came back for days. Oh, he's a grownup, he can do what he wants, but sometimes he comes home disheveled and looking like he hasn't slept in forever."

"Does he talk to you about things?"

"Not much. I've tried, believe me. Ted was the model child growing up. Polite, respectful. Oh, he was always athletic and good looking and he could get by on that for a while. Played baseball, football, basketball, soccer, you name it. And he was smart. You know he was offered a football scholarship to Stanford. They said he would have gotten in just on his grades alone. But they had already recruited a five-star quarterback; that's why he went up to Oregon. You know, schoolwork came easy to him. Everything just came easy to him. Maybe too easy."

"Sounds like the golden child."

"Yes, and Marvin, his dad, sensed that and tried to toughen him up. He'd pitch batting practice to him and intentionally throw at his head. Oh, he'd be wearing a helmet, it wasn't dangerous. But at the same time Ted was shooting baskets or throwing a football, Marv would quiz him on everything from math equations to world history to Peyton Manning's passing statistics. Made him think about multiple topics at once."

"So his father was involved with his sports career," I mulled, aimlessly.

"Oh yes. One night during his sophomore year, after Ted played poorly in a big game, his father made him walk home. Four miles. Uphill. Rode alongside to make sure he didn't call a friend to give him a ride. Marv had this idea that these tactics would somehow help him handle the stress that comes with being a pro athlete one day."

I didn't bother to ask how that one worked out. Some people's ideas of child rearing should be vetted through a professional. Ted Wade's dad seemed to think being tough on his son growing up would result in his son being tough-minded as an adult. When executed properly, and with the child knowing he was deeply loved, that strategy might work sometimes. When executed poorly, the results could be disastrous.

"It sounds like it might have worked to an extent," I said, trying my best to be ingratiating. "He was starting QB at Oregon. Played in the NFL for a couple of years."

"Yes, we're grateful for all of that. We just need to get him back on the straight and narrow. But it's much harder to do now. He's an adult. He doesn't listen to us anymore."

"He's his own person. Kids grow up and get to make their own choices."

"I know. Good and bad. But we've gotten off track. What was this about a shooting? What happened?"

"This is actually related to his agent. Or former agent. Gilbert Horne. I believe he's a relative."

"Gil?" she said incredulously. "Yes, he's Ted's uncle, my brother-in-law. Actually ex-brother-in-law. My husband's sister divorced him years ago. What's wrong?"

"I'm just trying to locate him. There was an incident a few days ago at the Horne residence. Someone fired a gunshot at either him or his wife. Maybe at both of them. No one was hurt, but we've been unable to locate Gil since."

Ellen raised her arms in resignation. "You know, I can't say as I'm totally shocked. Gil isn't the most savory person and doesn't run with the most upstanding crowd either. I was very concerned when Ted hired him as an agent, but that was Ted's decision. I think Ted helped Gil more than the other way around."

"How so?"

"Ted got some of his teammates to sign with Gil for representation. I think Gil leveraged the relationship."

"Leveraged is an interesting word."

"I could use others," she said, the bitterness starting to come out.

"Gil was probably not the best role model," I agreed.

"No, and once Ted signed that contract, the problems seemed to spiral out of control. I think in college, his life was very structured. Once he moved out into the real world, Ted went under Gil's wing and began to make bad choices."

"When was the last time you saw Ted?"

"Yesterday," she said. "He didn't come home last night. But like I said, that's not unusual."

I tried to find a few reassuring words. Not many sprang to mind. I looked around the magnificent living room and marveled at it. "Anyway, it looks like Gil negotiated a good contract for Ted. I imagine that helped him buy this house."

Her eyes widened. "Gil nothing. This is the home Ted grew up in. He went to Peninisula High School. He got a big contract, sure, but a lot of that money is gone. That's why he's back living with his parents."

I drew in a breath. "I'm sorry. I made the mistake of assuming the money he got from the NFL bought this house. It's very impressive."

"It is a very nice house," she agreed, with a measure of pride. "But you don't have to be a football player or a get-rich-quick artist to buy one of these things."

"Okay," I said, looking out at the gorgeous view of the Pacific and starting to wonder myself. "What's the secret?"

"No real secret," she told me. "My husband worked his way up the corporate ladder. He's retired now."

"What type of work did he do?"

"He used to be President of Nissan."

I drank this in. No real secret to living in luxury. Just get a cushy job that pays you millions of dollars.

*

It's unusual to find a football coach at home at almost any hour of the day. But when I called Johnny Cleary's number, he picked up and said he was indeed at his house in nearby Rolling Hills. A Tuesday afternoon in April is usually not the busiest time for the head coach of a major college football program. The annual spring game was coming up, which meant spring practice was almost over, the seniors' pro days had been completed, and the NFL draft was still a week away. But there are always things to do, be it check in with future recruits, review tapes from the spring practices or be available for interacting with wealthy alumni. Following the USC Trojans' 12-1 record last season, punctuated with a No. 3 national ranking, Johnny Cleary apparently felt he had earned an occasional afternoon off.

Johnny's house, while very nice, was nowhere near the grandiose estate the Wades lived in. His was a two-story structure on a good size lot, with a garage that would house only a pair of vehicles. The driveway was nowhere near as long as the Wades' so I parked my Pathfinder on the street.

"Welcome," Johnny said, as he ushered me in. "I've been meaning to have you and Gail over. I feel especially bad about it since I'm slated to be best man at your wedding."

"Just prepare a good toast," I smiled.

"Oh yeah. I've got some things in mind," he smiled back, albeit a tad devilishly.

"Uh-oh. I think I'll need to vet this."

"Nah, you'll be fine. A little humility never hurt anyone."

"I'm sure you're learning about that. Mr. Celebrity."

"Oh yeah. Being in the public eye has its downside. People I don't even know walk up to me now and act like I'm their best friend. Or have a special play they think I should run."

We walked into his back yard and sat down on lounge chairs. Johnny poured me a glass of iced tea. I looked out beyond his ranch-style redwood fence and saw vestiges of the ocean in the distance. I guess this is what realtors meant by a partial ocean view.

"You played pro football for 10 years," I said. "So people knew who you were. Back in the day."

"Yeah, but back then I wore a helmet and hardly anyone saw my face. Even as an assistant, I was pretty much anonymous. Now the TV camera pans over me a few dozen times every game."

"Just wait until you win a national championship," I said. "Your life will really not be your own."

Johnny smiled a relax smile. It was always better to see him during the off-season. "I'd live with those consequences," he assured me. Many years ago at USC, Johnny had been among the best cornerbacks in the nation. He played a position at which any failures were highly prominent and success meant remaining relatively inconspicuous. The level of preparation Johnny went through as a player ultimately reaped big dividends. In addition to making him into a great player, his tenacity made him well-suited to be a football coach later in life.

"So to what do I owe the pleasure of your visit?" he asked. "Not that it isn't good to see you. It's just that social calls aren't really in your DNA."

"Or yours," I added, and we both laughed. I had known Johnny for over 20 years and we had played together in the secondary at USC. We could go a long time without seeing one another, but when we did, the easy familiarity returned immediately. Friendships like these were golden. And rare.

"I'm working on a case," I said.

"Big surprise. Who's in trouble now? Hopefully not one of our guys again."

"Nope. It's actually an agent. Gilbert Horne. Someone tried to shoot him the other day."

"And you're looking for the guy who did it."

"I am."

"Bet you have a long list to go through," he laughed. "I'm glad I have an alibi."

"Yeah, there seems to be more than a few people unhappy with him."

"We've had nothing but problems with agents and their runners. I finally had to close off practices just to limit their access to players. Horne was one of the reasons."

"I imagine he was aggressive. But I'm also looking for Horne himself."

"Who's your client?" Johnny asked.

"Cliff Roper."

"Jesus" he said, shaking his head.

"Yeah, another prize."

"I'm glad my primary concern these days is beating Stanford and Oregon. Mostly that is. Keeping the agents away from the players has become a regular part of a head coach's job these days."

"I know you had a problem with Cliff last year."

"Yeah, and I appreciate your getting him out of my hair. Trying to blackmail a player into signing with his agency was disgusting. How can you have him as a client?"

"I could be wrong, but I think he may have been wrongly accused here. The world can be complicated. Not all the bad guys are bad all the time."

"And you think that's the case with Roper?"

"Maybe. Call it a gut-level hunch. And there really are quite a few other people who have motives here."

Johnny stretched his body and then relaxed. "Anyone you want to talk about?"

"How about some of his former clients? Patrick Washington, Oscar Romeo, Ted Wade. Maybe Brendan Webster too."

"Know 'em all. They're from the region. The first three played up at Oregon, I guess that's the connection, Horne went to law school there. We tried to recruit all those guys."

"Thoughts on them?"

"Sure. Patrick was the stud. Big, athletic, dominant. Anytime you can pile protoplasm that high, you're willing to take a chance, but Patrick was a sure thing. Hurt to see him pick another school in our conference, but that's how it goes sometimes."

"Can't land every one."

"Nope. And every other school recruits hard these days. College sports has hit the big-time. The money involved now is just off the charts."

"What about the others?"

"Let me think. Oscar was a big-time hitter, always the hammer, never the nail. Guy was strong as an ox, loved to light things up. Any receiver running a crossing pattern had to be wary of Oscar. He'd lay in the weeds and launch himself into the receiver when the ball arrived, sometimes a little early. He got flagged for a lot of penalties at Oregon. Still does in the league, and now they're taking a big stand against spearing. Too many concussions, on both sides of the ball. I sometimes wonder if Oscar didn't get his bell rung too many times himself."

"I know that from my own experience," I winced. "Two big, quick guys banging helmets when they're coming at each other at full speed. Both of them pay a price."

"True. Even quarterbacks aren't immune to this, but the league tries harder to protect them."

"What do you know about Ted Wade?"

"Oh, he was a guy we really wanted. He had the classic build, 6-foot-5, about 240 pounds. Definitely a specimen. Smart kid, fast, had a good arm. Should've made it in the

NFL but something happened. Too much partying, I don't know. Rumor was he used a little too much HGH."

HGH stood for Human Growth Hormone and was not an uncommon supplement for athletes these days. Guys who took it were quickly able to bench press far more weight than they ever could without it, and as a result their bodies soon became taut and ripped.

"And Brendan Webster?"

"Great athlete, sad story. Injuries took him down. I see him with a few of our former players sometimes. More of a hanger-on these days. So what does this all have to do with Gilbert Horne?"

"All these guys were represented by him at one point. And it sounds like he didn't do such a good job at it."

"Generally not a reason to shoot someone," Johnny pointed out wryly. "But when there's a lot of money on the table, things can get ugly. Especially if there's something personal at stake."

"For some guys, there's nothing more personal than money."

I thought back to when Johnny and I played together at USC. Our ultimate goal was to go into pro football. Playing in the NFL has been called a really bad job that pays really well. But for us, money was just one motivating factor. There was also the challenge of seeing how good we were, and whether we could succeed at the next level. And there was nothing quite like basking in the deafening cheers of a packed stadium.

Relative to the times, good players made a nice living back then, but it was peanuts compared to the huge contracts being thrown around today. Johnny played in the league for 10 years, but my football career was derailed by a knee injury, chasing a car burglary suspect across the USC campus during my final semester. It led me into a satisfying career in law enforcement, but lucrative would never be a word to describe it. Whatever regrets I had had vanished many years ago. Sometimes your path in life is pre-ordained.

"I could see where any of these guys might throw a few punches if they got steamed," Johnny said. "I'm still having a problem thinking a shooting could be financially related. Now I'm not saying one of them couldn't have been involved in this. But if they were, there was probably something more at play here."

"You have some good detective skills there, Coach."

"I'll let you play the gumshoe role. But did you drive all the way down here just for this?"

"No, I was in the neighborhood. The connection with those guys is Ted Wade. I just came from his house; he lives nearby. Horne is his uncle. "

Johnny looked off into the distance. "Last I heard about Ted, was he was checked into Betty Ford."

I looked at him. "Didn't know he was in rehab. His mother said he had problems, but I'm surprised she didn't mention that."

*

The drive back down off the peninsula was a little faster than it was going up. It was mid-afternoon, and before heading home, I decided to take a detour back to the Horne residence in Laurel Canyon. If nothing else, I was going to give Cliff Roper a day's work for a day's pay.

I doubted April Horne wanted to talk further, so I decided to park nearby and see if anything might happen to make my trek back to Laurel Canyon worthwhile. I pulled into a space up the street that offered a clear view of both the front door and the empty driveway. I whittled away the time listening to sports talk on the radio. The hosts were busy debating which college players would be taken in the first round of the NFL draft. Nothing happened for an hour, except the blathering of radio hosts needing to fill air time. Then something did.

A pair of near-identical Mercedes pulled into the driveway. April Horne got out of a white one, Gilbert Horne emerged from one that was silver. Both had paper license plates, indicating the vehicles were new. Almost immediately the pair began to argue. Gil Horne was gesticulating wildly with his arms, April stood with her hands on her hips. I rolled down my windows as the argument escalated into a screaming match. No real information was being disseminated, just the mutual feeling that the other person was not morally fit to crawl with snakes, and had a long way to go before achieving the status of a cockroach. A few neighbors walked outside to get a better glimpse of the ruckus. Finally, April stormed back into her white Mercedes and peeled away, and Gil stalked into the house. The neighbors walked back into their homes, looking a little disappointed that more of a show was not going to be performed.

I waited a few minutes and then rang the doorbell. Little would be gained by going after April. But apparently little was going to be gained by trying to speak with Gil either. After a solid 10 minutes of leaning on his doorbell and knocking loudly, I gave up. Either he was wearing ear plugs and sound asleep, or he was simply not in the mood to speak with anyone. No matter. I could always come back tomorrow.

The rush hour drive home was long and weary. I got back to the apartment before Gail, so I started making dinner. I chopped onions and peppers and tossed them into a pan with a few dashes of olive oil, then sautéed them until they were soft and tender. Taking the pan off the stove, I waited until Gail got home before I resumed cooking, grilling some chicken-apple sausages and slicing into the loaf of rosemary bread I had picked up from La Brea Bakery earlier in the morning. We ate, talked about the events in our day and then snuggled on the couch for a while before going to bed.

I slept later than normal the next morning. Apparently Ms. Linzmeier was sleeping in also. Up at 6:30 a.m., I went into the kitchen to start brewing a pot of coffee. At that point my phone buzzed. It was a local number, but one I didn't recognize.

"Yes?"

"Burnside, this is Roper."

"Good morning. Early for you, isn't it?"

"Let's just say the night hasn't ended."

"Uh-huh," I said, wondering what he had been up to now. "Good time?"

"You haven't heard?"

"I guess not."

"Geez, do you even bother to watch the evening news?"

I ignored the crack. "Not last night."

"I need you to go and talk to Honey."

"Who's that?"

"My daughter."

I didn't say anything. I wasn't sure what was more odd, that Roper had a child or that Honey was her name. My silence apparently spoke volumes, and Roper was remarkably good at reading minds.

"Yeah, I got a daughter, her name's Honey. She works for Disney. That okay with you?"

"What should I talk with her about?"

"About getting me bailed out of jail is what. I'm being arraigned this morning. She needs to get a hold of Silverstein, my personal lawyer. I already have a criminal attorney working this."

"Have you tried calling her?"

"She doesn't pick up my calls."

I wasn't entirely surprised. "Tell me what happened."

"I gotta explain this to you? Geez Louise."

"I guess you do have to explain this to me," I said, a little testily. "That is if you want my help."

"Gilbert Horne was shot to death last night."

My mind became instantly alert. "Where?"

"Where. At his house. Where else?"

"And the police think you did it."

"You're a genius."

"Did his wife accuse you?"

"His wife? April's not accusing anyone of anything."

"How's that? I'm surprised she's not a suspect."

"That would be nice," he growled. "But she's dead too. Police say the same person popped them both. And they think it was me."

Eight

Honey Roper lived in Burbank, near Toluca Lake. She worked for Disney on the studio lot, but wanted to meet me at a nearby Starbucks. I surmised she didn't want her colleagues overhearing our conversation and I didn't blame her one bit.

I arrived at 8:30 a.m. and while the line to order coffee was long, many of the tables were empty. At one table however, I saw a strikingly pretty young woman sitting alone and nursing a latte. She looked young, and had a lean, athletic build. Everything about her was simply beautiful. Large, china blue eyes, an exquisitely cut mouth and long, shimmering, dark blonde hair. She was wearing a blue sweater which accentuated her eyes, but her face had an unusual intensity to it. I wasn't sure if that was natural, or just brought on by recent developments.

"Hello, I'm Burnside."

She stood up immediately and shook my hand firmly. Her long legs made her taller than I had thought. "Thank you for coming out here," she said with an air of seriousness.

"No problem. I'm doing some work for your father, I'm a private investigator. You heard about what happened?"

"I just went on the net a little while ago. I read about it."

"Sorry."

"No, it's okay. In fact, I'm kind of used to it. This sort of thing happened to Dad before. When we lived up in Vegas."

"How'd you deal with it?" I asked.

"Mostly pretended it didn't happen. I had some real problems obviously with Dad's behavior. My mom divorced him a few years ago; it wasn't a pretty episode. But in the end, your dad's your dad. You only get one and you have to accept him for who he is. In school, a few kids poked fun. But others were a little scared of me. I actually think it gave me some street cred."

"Guess it depends on what crowd you run with."

Honey took a sip from her latte. "When I was in high school, I hung out with some kids that were from, well, I guess you'd say the wrong side of the tracks. I drifted away from them when I got to college, UNLV. Played on the women's basketball team there. That helped provide some separation."

"What did you study?"

"I earned a degree in business; I was planning to go work for one of the casinos. Then Dad moved his operation to L.A. So I figured, well, there would be more opportunity out here."

"So you wound up at Disney. From gambling casinos to kids entertainment. Quite a leap."

"Maybe not so much," she pointed out. "I work in marketing. I write ad copy for feature films that are being released theatrically. It's interesting work. But in the end, I just help promote a film. The product I work on is a means to an end."

"Which is?"

"Moving up the ladder. Getting ahead. I guess in some ways I take after Dad. Hopefully just the good ways."

"I've only just met you, but you seem to have a lot of maturity and perspective," I acknowledged. "And you seem well-grounded. All things considered."

Honey laughed for a moment, displaying a sweet smile, but just as quickly she took it away. Her face suddenly became serious again. "When you grow up in Vegas, you grow up quick. I guess I grew up quicker than most," she said, and then paused. "So what was it you wanted to drive here and talk with me about? You're cute and everything, but I'm sure you're busy."

I looked at her for a moment. Honey was as engaging as her father, but without the thorny personality. Her rapid movement from topic to topic was unusual but intriguing. "There are a couple of things I need to discuss with you," I started. "First, what do you know about your father's business partner?"

"Gil?" she said, wrinkling her nose. "More than I'd have liked. He's been hitting on me since I was 16. One time when he was drunk he even exposed himself to me. I finally told him to stop it or I'd twist his johnson into a pretzel."

I burst into laughter. "That got his attention I'm sure."

"Well, yes it did. Sorry for the graphic description," she said.

"They probably don't talk that way at Disney."

"You'd be surprised."

"Okay," I said, having trouble keeping a smile off my face. "But seriously. I don't think your dad did this. I really don't. It just doesn't add up."

"Thanks. I don't think so either. And not just because he's my dad. Who would want to shoot both Gil and April? My dad didn't like Gil, didn't respect him. But Dad would never do this. He once told me the only reason he stayed with Gil as partners was because Gil was bringing in business. It was an interesting lesson for me."

"How so?"

"That you can choose to work with someone you don't like. The business world is simply about money. If someone is helping you financially, you put up with them."

"Interesting lesson indeed," I said, growing more and more impressed with Honey Roper.

"Absolutely. But was there anything else you wanted to talk about? I'm going to have to figure out where Dad is and go see him. That's what family does. Be there when they need you, although I'm not sure what I can really do beyond provide moral support."

"Yeah about that," I said with a frown. "There's something else we need to discuss. It's actually the main reason why I'm here."

"What's that?"

"Your dad needs you to bail him out of jail," I said.

Her big blue eyes suddenly grew even wider. "Really? I'm not sure how I'd do that. I don't have that kind of money. I get the feeling Dad's bail is going to run into six figures," she said, and then added wryly, "at least it did last time."

"He's got a plan."

She gave a quick laugh. "That's Dad."

"He told me the title to his house is in a trust. The trust includes both your names."

Honey stopped laughing and gave me a bewildered look. "That's news to me."

"I suppose that might be true," I said. "Anyway, he wants you to use the house as collateral. He said that as co-trustee, you can sign the paperwork. Once that happens, he'll make bail and be released."

She thought about this for a moment. "Okay," she finally said. "I know his personal lawyer, Jack Silverstein. I can have him run the paperwork and I'll sign what I have to sign. Good lord."

"What?"

"My Dad put me on the title to his house and he didn't say anything to me."

"It's strange. When you set up a trust I thought all parties had to sign. Surprise you?"

She stared down at her cup for a long minute. I sensed I had touched something within Honey. She took a deep breath, and then stood up to leave. "No," she said. "I suppose it doesn't. He's forged my name before."

I walked with her out the door and over to her car, a silver Honda Civic. "So let me ask you something. If your dad wasn't involved in all this with Gil, who do you think might have done it?"

In an oddly fascinating way, Honey pushed her lower lip forward in the exact same manner that Gail did when she was thinking deeply. It was adorable and added to Honey's allure. But I had to be careful. If I were 20 years younger, I'd probably start to get smitten. I still might.

"Gil and April had a marriage that was going south," she said. "Gil cheated. I'm sure he always cheated. Guys like him never stop at just flirting. I think there were a few women at the dealership he was involved with. But I know there was one woman in particular, even Dad commented on her once. He said she would have been good for him. She works at his dealership, but I don't think she'll talk to you."

"Why not?"

"On account of she's married. She was his assistant. I think her name might have been Betty."

*

I stayed off the freeways and took Laurel Canyon over the hill and into Hollywood. I didn't bother driving up Lookout Mountain. The forensics team was probably still doing their investigation at the Horne residence.

When I got to the Hollywood Division, it was buzzing. A lot of people were moving around, there seemed to be activity everywhere. I asked for Detective Mulligan but he had not come in yet and my former colleague, Rick Taggart, was still on vacation in Maui. I asked the harried assistant to the chief of detectives if someone could call me today, and that my name was Burnside.

"Did you say Burnside?" she asked, suddenly stopping and focusing on me.

"I did."

"One moment," she said, and picked up the phone. "Mr. Burnside is here ... no, I mean he's right here ... yes, he's standing in front of me."

She moved the phone away from her ear, looked at it oddly and placed it back onto the cradle. "Someone will be right out."

It took only about 10 seconds, which for the LAPD was the equivalent of moving at the speed of light. A tall, well-built man wearing a black shirt and gray tie approached purposefully. He sported a deep tan, and his shiny black hair was combed straight back. He wore a gold shield pinned to his belt, on the left side of the buckle. A Glock 22 was sitting in a holster, clipped on the right side.

"You're Burnside?" he asked.

"Oh yeah. Been Burnside all my life."

He looked at me for a long second. "Follow me," he said brusquely, and turned and walked down the hall without so much as looking back. I suppose it would have been quite easy for me to stop and walk in the other direction, but my interest was now sufficiently piqued.

I trailed him into a nondescript office with a table and two black metal folding chairs. The room was institutional. The bottom portion of the walls were painted dark green, the upper portion were more of a sea green. It looked like neither had been painted in a while. On one side of the room was a window facing an alley. On the other side, a large mirror measuring three feet square hung against the wall. I knew from experience that this was a two-way mirror and there was someone behind it observing and taking notes. They might also be recording the session.

The detective pointed to one of the metal chairs. "Sit," he directed. "I'm Jim Johnson."

"How nice for you."

He looked at me. "Are you going to make this easy or hard?"

"I don't know yet. Are there any other choices?"

He stood up and walked around the table and folded his arms across his chest. He was about 6-foot-2 and looked like he weighed a little over 200 pounds. His face was as placid as his body was solid.

"Tell me what you know about Gilbert Horne."

"He's dead."

Johnson slowly turned his head from side to side. "You're a real smartass. I heard about you. Got kicked off the force a few years ago. Now you're a free agent. Representing scum."

"It's a living."

"That's some living," he sneered. "Cliff Roper is your client? Is that how low you've fallen?"

"I don't choose to look at it that way," I pointed out.

"Oh, and how do you look at taking on a double murderer as your client?"

"He wasn't a murderer when he hired me. And I'm not so sure he is now."

Johnson walked back to the other side of the table and sat down and glared at me for a long minute. Why he stood up in the first place was beyond me. Maybe he thought it added drama to the scene and would make me uncomfortable. If so, he had a lot to learn about me.

"Well let's just take a look at this, shall we?," he snarled. "The Hornes were murdered by someone using a Glock. Their bodies were found in their living room with no trail of blood. The shooter was kind enough to leave the Glock outside the crime scene. We found it in the bushes. When we inspected the gun we ran the serial number and saw it was registered to Cliff Roper."

"And your point is?"

Johnson shook his head. "You need everything spelled out for you?"

"Sure. Spell it out," I retorted. "And while you're at it, did it occur to you how stupid your whole theory is? If it had really been Cliff Roper, leaving the gun behind would have been the dumbest thing in the world for him to do. I'm sure you dusted it for prints, and I'd bet anything that Forensics comes back with nothing. I'm sure it was wiped clean."

"Oh you're sure," he smirked. "We've got this case wrapped up. Just need to put a bow on it."

"What does that mean?"

"It means it's easier to move on with a confession. But your stubborn client would rather risk lethal injection than cooperate and get a sentence of 40 to life."

"Maybe he didn't do it."

"Sure. And pigs fly too. The gun was allegedly stolen out of Roper's safe, but he never filed anything with the police. The Hornes were shot at the other day by a Glock and we found a bullet lodged in the wall. And Roper has no alibi that will hold up. Got any more smart answers?"

"I didn't know pigs could fly. They don't usually move too fast. Especially in this Division."

The sneer on Johnson's face stayed there. "I want to know everything you've got on this case," he said. "You hold anything back and I'll not only pull your license but I'll have you charged as an accessory to murder. You and Roper can grow even friendlier up in San Quentin."

At that point I decided to refrain from making further witty observations. And over the next four hours I explained, in excruciating detail, what my role was in the case, as well as my movements over the past two days. I repeated it again for Johnson, and then two more times for two other detectives. Finally, Johnson walked back into the room.

"Well, hello again," he said sarcastically. "You still comfortable in here? Get you a nice sandwich? Bottle of pop?"

"I'm fine," I lied. They weren't going to bring me anything, so there was no point in letting them think I was getting worn down.

"Been a long morning for you," he said wryly, the hint of a smile crossing his thin lips.

"Sure," I said. "Or is it afternoon by now?"

"It's 2:30," he smiled. "Don't worry, I'm your last stop of the day. Anything more you care to disclose here? Before you're in so deep that you can't get out?"

"Nope," I answered. "But like I told you earlier, the only thing Roper did was hire me to find out who took a shot at the Hornes last week. It wasn't altruistic, and I know Roper was a person of interest. He had a breakup with Horne and he wanted to dissolve their partnership. Came at a bad time for Horne, he owed money on what was probably gambling debts. And his car dealership wasn't doing well. He lived in the fast lane, but a lot of what he lived on was borrowed. Not unusual. Not in L.A."

"Sure," he said. "But you have to recognize that the reason for Roper's arrest is that we have evidence. And a motive. And a murder weapon."

I stared at him for a long moment. "When you think it through, do you really believe it made any sense for Roper to take this action now? He knew the police were targeting him, that they had identified him as a possible suspect in the shooting last week, that they knew the gun used was the same as the one he had owned. It would have been insane for him to move forward and do this."

"You know the routine," he said. "You were on the job for a long time. Great reputation I hear. Well, until the end anyways."

I gave him a look. "Okay, you read my file, you did your homework. I had a bad time of it in the end. The department suspended me. And when I got exonerated, well, things changed. I wasn't willing to play by the rules any more. Sure, that attitude got me kicked off the force. But it also set me on a new path, one where I wasn't going to take the easy way out just because it was expedient."

"What would you have done?"

I looked at Johnson and then took a look at the two way mirror and spoke to the mirror. "I'd have done some good detective work, because that's what I was paid to do. What I wouldn't have done is take the easy route just because it's there."

Johnson tried to nod sympathetically. It wasn't easy for him. Being nice didn't come naturally to most cops. I knew that from personal experience. "Your prints are all over the Horne's house," he said.

I rubbed the bridge of my nose. "Again, that was because I was there yesterday morning, talking to April."

"And you came back in the afternoon just to sit in your vehicle and watch the house."

"Yes," I said, not liking at all where this was headed.

"You would understand how we might wonder about your involvement here."

"And I'd have to be a really stupid assassin to visit the victims' house multiple times in one day before going inside and pulling the trigger on both of them."

"You're insisting Roper's innocent. Maybe he is. Maybe you're not."

"And maybe," I sneered, "you ought to come back with some concrete proof, rather than some half-baked innuendo."

"You made a good point a few minutes ago."

"I'm sure I did."

He ignored the crack and continued. "You said we should do some more detective work."

"No," I reminded him, that cantankerous feeling rising back to the surface. "I said you should do some *good* detective work. I'm not sure you know the difference."

Johnson gave an ugly laugh. "You've got a big mouth. But we're letting you go. For the time being that is. And yes. That's only because we don't have anything concrete on you just yet. Maybe your client will throw you under the bus after we finish grilling him. But if I were you, I'd come clean now rather than later. You got anything to tell us, it's in your best interest to put it on the table early."

The only thing I wanted to put on the table was Johnson's head with my fist bearing down on it. Instead I told him I had nothing further to share. And as I left, I thought about the wisdom of taking this case and began to feel as if someone had handed me a stick of dynamite with the fuse lit.

Nine

I found myself leaving the Hollywood Division a little hungry, so I absently bought a sandwich from a vending machine on the way out. I took two bites and kicked myself for not remembering how bad the food was there. Tossing the remainder in a trash bin, I climbed into my Pathfinder and thought about my day thus far.

The Horner murder case was SOP for the police, standard operating procedure. Take the easy way out, find the path of least resistance. By charging Roper, they'd wiped a double murder off their plate and handed it over to the City Attorney for prosecuting. Whether the City Attorney was actually able to move forward successfully was of little concern to them. What was important was that it looked like they had quickly solved a crime. If the prosecution failed to convict Roper, that was their problem.

So all of a sudden, my investigation was no longer limited to my client, Cliff Roper. I was now faced with the need to exonerate myself from any wrongdoing. My thoughts drifted first to Johnny Cleary's beautiful Palos Verdes home, and then to the even more palatial estate of his neighbors, the Wades. I began to wonder about my career choices. I worked as hard as anyone, but while they lived in the lap of luxury, I lived in a rent controlled apartment. It wasn't too late to try a new line of work, but making a radical career change just to earn more money was a dubious move.

I struggled to change the focus of my thoughts. Sometimes when I distance myself from a knotty problem for a while, creativity blossoms and fresh thinking begins to take shape. And with that, I recognized I needed to pay some attention to Harold Stevens' case, that of the questionable burglary victim, Noreen Giles. I checked her address and discovered she lived only about a mile from the Hollywood Division. It seemed like a good stop before I went back to Santa Monica.

Will and Noreen Giles lived on a tree-lined street near Melrose Avenue. It was a nice enough neighborhood, albeit nothing fancy. This was a slice of old L.A., wedged between the wealthy Hancock Park zip code featuring stately manors, and an inner-city working class neighborhood lined with rundown apartment buildings. Hancock Park was one of L.A.'s toniest neighborhoods, and had numerous Tudor-style homes and well-maintained properties. The street the Giles lived on was more pedestrian, with older, smaller homes that were nicely kept up, built back in the 1920s. Their house was beige with a red Spanish tile roof. A sign promoting GSL Security Systems was hammered into the lawn. The sign was wrinkled and weather-beaten, and it looked like it had been there for quite a while.

I rang the doorbell and a nicely dressed, middle-aged woman with shoulder-length auburn hair appeared. She was wearing slacks and a white top, nothing special except for a stunning emerald necklace that draped her neck.

"May I help you?" she asked pleasantly.

"Hi," I said. "My name's Burnside. I'm an investigator working with the Differential Insurance Company. I'm looking for a Mrs. Giles."

"Oh yes," she exclaimed, and motioned with her hand. "Come in."

Unlike the reception I received at the Hollywood Division, this was a nice change of pace. Noreen Giles ushered me into the living room, where she had me sit down on a green leather couch and offered me some coffee. The room was small but nicely appointed. The taupe carpeting appeared new, and a pair of crystal lamps sat on pecan end tables on either side of the couch. A couple of small chairs were situated in each corner.

"No thanks. I've reached my limit for the day. Anything more than six cups and I get too jittery."

"I'm a coffee addict," she bragged. "I drink it all day long. Even before bed. Doesn't affect my sleep."

"I've heard about people like you. I'm envious," I said, at the same time wondering what the point was of drinking regular coffee right before you went to sleep.

"It's interesting," she said. "It gets me going through the day, but by nighttime I get a serenity that's very nice."

"You're one of the lucky ones," I commented, knowing that caffeine was a drug and we were both addicted, just with different levels of tolerance.

"Oh yes," she gushed. "I know. Lucky indeed. So what is it you need from me today?"

"Just a routine follow up. Why don't you tell me about the burglary you had here."

"Not much to tell," she said. "It was daytime, we were gone, it happened sometime between 10 a.m. and 2 p.m. We were at work. They smashed the sliding glass door in the back. They took our TV and sound system, a few paintings from the walls, a little cash, and of course, all the jewelry. They seemed to know right where it was."

"Where was the jewelry?"

"I had it hidden in a shoe box in the walk-in closet. I must have 50 boxes of shoes, but they went through each and every one of them. They took it all too. Some really lovely pieces. A couple were heirlooms, been in the family for generations. Irreplaceable."

"You should check some of the local pawn shops," I suggested.

"I have. Nothing's come up."

"Can you show me the sliding glass door where they entered the premises?" I asked, standing up.

"Of course," she responded and I followed her down a narrow hall, highlighted by a low, curved archway. The house was indeed older, probably built close to a hundred years ago. There was no central heating, just a furnace in the middle of the house, tucked away inside a closet, and connected to a few floor vents nearby.

Mrs. Giles led me into a small back room which was furnished with a desk and a credenza and a filing cabinet. Everything was neat and tidy. The replacement glass had already been installed, and not by the best craftsman. As I opened and closed it, the sliding door did not feel like it was rolling properly on the rails; a rattling sound was evident, and the glass itself was not flush with the frame.

"I noticed you had a sign for a security company out front. Do you still use them?"

"No. It's been there a while, before we moved in. We just started living here this year, since January. My husband and I are realtors, and business has been slow. We should have signed up with the security company, but you know, hindsight is 20-20."

"I'm sure it is," I said, recalling a coarse joke about how hindsight may indeed be 20-20, but it's hard to look through that little hole.

"So," I said, "they smashed the glass door, came in, took the items and exited the same way."

"Yes. Very simple."

"Any witnesses? Neighbors?"

"No, not a one. No one heard a thing. My guess is they used a baseball bat wrapped in a towel. Keeps the sound down. It's the smashing of glass that gets people's attention."

My eyebrows shot up. "Why do you say that?"

"Oh, well, I don't know for sure, mind you. Just a guess. I heard that's how burglars work," she said, suddenly apprehensive about details. "I think I read about it in a magazine."

"Sure," I said. "But I must say that's a lot of expensive jewelry to have around the house. Even it were hidden in a safe."

"Oh, I know, isn't it? But well, I'm in real estate, just like my husband. We sometimes have to show off a bit to let clients think we're successful. That's the main reason I kept it handy. To wear it."

"The image can be the reality for some people," I remarked.

"Oh, that's so true!" she cried. "Especially in this town. If you look successful, people just assume you really *are* successful. Who has the time to investigate?"

I responded by smiling. One person in particular had the time.

"So do you see any problem with getting our claim processed quickly?" she asked, smiling back at me.

I gave her a noncommittal answer, mostly because I didn't have a good answer. "Quickly is hard to say, that's up to the claims people, you know how they operate. But nothing here seems out of the ordinary."

"Oh, good. You know getting burglarized is quite traumatizing. We just moved in here and we're wondering if we should even stay."

"Where are you from?"

"Nebraska. We moved here years ago when the real estate market was hot. We figured we'd take advantage of it. You know, make hay while the sun shines. But we're actually thinking of going back to Omaha after this. Too many lean years."

"Understood," I said, and we started walking to the front door. "Big cities have their share of crime. I'll file my report, although I may need to come back for a few more questions."

"That's no problem. It's better if you call first, I'll make sure Will's home too."

I rarely set appointments when I was investigating. Seeing people when they least expected it was a good way to gauge things. "By the way," I said as I was leaving, "that's a gorgeous necklace you have on. I guess the thieves didn't get that one. Is it emerald?"

Noreen Giles opened her mouth in surprise for a moment. "Oh," she exclaimed. "No. This isn't emerald. Costume jewelry. Just looks like the real thing."

I smiled at her as I walked off. "Sometimes that's almost as good. Maybe even better."

"How's that?"

"Most people can't tell the difference. And you don't have to worry about it getting stolen."

She gave me a long look and swallowed hard. "Good point."

*

My route back home took me past Pink's Hot Dogs. I briefly thought of stopping there for lunch, but the combination of a long line and a less-than-healthy meal convinced me to keep driving. I went back to my office first, and figured I'd grab something nearby. But as I approached the door, there was a hulking figure waiting outside in the hallway. He was big, blond and didn't look happy.

"May I help you?" I asked.

"I'm looking for Burnside."

"You found him. Who are you?"

"I'm Ted Wade. I hear you've been looking into me."

I opened the door and we sat down. I moved behind my desk; Ted Wade sat in a chair I had bought from a former neighbor who was evicted for not paying his rent. The chair had looked comfortable at the time, but clients told me it wasn't very cushy. I opened the bottom desk drawer and left it open. Inside was a .38 special.

"What I've been looking into," I began, "is the shooting incident at the Horne residence. It's now morphed into murder."

"Why were you talking to my mother?" he asked, ignoring what I had just told him.

"Because you weren't home."

Ted Wade thought about this and nodded slowly. He was dressed in white pants and a bright blue Hawaiian shirt. His shoulders were broad, his thick arms were large and muscular, and his hands were big. His jaw was square and even his face looked solid.

"I'd like you to stay away from my parents," he said.

I gave him the once over. "I don't know that I'll need to talk with them any further," I said. "You, however, are another matter entirely."

A look of confusion flashed across his face. "Why do you want to talk to me?"

"You're Gilbert Horne's nephew," I remind him. "He was your agent. You introduced him to other football players who became his clients. These players were upset with how your uncle was representing them. He cost them money. So someone tried to shoot him the other night and yesterday someone killed him. That's why I need to talk with you."

"Oh. Have you found out anything?"

"Just that there were a number of people who had beef with him."

"Who hired you in the first place?"

"That's confidential," I said, starting to wonder who was going to be asking all the questions here. "But why don't you tell me about your uncle. You helped him sign some of your teammates at Oregon."

Ted Wade rubbed his eyes and looked tired. "All I did was make the introduction. Patrick and Oscar were the big fish. They were the two who hit it big in the NFL. They're just crying because they're not grabbing every last dime they could. My uncle negotiated great deals for them when they got drafted. He also helped a few other guys out, Ricky Catalano, our strong safety, Tony Clifford, our kicker. There were more. But most guys don't last long in the NFL. It's super competitive. Sometimes you make one mistake and that's it. Or you get injured and you're out."

"I thought the teams don't cut guys if they're injured. Part of the union contract."

"Unions," he said derisively. "They don't do squat except collect dues. The teams get around that rule by helping a player rehab from their injury as quickly as possible. Then they cut them."

"Got it," I said. "Does Catalano or Clifford live in L.A.?"

"Catalano lives in Orange County."

"And Clifford?"

"Lives up north. Heard he owns a pot farm. Typical kicker, real weirdo."

"Okay," I said, smiling to myself. Kickers were never full-fledged members of a football team; their roles were very different and their skill sets unique. The best football players were big, strong and fast; the best kickers were often short, slender, and not especially athletic.

"You really think a football player did this?" Wade asked.

"I dunno, kid. I really don't. These guys were angry and they had motive. But so did some other people. Your uncle had money problems. And women problems."

Ted's eyes lit up. "Who?"

I looked past him. "Can't say. But it sounds like more than a few. And the fact that his wife was also killed makes this case even more complex."

"Yeah," he said. "The only one who'd have wanted to kill April was probably Uncle Gil."

"Why's that?"

"They had a bad marriage."

"So I heard. But that's usually fixed by divorce, not murder."

Ted's mouth tightened. "I'd like to hire you," he said.

I frowned. "To do what?"

"To find out who did this."

"I'm already hired, kid. I'm working the case."

"Yeah, but I want you working for me."

"Can't do it," I said, shaking my head. "Conflict of interest."

"What do you charge? I'll pay you double your rate."

As much as I'd have liked to get paid multiple times for working the same case, this was not really kosher. And something smelled more than a little funny here. Nephew of the deceased, friendly with players who detested his uncle, and a substance abuse problem did not mix well. And then I thought of Gail and the cost of our upcoming wedding. And then I thought back to my own code of ethics.

"I'll tell you what, kid. I'm not going to take you on as a client, so you don't have to pay me. But if you want to help me unravel this case, you can tell me everything you know about Patrick Washington, Oscar Romeo, Gil's other clients, whoever might be of interest here. Anyone you know who came into contact with your uncle. Anyone who might have anything to do with what happened. Deal?"

Ted looked confused, and more than a little hesitant about agreeing to snitch on his friends. But I think he knew that anything besides acquiescing would raise red flags about him.

"I guess so," he finally managed. "But just don't talk to my parents again, okay?"

I smiled and didn't say anything. Or agree to his request. I had the odd feeling that I had better start carrying my .38 special with me on a regular basis. I also had the feeling the Wades might indeed get another visit from me. If for no other reason than to find out how one can become a high-level executive and retire in P.V. with a large, ocean-view home.

Ten

It had been another long and trying afternoon. I attempted to get on Duncan Whitestone's calendar today at Bay City Motor Cars, but was only able to secure an appointment for the next morning. Betty was extremely upset on the phone and there was nothing I could say to her that would make the pain of losing Gil go away. I tried to assure her that justice would prevail, but that was of little consolation. When someone you care about is taken from you so suddenly, little else is important. Hanging up, I thought about the people I cared about, and startlingly I found my thoughts drifting to the lovely Honey Roper. I quickly decided that these thoughts needed to go in another direction. Since I never got around to eating lunch. I called Gail to see if she was up for an early dinner tonight. Comfort food was on my mind.

"I think I need a better idea of how you define comfort food, *amigo*," she said.

"How do *you* define it?"

"Growing up it was meat loaf and mashed potatoes. Mom had it down to a science. And apple pie for dessert. Once I was in college, good meat loaf was hard to find. Comfort food became hot wings."

"Sounds like you were a real rebel."

I could feel her grin through the phone line. "You have no idea," she said.

"Well let's see. Hot wings doesn't do it for me. How does Chinese food sound?" I asked.

"Is that really your comfort food?"

I thought for a moment. It used to be, but that was back when L.A. had a lot of old-style Chinese restaurants. Good cashew chicken, chow fun noodles and velvet shrimp were getting harder and harder to find these days. In fact, my favorite Chinese restaurant was located downtown, and the last thing I felt like doing was battle traffic for an hour each way. For comfort food.

"How about a hamburger and a beer?" I asked.

"That sounds like my guy," she said, her smile still shining through the phone.

"I'll meet you at Father's Office. How about 6 p.m.?"

"Well all right then."

Every neighborhood should have a place like Father's Office. Many years ago, it was a dive bar along a quiet strip of Montana Avenue. It derived its name from Prohibition days, when some men who were en route to a speakeasy would tell their families they were going to work. Over the years, this dive bar transformed into a very hip tavern, featuring a myriad of craft beers and gourmet dishes.

The crown jewel on the Father's Office menu was the hamburger, dry aged and grilled perfectly. It was nestled in a bed of caramelized onions, gruyere cheese and bacon, all on a soft roll. It may not have been made as lovingly as my future mother-in-law's meat loaf, but it was a perfect gastronomic invention. And the added benefit was that it was just six blocks from my apartment. Our apartment.

I arrived a few minutes before Gail and secured a table near the bar. Some nice upgrades to the decor had been made over the years, but the low lighting maintained a dark ambience. Ordering an icy Sierra Nevada pale ale, I'd taken a few sips when I noticed my beautiful *fiancée* had presented herself in the doorway. Before she could enter however, the bouncer insisted on seeing her ID. It took a few moments of hunting through her purse before she could find it and join me.

"Well, that was awkward," she said, sitting down and looking splendid in a black pantsuit and a white top. Her chestnut brown hair fell a good six inches past her shoulders.

"I would think it'd be quite flattering," I smiled. "You still can pass for a teenager."

"At 31, I do believe I'd prefer to pass for a grown woman."

"It is uncanny," I said, taking another sip of ale, "how such a poised, professional woman can still maintain such a youthful persona."

Gail smiled her million-dollar smile. "For a tough guy, you have quite a way with words."

"I haven't been so tough lately. In fact, it's been quite a while since I engaged in any fisticuffs."

"And I'd like to say how proud I am of you. I can only hope it stays that way."

I shrugged. "I'll do my best. But just so you know, nothing lasts forever."

"You're not hard-wired to fight people. And your ability to use words rather than violence will serve you well. Especially as you get older."

"I'm glad you noticed my ability to speak extemporaneously."

Gail threw back her head and laughed. "Of course I did. That's one of the things I admire about you. You're strong, but you're smart too. You know a lot of big words and you know how to use them. I met a lot of smart men in law school and I meet more of them now at the office. Men who are very glib. Plenty of them work out and they stay in good shape. But a lot of their toughness is bravado. They're physically strong, but when you push through that emotional layer, they often have the fortitude of a wet paper napkin."

"Don't tell me you dated other men when you were away at law school."

She gave a half-smile, which was still extraordinarily appealing. Her soft gray eyes had a twinkle in them, the kind a mischievous little girl might display. "I admit I went out with a few guys. You and I weren't engaged back then. And the separation was an extraordinary test for us."

"And ... "

"And nothing, *senor*. I dated a bit but it rarely got past the first date stage. And I did not have any affairs or anything else your wild imagination is going to conjure up."

"Okay," I smiled. "I'm not asking you for anything here."

"No?"

"Well ... maybe a little reassurance."

"And you? Men are the ones more known for straying."

I held up my hands. "My heart was pure when you were away."

"That's good," she said. "I'll think about whether I want to believe you."

I smiled some more and drank some more ale. There were a lot of benefits to having a really smart, savvy woman in my life. The downsides occurred when they shined that intellectual high beam on you. I excused myself and went over and bought Gail a Sierra Nevada of her own and then ordered cheeseburgers from the bar. I was familiar enough with the chef's rules for customers, so I didn't bother to ask for any changes to how the burgers were prepared. On my first visit here, I asked them to hold the bacon but was told the chef doesn't do that and they suggested I order something else. Lesson learned. Two gooey cheeseburgers arrived about 15 minutes later, just in time for another round of ale.

"You know, we have to set aside some time for wedding planning," Gail said.

"All right," I agreed. "Anything in particular?"

"You'll like this part. Tasting wedding cakes. And also tasting *hors d'oeuvres* for the reception."

"That sounds like fun."

"It will be. Not everything about planning a wedding is hard work."

"Good to know," I said, having resigned myself to letting Gail have the green light to do pretty much anything she wanted. I decided that there would probably be a few things I'd need to draw a line in the sand on and not budge. But for the most part, I had observed that good marriages worked best when the wife got her way most of the time. Sexist as that might sound, it struck me as the best path to follow.

"So tell me about your day, sweetie," she said, as she looked around the table for something.

"What do you need?" I asked.

"Just ketchup."

"Unfortunately they don't allow it in here," I said, picking up my burger and taking a bite. "Chef's rules."

Gail gave a sad smile. "All right. When in Rome," she said, and dug in herself. Smiling and nodding at the same time signaled that she could live without the ketchup.

"It's important to be open to new ways of doing things," I said.

"Indeed."

"So you've seen the headlines about Gilbert Horne I take it."

"And heard about it at the office. That's what everyone was talking about today."

"What does the City Attorney's office think about their case?"

Gail put her burger down. "You know I can't discuss that with you," she said.

"All right, I'll do the talking."

"That works for me."

"I met with Roper's daughter this morning and she's arranging bail."

"Already done. Roper's out."

I smiled to myself. No surprise that Honey Roper moved quickly. "And I spent the better part of the day with the distinguished detectives at the Hollywood Division. It seems they have this idea that a certain smartass private investigator had something to do with the double murder."

Gail's eyes widened. "You've got to be kidding."

"Nope. Apparently they are wondering why I was identified a number of times yesterday at the Horne residence. And why April Horne had my business card in her possession. And why I was representing Cliff Roper."

"Circumstantial evidence," she said. "They have nothing. It sounds like they're just fishing."

"It also sounds like they themselves may have some doubts about Cliff Roper's involvement. They wouldn't admit it, but finding Roper's gun at the crime scene is just a little too convenient. The key issue here is who broke into Roper's safe and took his gun with them."

"Inside job."

"In some ways, absolutely. But that still doesn't rule out a professional here. And the person who was most likely to have the combination to the safe was Gilbert Horne himself. At first I thought this could be a murder-suicide case, but neither Gil nor April's prints were on the gun. Neither were wearing gloves. And the gun itself was found outside the house, away from the crime scene."

"So someone took the gun off of Horne."

"Or he gave it to them for some reason," I added.

"And where does that leave you?"

I took another big bite of my cheeseburger, chewed slowly, washed it down with some more ale and then smiled at my lovely *fiancée*. Everyone has their own comfort foods and this burger was one of mine. I hoped it would also become one of Gail's. The more things a couple can share with each other, the stronger their bond can become. And the stronger their bond, the better their relationship. I had read somewhere that the best relationships were those where the window between a couple and the outside world was raised, but the window between the couple themselves was always down. Gail and I worked in a similar field and that was bound to cause a conflict at some point. How maturely we dealt with that would help determine how much of a window would exist between us.

"I'll be fine. I have an alibi for where I was at the time of the murder last night."

Gail smiled that extraordinary smile again. "Indeed you do."

"And someone might inquire about that at some point."

"I'll be happy to testify on your behalf," she said, playfully. "I have intimate knowledge regarding your whereabouts. Although I may need to be discreet about your exact position."

Eleven

While it was still the end of April in Southern California, we had already entered that period called May Gray, which would soon evolve into June Gloom. The morning skies were dim and overcast, as the marine layer continued to throw its cloud cover across the region. Over the next two months this pattern would be repeated, and the sun would usually burn its way through by the afternoon, doing so earlier and earlier. But for now, the mornings were depressing. The mood did not get any better when I walked into the offices of Bay City Motor Cars.

Betty Luttinger was seated at her desk, working on the computer, and didn't notice me until I was standing in front of her.

"Good morning," I said, clearing my throat.

"Oh yes, Mr. Burnside," she jumped, and turned suddenly toward me. "Mr. Whitestone is in conference at the moment. Please have a seat."

I glanced over at the pair of uncomfortable looking chairs nearby and decided to stand. "How are you holding up here?"

She sighed a deep sigh. "It's been very hard. Everyone is in shock. It's so sad. You see these types of things on the news all the time, and you just never believe they'll happen to someone you know."

"I'm sure it's been painful."

"Gil had his demons, but he wasn't a bad man. He just couldn't say no to certain things. He had one of those personalities."

"Any thoughts as to who it might have been?"

She pulled out a tissue. "Ordinarily I would have thought his wife. And I think it still might be related to her. She was fooling around with some guy. A football player."

I stared at her. "You know who that was?"

"No," she said. "Someone had mentioned it."

"Really?"

"Well ... someone at the dealership knew about it," she said quickly, almost too quickly. "I heard about it through the grapevine."

At that moment, the office door opened and two men emerged. One had white hair and was dressed in a finely tailored gray suit with a burgundy club tie. The other wore khakis and a short sleeve shirt, light blue, with narrow maroon stripes intersecting and forming a box pattern. His arms were the size of tree trunks, and hairy as an ape's. I approached the man in the nice gray suit.

"Mr. Whitestone?"

"Yes," he replied.

"The name's Burnside. I'm hoping to have a few minutes of your time."

He looked at me evenly. "Is this about Gil?" he inquired.

"It is."

"I see. Ike, can you give me a few minutes?"

The man with the big hairy arms said of course. "I'm Isaac Vale by the way." He stuck out a massive hand and I shook it, regretting it instantly. I checked to see if I still had any bones intact in my fingers.

"You have a mighty good grip there," I commented, making a fist and releasing it. "I don't think I'd want to get in the ring with you."

He smiled. "Thanks. I run the service department. Still have to get my hands dirty sometimes. Keeps me fit."

"Any relation to Christy Vale?" I asked.

"Yeah, that cutie's my wife. How do you know her?"

"I was in here a few days ago. She tried to sell me a Porsche."

Isaac Vale laughed and shook his head. "Yup. That's Christy. She's a great salesperson."

"I could tell."

"I sometimes have to remind her to stop selling all the time. That not everyone is a prospect."

That was certainly true for me. It would be quite a while before I could come to close to affording one of these vehicles. Especially if they were expecting me to pay six figures for a car with no back seat and a tiny trunk.

Duncan Whitehead spoke. "Why don't we take this into my office. Betty, hold my calls."

We moved inside his spacious executive-style office, replete with a large desk and two comfy looking chairs facing it. There was a couch off to one side and a flat screen TV mounted on the wall. The TV was turned to The

Golf Channel. The walls were wood-paneled and there were no windows. While the indirect lighting made his office rather dark, a bright lamp next to his laptop made the desk practically glow. Not that it was necessary. Duncan Whitestone's desktop was clean and bereft of anything that looked like work, save for a gold pen stand and a gold letter tray with a grand total of one sheet of paper sitting in it.

"So I'm not sure how I can assist you, Mr. Burnside. I told the police everything I know about Gil. Which honestly isn't that much regarding this ... incident. And I understand they've already made an arrest."

"Yes, but I'm not sure that arrest is going to stick. Let me ask you something," I said, trying to steer the conversation. "How did you originally meet Gilbert Horne?"

He smiled paternally. "My previous partner, Coleman, sold his share of the dealership to him. Cole was having financial problems."

I took notice of the minor detail he omitted, the part about losing his share of the dealership in a card game. "I understand that Gil was having some money problems too."

"Lately, yes. A few years ago he was flying high. But cars are an up-and-down business, especially these luxury models. We do great when the economy is hot, we take a beating when there's a downturn. Not everyone can weather the storm."

"So you were aware of Gil's financial situation."

"We were partners. Of course."

"How was he planning to get out from under this?"

Whitestone shrugged. "Can't say as he had a fully formed plan. He wanted me to buy out his share of the dealership, but that was problematic. The value of the lot has gone down along with the economy. And my own financial situation isn't great right now. I couldn't bail him out."

"What options did he have?"

"Not many, unfortunately. Gil had been tapping into the equity from his home, so that was off the table. In fact he was even having trouble meeting his mortgage payments. His sports agency wasn't generating the income it used to. Plus he was having problems with his partner over there. That Roper fellow, the one the police apprehended."

"Did you know Cliff Roper?"

"I met him a few times, he leases his cars through us. Or used to, I guess. Now we'll probably have to repossess them if he goes off to prison. Never was my type of guy. Untrustworthy. Nothing that comes out of that guy's mouth ever struck me as believable. I, uh, wouldn't put anything past him."

"Any of Gil's clients come in here to do business? Football players?"

"Sure. In fact those guys were actually keeping him afloat lately. Some of his clients get their vehicles through us. And of course Gil got the commission, even though he's a partner here."

I had an idea. "Let me run a few names by you. See if they mean anything. Ted Wade?"

"Yup, he got his Porsche Boxster here."

"Patrick Washington?"

"Oh yeah. Can't miss that guy. It's like seeing a circus freak walk in. We called him Twins because his body was big enough to hold two people."

"That's funny," I said without smiling. I'm sure Patrick would be pleased to know this. People to whom he paid a small fortune were snickering and calling him names behind his back. "Patrick wasn't buying sports cars, was he?"

"Sure was."

"He's such a big guy. How'd he fit in them?"

"He'd buy two. Then we'd send them out to a shop that would cut them into pieces and then build a front seat he could fit into. Then they'd weld it all back together."

I smiled. When you had enough money you could do almost anything. "How about Oscar Romeo?"

"Sure, Oscar and his Lamborghinis," he smiled.

"He has more than one?"

"No, he just gets a new one every year or two. Trades in his old one. One of our best clients. In fact, he stopped by the other day to look at this year's models. Quite an outgoing guy. And he knows cars. Everyone on the lot loves Oscar."

"Anyone ever have a beef with Gil?"

Duncan Whitestone pursed his lips at this sudden change in direction and hesitated. He looked down at his empty desk. "Not that I can recall."

"That's not exactly a solid answer."

"I can't say anything more," he said standing up, indicating our time was running out. "Other than Gil's personal life spilled over into his business life. Never a good mix."

"Mr. Whitestone," I said, standing up myself. "If there's anything you know that would help us in this investigation, now is the time to say it."

"Mr. Burnside, I think I've told you enough. More than enough, really."

Twelve

I had turned off the ringer of my phone before I entered the dealership, and saw I now had a voice mail message. The message was from Cliff Roper. He said he wanted to see me at his office. Now.

Ordinarily, having my own P.I. agency meant I didn't need to kowtow to anyone. The absence of a boss had been one of the big upsides to my job. But the downsides included an inconsistent stream of income, so in a sense, anyone who hired me became my boss. And if someone who hired me happened to pay me an upfront premium in cash, they were sometimes given license to become my *demanding* boss.

Cliff Roper's offices were located on Sunset Boulevard, in an area that had become urbanized over the years. His sports agency was located on the 25th floor of a high-rise tower, one that looked plush and impressive. As I exited the elevator, even the air smelled better. I approached his latest cupcake receptionist, handed her my business card and said that Cliff was expecting me.

"Oh yes," she squealed. "Mr. Roper said to bring you right in!"

I smiled at her exuberance and followed her. She practically skipped down the tiled hallway and ushered me into his office, closing the door behind me. Roper was on the phone in mid-conversation. Or perhaps in mid-monologue.

"Kid, I've been on the phone with Dallas and they've got you down as their 4th round pick. They're not penciling you in, they're putting you in in ink, kid. I said Ink! Dallas is perfect for you, their tight end is getting old and his backup's a putz ... yeah, yeah, you'll get a signing bonus no matter what. Hey don't worry, I'm looking out for you."

Roper finally noticed yours truly and motioned for me to take a seat at his conference table. I listened to him wax rhapsodic as I gazed out at the smoggy view of Beechwood Canyon.

"Okay kid, don't stop your workout regimen, there's OTAs next month and you need to be ready ... how do I know what OTA stands for? Look, all you need to know is it means spring training camp. Me? I'm good, don't worry about me, you worry about you. Yeah, I'll talk to you, bye ... Hey Burnside, let me just take this last call ... Jalen, great to hear from you, buddy. No, no, that stuff in the papers was all a big mistake, it's bullshit, we're taking care of it. Mistaken identity ... Ha! You been there too? Yeah, the government, man, you nailed it, they can't get anything right. Hey, I literally just got off the phone with Miami, they have you on the board, but they know you're a sleeper, so they're holding their powder. You're looking like a 5th rounder, 6th at the latest. You're gonna love South Beach, the pussy there's the best in the world ... I'm excited for you too. Keep pumping that iron, you gotta be at your best when they bring you in next month for OTAs. Yeah, sure, when I know something, you'll know something. See ya."

"Well, look who finally turned up!" he exclaimed, taking off his headset and walking over to me.

I smiled. With Roper there was not much more one could do. "I just got your message," I said. "You only called me an hour ago."

"Time is money, my friend. I've been doing damage control all morning. The NFL draft is right around the corner and the timing of this crap is terrible. I have to talk to every single client and reassure them."

"Sounds like you have a bunch of guys about to get drafted."

"Drafted my ass," he snorted. "Most of these guys are going the free agent route. If they get drafted it'll be a miracle. Yeah, yeah, I know, I'm telling 'em they're on the board for sure, and one or two of them might actually slip in. But the rest won't. It's a numbers game. Only seven rounds in the draft, so only a couple hundred players get picked. My job is to place them as free agents with the clubs where they've got some chance of sticking, even if it's just on special teams. Most of them will get cut, but a couple always seem to make the roster. I gotta keep their spirits up. You believe this? Strongest guys in the world and they're the most insecure wusses you can imagine."

"You have anyone that might go in the first few rounds?"

"I got one kid out of Stanford, a left tackle who may go. But when the NFL hears Stanford, they think he's too smart or too soft. Teams are always looking for dirt on guys, any scuttlebutt that makes them nervous about picking them. I gotta convince them otherwise."

"Good thing you've got a golden tongue."

"Yeah, yeah, that may not be enough this year. I'm heading down to the spring game at USC on Saturday to check out next year's crop. Got to plan for the future. There were a couple of seniors I was about to poach from another agent, but then this nonsense with Horne comes up. Guys are worried I may go to jail. The draft is next weekend so no one's going to move around until this crap gets worked out. And that means you doing your job properly."

"Which is?" I asked, eyebrows raised.

"Getting me off the hook."

"Ah, that part of the job."

"Yeah, yeah. I hear the cops hauled you in for questioning too. What'd you tell them?"

"Not much to tell," I said. "They were mostly interested in why I was spending so much time outside Horne's property the other day. I spoke with April in the morning and then came back later in the day to monitor the house. I saw Gil and April come back."

Roper's face tightened. "You saw Gil? What'd he say to you?"

"Nothing, I didn't have the chance. He immediately got into it with April and they were arguing in the driveway. Then April jumped back in her car and peeled off. Gil marched into the house."

"You didn't talk to him?" he asked incredulously.

"I tried. He didn't answer the doorbell. Ten minutes of leaning on it. *Nada.*"

"So what? You couldn't have just up and left?"

"I wasn't going to spend all night there."

"Considering what happened, you probably should have," he said, pointing a finger at me. "I'm paying you a lot of dough."

"And I'm trying to earn it," I said evenly. "If I knew the two of them were going to be shot to death later that evening, then yes, I think maybe I would have stuck around. But I don't have psychic powers."

"Yeah, yeah. Everyone's got an excuse," he said disgustedly, looking out the window. "So tell me what you got this week. Who do you think popped him?"

I took a deep breath. Talking with Roper made me feel like I was always coming up for air. "Right now we're looking at three areas," I said. "Gambling debts, angry football players, jealous women. All of those are on the table."

"Tell me something I don't know. Horne would bet on when a light would turn red. One time I was leaving for the airport and he hands over 10 bucks and asks me to stop at one of those Mutual of Omaha kiosks. Wanted me to take out a life insurance policy, three hundred grand payout if my plane goes down. Wanted me to name him the beneficiary of course. What a degenerate."

"That sounds like a losing bet."

"You think? I just used his 10 bucks to tip the skycap."

"Definitely a better idea," I agreed. "Tell me something. What do you know about Ted Wade?"

"Horne's nephew? He helped Horne get most of his clients. Played a little bit in the league, but he wasn't cut out for it. Hey, I didn't even consider Ted. He might be in on this, you think?"

"Not sure. But the more I dig, the more I start to wonder."

"Ted's a stoner and he's got mental problems. His dad's a piece of work too. Thought he was grooming the kid for the NFL, but all he did was mess up his head. You hold the reigns too tight, the horse is going to buck after a while."

"You knew him well?"

"I know everyone well," Roper said with a dismissive wave of the hand. "Who else you got?"

"There's a woman at his dealership. Betty Luttinger, his assistant. I think you know Gil was having a fling with her."

"Of course I knew that. Everyone at the dealership knew that. Half the Westside knew that. The problem here is that Betty Luttinger wouldn't kill a cricket. Much less Horne. That's one of her problems. She'll suffer in silence. Some people are like that."

That's some problem, I thought to myself. "What do you mean suffer in silence?"

"Betty was in love with him. Don't ask me why. She was probably good for him too. If he had half a brain, he'd have dumped that gold digging whore he was married to and tied the knot with Betty. But my partner unfortunately didn't have half a brain."

"There were other women, also."

"Who?"

"I'm just starting to dissect that part. He met some of them at the Seaside. Don't have names yet, they seemed to come and go."

"Uh-huh, look. This is all great stuff, my ex-partner was a horny bastard who'd sleep with anything that moved, but I think his situation had to do with money," Roper declared. "Or the lack thereof. I think you need to focus on his gambling debts. You find that big gorilla from A&M? Brendan Webster?"

"No," I said, pointing out, "you wouldn't tell me who he works for."

Roper hesitated. "Look these guys are no-nonsense. If they find out it was me who passed their names on to someone in law enforcement, they won't be happy campers."

"So what? Don't tell me Cliff Roper is scared of something."

"I'm not scared of jack shit. I just may need to, uh, use them at some point. I don't want that relationship to get, you know, strained."

"What if they were behind the Hornes getting whacked?"

Roper pondered the thought. "Be nice if they could slip through the cracks," he muttered.

I looked at him incredulously. "Look, double murders just don't go away. There's no statute of limitations. I thought you hired me to get to the bottom of this."

"No, I hired you to help get me off the hook. And I know all about statutes of limitations. And I know about double jeopardy too, so when I'm found not guilty, the City Attorney doesn't get to try me again."

"You're well-versed in the law."

"Three years of law school does that."

"Now that's a surprise," I remarked. Cliff Roper had all the earmarks of someone who had graduated from the College of Hard Knocks.

"Why's that? I'm an agent, I need to read contracts. Law school helped. I never bothered to take the bar, never actually practiced. But I know about the law. Comes in handy."

"You're just a jack-in-the-box of surprises, you know that?" I said, shaking my head. "Where'd you go to law school, Tijuana?"

"Hey, hey, hey. No need to get nasty here. I have feelings too, you know."

I put my head back and took a deep breath. Time to float the bulls-eye question. "Did you shoot Gilbert and April Horne?"

Roper stared at me. "I don't believe you just asked me that."

"I need to know."

"Why do you need to know?"

"Because if I'm going to keep going down this path, it better be for a good reason. And accepting a big pile of money just isn't a good reason anymore."

Roper continued to stare at me and then pulled out his iPhone and moved quickly through it. Picking up a piece of paper, he wrote down an address. "Here's where you'll find Brendan. He works for the Rooney Brothers."

I looked at the paper. It listed the name and address of a bar in the Valley. "What is this?"

"Geez, do I have to spell everything out for you? It's the Herman Room. Call it their office. You can find them there most days. But you need to be careful how you approach them. They're meatheads and they have a short fuse. Make up a story, but keep my name out of it."

I rubbed the piece of paper in my hand. "You didn't answer my question."

"What question's that?"

"Did you do it?"

"Do what?"

"Shoot. The. Hornes," I asked, starting to get a little exasperated.

Roper looked out the window for a long while before speaking. "I did not shoot the Hornes," he said. "I did not kill the Hornes. I had nothing to do with their deaths. I had nothing to do with the Lindbergh kidnapping or the JFK assassination or the 9-11 attack. I am as pure and innocent as the fucking driven snow. You happy now?"

I looked at him and gave an approving nod. "Maybe just a little."

Thirteen

I drove out of the subterranean garage in Roper's building and pulled onto Sunset. Sometimes in L.A., your plans are simply dictated by where you happen to be. Traffic is such that if you have a piece of business nearby, you take care of it. And I had some unfinished business in Laurel Canyon.

Turning onto Lookout Mountain, I drove up about a mile and parked across the street from the Horne residence. I then did a double take at the car parked ostentatiously in the driveway. A bright blue Lamborghini. I waited about 20 minutes in my vehicle before Oscar Romeo emerged from the house, wearing a black t-shirt and jeans and carrying a large envelope. I got out of my car and approached him.

"Hey there."

Oscar was about to open the driver's side door and stopped. "Mr. Detective. You get around."

"As do you, I see."

"I just had to retrieve some documents," Oscar said, holding up the envelope. "Roper's staff wouldn't help me, they said all of Gil's files had been shipped to his house."

"What did you need?"

"Endorsements contracts. My own contract with the Chargers. Things you trust your agent to keep for you. I never actually got a copy of these from Horne after I signed. He said he'd send it, but it never happened. No surprise. He was a lot more interested in getting his commission right away."

"You have a new agent?"

"Nope, still evaluating them. I'm going to be a lot more selective this time around."

"You could have stayed with Roper," I suggested, curious as to where that trail would lead.

Oscar gave a laugh. "Yeah, sure. What do I do when he gets convicted of murder? Not the best time to go under his wing, you know. Plus I got my brand image to consider."

"Brand image?"

"Yeah, man. I'm the All-American kid. My father's part African-American, part Italian. My mother's part Samoan, part Mexican. I got a little bit of everything in me. Just like America."

"So you can't get caught up being represented by a guy on trial for double murder."

"Man, you got that right."

"You think Roper did it?" I asked.

Oscar cocked his head for a moment. "I dunno. Maybe not. Doesn't really make sense, but not a lot of things make sense in this world. Who knows."

"Sure," I agreed. "Who knows. Hey, I wanted to ask you something."

"What's that?"

"Did Gil ever talk to you about being involved in business dealings with Brendan Webster?"

Oscar cocked his head once more. "He never said much, but Gil was Brendan's agent. I think he was trying to move Brendan into a different career. He also set Brendan up with a side job working for the Rooneys."

"What exactly do the Rooneys do?" I asked.

"Little of this, little of that. They handle security sometimes. I also heard they run a bookmaking operation on the side. Brendan made collections for them. Kind of funny he wound up having to collect from Gil. "

"What would happen if Gil didn't come up with the weekly vig?"

Oscar gave the palms-up sign. "No idea."

I turned and looked admiringly at the blue Lamborghini. "Great machine," I said. "I don't think I've ever seen a color like that on a car."

"Yeah, these cars are the best. The color's custom. That's one of the beautiful things about the Lamborghini. You send them a color chip and they match it."

"Nice."

"I once had a Hot Wheels toy car that looked like this. It's pretty cool. Now I can get a real car with the same color. Every kid's dream come true."

"Well, you earned it."

"Oh, I did. Got more than my share of bumps and bruises and sprains. Funny thing, though."

"What's that?"

"A ride like this sets you back almost five hundred, and the trade-in only gets you so much. I was counting on that shoe contract to make up the difference. Looks like I'm gonna need to make All-Pro next season. Then I can go in and renegotiate my deal. Hopefully with an agent who knows what he's doing. Finding a good one's going to be important."

Five hundred meant five hundred thousand. Half a million dollars for a car. I looked at my eight year old Pathfinder. Nowhere near as sleek or stylish, nowhere near as comfortable, but it got me to and from my destinations. A long time ago I had dreamed of a pro football career, but even back then, the money for the top players wasn't anywhere close to this level. The stakes were a lot higher for these guys now.

"Good luck with that, Oscar."

He nodded goodbye, hopped into his grossly expensive toy and turned the engine over. It emitted a low roar, more like a throaty growl than the sound of an internal combustion engine. He pulled onto the road and sped off quickly around the bend.

I walked down the road and began knocking on doors. Finding a front door was never easy in this neighborhood. The houses were often shrouded by foliage, and the front doors were sometimes behind a locked gate, up a flight of stairs or on the side of the house, not out in front.

Most of the neighbors I encountered expressed shock at the tragedy of the other night, but knew little about the Hornes and their lifestyle. They said the couple came and went at odd hours, and had a regular flow of visitors; the neighbors would occasionally hear raised voices coming from the house. But nothing that led them to believe it could ever lead to this. I was learning nothing new. And then I met Barry Hamlin.

Barry Hamlin was the type of Angelino I had expected to find in Laurel Canyon. He had written and sold a dozen screenplays, had made a lot of money, but had never seen any of his scripts actually produced. A real estate agent when the screenwriting wasn't going well, Barry was a stocky, middle-aged guy with a good bit of stomach fat, short, cropped hair and neatly trimmed beard.

"This area's a nice place to live," he confided. "It'll be nicer now that those people are gone. Not to besmirch the dearly departed, but they weren't the best of neighbors."

"In what way?"

"In every way imaginable. They were loud, obnoxious, fought all the time, had raucous parties, and people were coming and going at all hours of the night. They didn't respect their neighbors. Hell, they acted like they didn't have any neighbors at all, except when they needed a favor."

"Bet you got a lot material for a script," I speculated.

"Oh yeah, for a fact. My office window faces their house, so I saw quite a bit. I just hope someone doesn't do a documentary on them first."

"Lookout Mountain would be a good title."

"Ha! You're right, I think I'll steal that one!"

"Steal away," I said, thinking I could probably write some good murder mysteries myself, but I'm too busy living smack in the middle of them.

"That's a good one," he laughed. "You probably have a lot of stories to tell. We should sit down sometime. I'm always up for partnering with someone on a script. Good material's not easy to come by."

"I'll keep that in mind," I said, and made a mental note to forget it as soon as possible. For a private investigator, discretion is critical and blabbing about confidential matters to a writer would be the ultimate breach of trust. "Anything you can tell me about the other night?"

Barry struck a pose as he pondered this. "Just like I told the police," he declared. "It was a typical night there. A couple of Porsches came and went, some hot women dropped by. And men too by the way, real buff. I don't know how they knew all these people but it was like a modeling agency over there."

"Anything different about the other night?"

"Well, sure. About 9:00 p.m. I heard a few pops and their dog started barking. I'd like to shoot that damn thing myself, she just barks for hours when they're gone. But this time there seemed to be a real urgency to her yapping. It was non-stop and she sounded alarmed. I guess someone finally called 9-1-1 just to get her to shut up. But when the police came, they went inside and next thing you know there's a dozen cop cars clogging up the street."

"You see anyone in particular come or go that night?"

"It was too dark, I barely made out much. Oh yeah, that Lamborghini that was here earlier today. He was there that night."

I drew in a breath. "Okay. Anyone else?"

Barry Hamlin again posed as if he were deep in thought. "No, just the usual," he finally said, and then an angry expression formed on his face as he looked past me. "Aw, shit. Not you again."

I looked over and a very tired, very raggedy black cocker spaniel came walking slowly up to us. She was a small dog, maybe 15 pounds at the most. Her black fur was thick and matted, and she had long floppy ears. She started toward us at first, wagging her tail, but jumped back quickly when Hamlin picked up a rock and was about to throw it at her. I grabbed his arm before he could let it sail.

"C'mon, stop it. I'm sick of that mutt. I'm gonna take her out now!"

"What the hell for?" I asked, struggling to wrench the stone out of his hand.

"Damn thing barks all night and tears into the trash cans all day," he panted, as I finally jerked the stone away from him. "She's a total pain in the ass. Just like her masters. Except she still keeps hanging around."

I glared at him. "I would guess if you were a kid and the people taking care of you were suddenly gone, and you had no one to feed you, you'd be doing the same damn thing as she is."

He dusted himself off. "I'm calling 9-1-1. I had to listen to her howl all last night. I got work to do."

Yes, I thought, writing screenplays for movies no one will ever go to the theatres and watch. "I'll take her over to the shelter," I said. "No sense tying up the emergency lines."

I gave my card to Hamlin and told him to call me if he remembered anything else. Hopefully the call wouldn't be an invitation to share police files for his next script. I looked over at the cocker spaniel and remembered her name was Chewy. I called her name and extended my hand for her to sniff. She walked over tepidly and began licking my fingers. I opened up the Pathfinder and reached inside for a bottle of water. Pouring some into my cupped hand, I offered it to her and she lapped it up quickly.

Hmmm. I had an idea. I opened up the door wider and she looked up at me. "Go on in," I said. After a moment's hesitation she jumped into the Pathfinder and lay down on the front passenger seat.

"You're okay with riding shotgun?" I asked her.

Chewy responded with a big yawn and curled up in a ball. I drove slowly down Lookout Mountain, and by the time I turned onto Laurel Canyon Boulevard, Chewy was sound asleep.

Fourteen

In addition to being a rustic outpost within a big metropolis, Laurel Canyon serves as a gateway into the San Fernando Valley. The scenery changed as Chewy and I wound our way down through the passes. At first, the shrubs and greenery masked entranceways to multi-million dollar homes and estates. There were also the occasional glimpses of the sweeping views of the Valley floor. Had it been a clear day, the drive might have been spectacular.

At the bottom of the hill lay Studio City, an upscale suburban community, replete with nice homes that were a bit less ostentatious than the ones tucked away inside the canyon. As we pushed forward into the Valley though, the homes became older and more pedestrian, eventually giving way to the industrial neighborhood of North Hollywood. The Laurel Canyon Boulevard of the Valley was lined with auto repair shops, warehouses and strip malls. Instead of mansions and gardens, we passed liquor stores, cheap nail salons and video game shops.

I turned left onto Sherman Way and continued to drive through a series of modest and then less-than-modest neighborhoods. Along the way I stopped at a large Petco and bought Chewy a collar, a leash, some dry dog food and a pair of bowls, one for water and one for food. After loading them in the Pathfinder, I looked to see if Chewy wanted a drink out of a real bowl. Her light snoring told me she had other priorities.

After a few miles I found the Herman Room in Van Nuys and parked in the small lot behind the gritty establishment. Exiting the Pathfinder, I left a couple of windows open a few inches for Chewy. As I approached the decrepit establishment, my nose wrinkled. At some point in time, the Herman Room might have been a decent place. There used to be a lot of these venues around L.A. These were the old-school bar and grills, where they served cheap steaks and cheap drinks. The interior was lined with faux wood paneling and they had those red naugahyde booths that inevitably developed cracks along the surface from excess wear and too little upkeep. A number of booths had strips of gray tape holding the seats together. The bar featured bottles of top drawer liquor brands, but the reality was the owner would often refill them every few days with generic booze. The clientele were usually more interested in getting drunk for a reasonable price, and rarely took notice of the product's quality.

I walked inside and was immediately hit with the stench of drinks that had never been properly cleaned up, as well as food that had been fried too long. The floor was covered with sawdust to give it a western feel, but that only served to give the owners a reason to not sweep up every day.

It was about 3:30 p.m., so it came as no great surprise

that the joint was empty. Behind the bar stood a very large, swarthy man wearing a cheap white shirt, red vest and black bow tie. He looked to be somewhere between 30 and 50 years old; he had one of those timeless faces for which fat did a good job of hiding his age. There were a pair of men seated at a table in the back. One of the men was well into his mid-50s, lean, with graying hair and a scratchy looking gray beard. The other was in his early 20s and was as big as the man behind the bar, but looked far more solid. He was deeply muscled and evoked a sense that he did nothing more than pump iron all day. The older man was hunched over an iPad, working on a spreadsheet. The younger one stared into space.

"You need something?" asked the older man, looking up from his spreadsheet.

I thought of telling him I needed a place for my new dog to urinate, and she'd probably find this room to her liking. But I figured I'd start off by playing nice.

"Is Brendan around?"

The two men looked at each other. "Who wants to know?" the older man demanded.

"Name's Burnside."

"What's your business?"

"It's a private matter. Just want to talk to him."

"Uh-huh. Well, Brendan's gone. He went to Mexico. Be back next week," the older man said, and the fat guy behind the bar began to giggle obnoxiously.

"Yeah," the fat man smirked, and laughed a stupid laugh. "Gone to Mexico."

"Maybe I should wait for him."

"Maybe you should go screw," the older man replied.

"Yeah," parroted the fat man behind the bar, his laughter now derisive. "Go screw."

So much for playing nice. "This is about Gilbert Horne."

"Never heard of him," the older man said.

"Don't you ever look at your TV?" I said, pointing to the old-style 25-inch box TV that was placed above the bar. "Or is that just there to figure out the betting line?"

The young guy began to get up, but the graybeard used his hand to signal him to sit back down. "You don't need to get involved in this," he told him. "Fernando, throw this douche bag out the door."

"I wouldn't try that if I were you," I warned.

The big man behind the bar laughed again and wiped his hands and came slowly toward me. He moved deliberately, not out of caution, but as if this were just one more boring thing on his to-do list. Sizing me up, he stopped next to me and decided he would give me a break. He pointed to the door.

"Get out," he ordered, with an air of finality.

"Make me," I responded.

"You're gonna get hurt."

"No, I'm gonna shove that laugh down your throat."

His jolliness no longer evident, the fat man reached out and tried to grab my left arm, but I was ready for him and drove my right fist into his solar plexus, followed with a left to the side of his temple. Groaning slightly, he gave me a sneer as if to say I was messing up his afternoon. Coming at me with a little more interest, he threw an overhand right, which I sidestepped as I moved my head back slightly. Off balance now, he tried to throw a punch with his left hand, but I blocked it easily. I grabbed his left wrist, and in one motion, ducked underneath his arm and twisted the wrist sharply behind his back. He yelped in pain as I jerked his arm high up his back. As I cut his left ankle out from under him, he started to fall and I grabbed the scruff of his neck and slammed his forehead against the wooden bar. His head bounced up for a moment and then down again, and the rest of his body went limp and slid down a bar stool, taking a second or two before ending up on the sawdust-covered floor.

Breathing heavily now, I turned to look back at the two men. "Got any more goons nearby, or do you want to tell me where Brendan Webster is?"

They looked at each other. "Again, what do you want with him?" the older man demanded.

"Again, it's a private matter."

Graybeard looked at the kid with the muscles. "Okay, go ahead. If he can take Fernando, maybe we can use him on something." He went back to working on his spreadsheet. The muscle-bound young man rose.

"Who are you?" I asked, my right hand starting to edge closer to my shoulder holster. There are only so many fights you can get into with bruisers before one of them lands a lucky punch. And with guys this big, one punch is all that's needed.

"I'm your guy. I'm Brendan."

I stopped. "You could have saved your friend a nasty bump on the head by telling me that a minute ago."

Brendan looked at me. "Mr. Rooney's the boss. I do what I'm told."

We walked outside and started down the block. It was warmer in the Valley, and considerably more hazy than it was in the L.A. basin. At the corner, we turned into a strip mall that boasted a hodgepodge of outlets. These included a shoe repair shop, a liquor store, and a pizzeria with a faded banner advertising its grand opening held a long time ago.

"Tell me about Gilbert Horne," I started.

"You a cop?"

I flashed my private eye shield at him and didn't answer the question directly. "Three guesses."

Brendan stopped. "Why didn't you just say so from the start?"

"Your boss would have been on the phone to his lawyer in two seconds. This way's more difficult, but it's better, believe me."

Brendan processed this, but I wasn't sure how much sunk in. "Do I need a lawyer?"

"If you shot Gilbert Horne and his wife," I said, testing the waters, "then I would say yes. Otherwise no."

"Okay. I didn't have anything to do with those murders. I heard about them, though. But all I did was make some pickups from Mr. Horne. He owed money to my boss. Lots of money. That's about it."

"How did he owe money to the Rooneys?" I asked.

"How else? Gambling."

"Sports?"

"Sports, horses, card games. I guess he was a good

poker player at one time. They say that's how he got that fancy car dealership in Santa Monica. I guess he thought lightning would strike twice."

"So you made the pickups from him at the Seaside."

"The what?"

"The Seaside," I repeated. I started to surmise that any line of work where Brendan would have to think hard would be problematic for him. "It's a hotel in the Marina."

"Oh yeah. Also at his house sometimes. He didn't always show up at the hotel when he was supposed to. Sometimes he didn't have the full payment."

"You ever work him over?"

He shook his head furiously. "No, never. I mean Mr. Rooney wanted me to, but the whole business was messy. I'd known Gil a while. He represented me when I was playing football. Still did after that. I didn't want to screw that up."

"He was your agent after football?" I asked. "For what?"

"MMA. He was arranging a few fights for me."

MMA stood for Mixed Martial Arts, the contemporary version of boxing, except with most of the rules thrown out. The two combatants went into a steel cage and were allowed to fight in almost any way they chose to. There was a referee there as well, but more for pretense than actual officiating. The winner was usually the guy who didn't get beaten to a pulp.

"How'd you get involved in that?" I asked.

"Tore up my knee in football. Texas A&M. This seemed like my best chance to make it in a sport."

"And I understand you played high school ball locally," I asked.

"Down in the O.C. but yeah. I guess that's kind of local."

"You happen to know some of Horne's clients? Oscar Romeo, Patrick Washington, Ted Wade?"

"Sure. Everyone knows them. Great guys."

"They had Gil Horne as their agent. Any problems you know of?"

"Yeah. I know Oscar and Patrick were pretty unhappy with him."

"Unhappy enough to shoot him?"

"I don't know. Maybe Oscar, he's got some issues. Not Patrick, he's all business. Both felt Mr. Horne wasn't doing the job. Heard they finally fired him. But I don't think it was just because of how he represented them."

"Oh? What else?"

"On account of Mr. Horne's wife. April. She seemed like a piece of work. I only met her a few times, but I've heard the stories. I didn't think she was all that hot, but you know, lot of guys like that type. Blonde, big boobs, gets high a lot. When she got high, she would get crazy. She tried coming on to me once, but I gotta keep business and bitches separate. Makes things too complicated, you know?"

"Yeah, sure, I'll bet," I said, doing my best to sound agreeable. "Can you remember any other guys she came on to?"

"Sure. I know about Ted Wade."

"Meaning?" I asked.

"Meaning Ted was poking April. It got complicated you know, him being Mr. Horne's nephew and all. But Ted's crazy. Drugs can make you do all sorts of crazy stuff. Sleeping with your step-aunt? That's just messed up."

*

It was around 5:00 p.m. when I pulled into the garage underneath my apartment building, and that was just when Chewy began to stir. She gave a big yawn as I pulled into the space next to Gail's Toyota. Fixing the collar around her neck, I attached the leash and led her out of the Pathfinder. She bounded toward the elevator and it was all I could do to keep her somewhat heeled.

I hesitated as we approached our apartment. Gail and I had not even seriously discussed having children. The idea of surprising her with a pet this suddenly began to make me a little uneasy. Women sometimes liked surprises, but sometimes not. This one was a wild card. And it had seemed like such a great idea a few hours ago.

I looked down at Chewy. "You be on your best behavior, you hear?"

Taking a deep breath, I entered the apartment. "Gail, I'm home," I called out in my best patriarch voice. Just like Ward Cleaver. Or maybe Homer Simpson.

"Hi, I'm in the kitchen."

"Can you come out here. I have a surprise for you."

Gail walked into the living room a moment later and stopped suddenly. Chewy wagged her tail. We both looked at her expectantly.

"Oh my," she said.

I dropped the leash and let Chewy give Gail a proper greeting. Her tail whipped back and forth and wagged even harder as she sniffed Gail and looked up at her. Gail reached down and tried to pet her. Chewy responded by licking her hand.

"Wow," Gail whispered. "I don't know what to say. Where did you get her? She's beautiful, but she could certainly use a bath."

"Um. She's an orphan."

"Meaning?"

"Her name's Chewy. She used to belong to April and Gilbert Horne. She was wandering the streets. Lookout Mountain. I felt sorry for her."

Gail drew in a breath. "You do have a penchant for taking in girls who need help."

I looked at her and couldn't say anything. My open mouth probably spoke volumes. Gail and I rarely talked about this painful incident from my past.

"Sorry," she said, recognizing the inadvertent sting of her words. "That came out wrong. I meant that you were sympathetic. It's actually a good trait to have."

About six years ago, I had made the biggest mistake of my career, and possibly my life. I had arrested a young runaway named Judy Atkin, for prostitution. She was a minor, 17 years old at the time, but could have passed for 12 or 13, she looked that innocent. When she was released, I took her in, the type of mistake no cop should ever make. I knew better, but I felt like I had the chance to make a difference in someone's life.

In the end, Judy betrayed my trust and I was arrested for pimping a child. She skipped town and that got me off the hook, so the charges were dropped. While she didn't directly cause to me to leave the police force, the episode paved the way for my departure. Spending time in county jail with the same scum I had been locking up for years was a life-altering event. I was a changed man after that, for the better and for the worse. The events that followed sent me down a new path and a new career. I had to believe they led me to this moment, to be here with Gail, and to be starting a new life with her. And for that at least, I had no regrets.

"I knew what you meant," I said to Gail, and drew her into my arms. "You don't need to apologize. I trust your heart."

She kissed me and I held her tightly for a long moment. And then I felt a pair of paws scratching at my leg and a low whimper. We looked down. Chewy wanted to be part of the hug.

"Okay, look," she said. "Are pets even allowed in this building?"

"I've seen someone else walking a poodle. That's good enough for me."

"Maybe you can show me your rental agreement," she said suspiciously. "I don't want to fall in love and then discover we can't keep her."

"Too late for me," I said, looking down at Chewy. Her mouth was open and she was panting happily. That meant she was hot and sweating, but I chose to interpret it as she was smiling and in a very happy mood.

I took over the dinner chores from Gail as she hunted down the rental agreement. I threw some penne in a pot of water and set it to boil. Gail had been heating up a marinara sauce, and I added some minced garlic. About 20 minutes later, we were ready for dinner.

"There's nothing in here saying you can't have a dog," she said, scanning my contract. "Just that you're responsible for any damage to the carpets."

"I'm good with that."

"There is one issue you may not have thought of."

"Which is?"

"We leave in the morning and come back in the evening. At some point during the day, Chewy is going to need to do some, er, business. Which of course brings up the matter of the carpets."

I took a bite of food. Chewy pawed my leg and looked up hopefully with a pair of soulful brown eyes. "In the short run," I said, "I can put some pea gravel out on the balcony. We can leave the balcony door open. A benefit of being on the third floor of a four-story building."

"And you think she'll make the connection with the pea gravel?" Gail asked dubiously.

Chewy pawed my leg again, and this time I got up and grabbed the bag of dry dog food I had purchased at Petco. I poured some into her bowl and set it down in the kitchen. "Maybe what we really need is a dog walker."

Gail thought about it for a moment. "Do you happen to know the owner of the poodle?"

"No," I said, "but I'm happy to go make the acquaintance. You never know."

After dinner, I walked down the building hallway and knocked on a door next to the elevator. A pleasant-looking woman in her 60s opened the door. Her name was Dorothy and though we had lived in the same building for 15 years, we never had an occasion to introduce ourselves. A nod and a hello was all most people here typically did. I told her about Chewy and asked if she knew of any professional dog walkers nearby.

"I wouldn't know. I'm the one who takes Skylar out for walks. Four times a day. She has a small bladder."

I had a thought. Ordinarily, handing a stranger a key to my apartment was anathema, but she had lived down the hall for years, and I got a good feeling from her.

"Might you be available to walk Chewy during the day? We'd pay you, of course."

"That could work. I'm retired so I'm home during the day. And I could always use a few extra dollars. Fixed income, you know. When do I get to meet her?"

I invited both her and her poodle Skylar over, and Chewy gave both of them a proper greeting. Within 10 seconds, Chewy and Skylar began playing, chasing each other around our apartment.

"She's wonderful!" Dorothy said. "I'd be delighted to walk her."

As Dorothy left, I put my arms around Gail. "I think we're forming quite a nice family."

Gail smiled and looked over at Chewy, who was now sitting on the couch, playing with one of my socks. "She does fit right in."

Fifteen

After making a number of attempts at jumping into bed with us, Chewy finally got the message that a *ménage* à *trois* was not going to be in the cards. Gail established the sleeping arrangements decisively; Chewy sleeps on the floor. When I rose at my usual 5:30 a.m., I discovered I had to step over our new roommate as she lay sprawled in our bedroom doorway. She heard me go past her and lifted her head up for a moment, before laying it back down on the carpet and falling back asleep. Not wanting Gail to have to walk her on the first morning, I shook Chewy awake and led our sleepy puppy outside for a few minutes to do her thing. She reluctantly complied, and after pouring some more dog food in her bowl, I felt free to start my work day.

I decided to go to my office first. I had some paperwork to catch up on, and it was too early to make any visits. I also thought I'd stop by a coffee shop for breakfast, not wanting to wake Gail and Chewy to the sounds and smells of bacon frying. Gail was not a morning person, but I was.

I pulled the Pathfinder out onto Montana, and was pleased to see there were no other cars on the road at this early hour. Driving three blocks, I was able to make the green light and turn left onto Ocean Avenue hardly slowing down. The dawn's early light was bright and blue, and it looked like it was going to be a nice, sunny day. I decided to take a glimpse at the sparkling Pacific ocean, so I turned right to go down the California Incline.

While its name had a dramatic flair, the California Incline was simply an extension of California Avenue, which runs parallel to and three blocks south of Montana. The Incline part refers to the steep drop that the service road takes as it descends towards Pacific Coast Highway. It was originally built over a century ago as a walkway for local residents to access the beach, but was later expanded to allow for auto traffic. Over the years, considerable erosion had eaten away at the underpinnings and there was talk of closing it down. That would be a shame, I thought. The California Incline offered a sensational, panoramic view of Santa Monica Bay, and it allowed you to see the shoreline twist its way out toward Malibu. On a morning like this, it was a beautiful sight to behold. But then things got very ugly, very fast.

It started as I approached the traffic light at Pacific Coast Highway. I tried to apply the brakes, but nothing happened. Nothing at all. I pumped the brake pedal with my right foot, and then pushed with all my might, yet there was no response. I tried to engage the emergency brake with my left foot and the vehicle seemed to slow down slightly, but not by much. As I rumbled down the Incline, the one saving grace was that it was very early and there were no cars in front of me. Still, the traffic light was red and I was faced with driving straight through it. As my feet kept trying to work the brakes, I turned my head back and forth in a pivot motion to see if there were any cars moving along PCH. I caught a glimpse of a small yellow sports car speeding south. I jammed my palm onto the horn and gave a half-dozen short honks, followed by two long ones.

The sports car slowed, which was fortunate for both of us. As I skidded through the red light and across the intersection, I spun the steering wheel back and forth freely in case I needed to jerk the vehicle out of harm's way. Nothing was in my path and that was both good and bad. The Pathfinder had picked up some speed going down the Incline and as it barreled along, I was faced with crashing into a cement wall or into the Javelin Club, an exclusive downtown group that maintained a private beachfront property in Santa Monica. Club members had access to a secluded beach where they could frolic in the ocean without having to swim next to the great unwashed. With less than one second to decide where to crash, I quickly chose the Javelin Club.

The parking lot to the Javelin Club was blocked by a chain that had a "Keep Out" sign attached to it. Unable to follow the directive, I smashed through the chain and went over a dip that sent the Pathfinder airborne for a brief moment. At that point I lost control of the vehicle and when I came down, it spun directly into a brick wall.

In some ways it was good fortune that the chain slowed my momentum, because when I finally hit the wall I was traveling at less than 10 miles an hour. It was bad luck otherwise because the chain did a number on my front end, breaking a headlight and damaging both the grill and bumper. I sat for a long minute trying to catch my breath and regain my thoughts. Thank goodness for seat belts. I swore at that moment I would never drive another car without being harnessed in. My psyche was shaken up, but otherwise it seemed I was uninjured. Unbuckling myself, I climbed out of the vehicle, feeling a bit woozy, but otherwise maintaining my equilibrium.

"Sir, are you all right?" yelled a young man running up to me. He was dressed in white pants with a white t-shirt.

"I think so," I mumbled. "I'm not so sure about my ride."

"Wow. That sounded awful. I heard the crash clear on the other side of the parking lot."

"I'm surprised someone's working this early," I said, still feeling a little wobbly. "But I suppose the Javelin Club keeps staff around for moments just like this."

"Sir, why don't you come with me," he said, leading me by the arm and guiding me inside a building. We walked into the main room, and he went and brought me a glass of cold water after sitting me down on a chair. A few minutes later a couple of patrol officers from SMPD came by. The Santa Monica cops dressed similar to LAPD officers, but the uniforms of the beachside cops were a lighter shade of blue. I told them what had happened and they dutifully wrote things down in a notebook. I agreed to stop by later in the day to fill out a formal accident report. They told me a tow truck would be by in a few minutes. When they asked if I thought I needed any medical attention, I politely declined and took another sip of water, which had now become room temperature. The cops left and a Javelin club official came by and asked if I would mind signing a statement saying the accident was my fault. I was still feeling lightheaded, but not so much that I couldn't tell him to shove his statement up his ass.

I called Gail and she swung by a few minutes later, clad in jeans and a sweat shirt. "Oh my. What happened?"

"My brakes didn't work."

"Had you noticed any problems with them recently?" she asked.

"Nope."

"Uh-oh."

"Yeah," I said. This didn't look like any accident. The person who did this wanted me to stop the investigation. But if the intent was to scare me into backing off, they had picked the wrong guy. If they were trying to kill me, they had used a very uncertain method. My guess was they were trying to send me a message. It was either the killer, or someone trying to help the killer. The more I thought about who this might be, the more my head started to swim.

I assured Gail I was fine to drive, although convincing myself took some doing. Despite some strong misgivings, she drove me over to a rental car agency and I selected a gray Toyota Highlander. It wasn't as big as my Pathfinder or as rugged-looking, but for now it would get me to and from where I needed to be. And the gray color wouldn't stand out if I needed to tail someone. The kid at the rental car desk asked me how long I'd need the vehicle.

"I don't know," I shrugged. "I was just in an accident. It'll take some time to do the repairs."

"Sorry to hear that," he said, as he finished the paperwork. "So I assume you'll be taking the collision damage waiver."

"Why's that?" I asked. "Your assuming I'm a lousy driver?"

"No, I'm just assuming you're a smart guy."

"Collision damage waivers are a bad investment," I pointed out.

The kid looked at me and then down at his computer. "It all depends on whether you think you'll be in another accident," he mused, in an absent sort of way.

"Can you tell me whether you get a commission on this?"

The kid pursed his lips. "Well, yes and no."

I started to laugh. "What does that mean?"

The kid smiled a shy smile. "It means yes I get a commission. But no, I'm not supposed to tell you that."

"Why are you telling me then?"

"You strike me as a man who values honesty."

"You're a perceptive guy," I laughed. "I'm sure you'll go far."

"I'm sure I will too."

"What are you doing working here, then?" I asked, not overtly trying to be a smartass, but these gems seemed to just pop out my mouth.

"I get my bachelors degree in June. This is just a way station. I've got plans."

I looked at him admiringly. There were a lot of paths to success. Even the wrong path could still get you to the right place. "Okay," I said, still feeling I wasn't thinking as clearly as I should. "You win. I'll take the collision damage waiver. Consider it my contribution to your career goals."

"All right," the kid smiled.

I turned to Gail and she was holding back a grin. She told me to drive carefully and to call her immediately if I experienced any problems. I kissed her goodbye and she went off to work. I needed to go to work too. I just didn't quite know where to start.

With cars on my brain, I decided to drive over to Bay City Motor Cars. I asked for Betty Luttinger but she was again out sick. Duncan Whitehead hadn't come in yet and Christy Vale was on a test drive with a customer. I thought of trying to make a few new friends, but wasn't really in a sociable mood. I was also starting to get a headache. I went back home, took a couple of Advil pills and laid down on the couch for half an hour. Chewy climbed up next to me and I absent-mindedly stroked her belly as I rested.

Feeling only slightly better, I looked up Betty Luttinger's address and phone number, and drove over to her apartment on the hill near Ocean Park and 11th Street. I waited in my car for a few minutes before dialing her number. Not knowing if her husband was home, I decided calling first was better than just knocking on the door.

"Betty?"

"Yes?" she answered meekly, her voice a little hard to hear on my phone.

"This is Burnside. The private investigator?"

Silence.

"Are you still there?"

"Yes?"

"I'd like to speak with you."

Another sound of silence.

"Can I come up?"

"Right now?"

"Yes, right now. I'm downstairs."

Another tone of silence.

"Are you all right?" I asked.

"No."

"Is anyone with you?"

"I'm alone."

I waited a beat to see if she was going to say anything else. Nothing came. I told her I would be there in a minute, and this time I didn't bother to wait for her long pause of silence. I ended the call, walked across the street and climbed a flight of stairs. The Luttingers lived in a small, older apartment building that held six units, three on each of the two floors. The building was painted a dark green and bore a resemblance to a cheap motel. There was no doorbell, so I rapped lightly on her door. Betty appeared about 10 seconds later, dressed in sweats, no makeup, looking morose. She glanced at me vacantly, and held the door open as a way of inviting me in. The apartment itself was spacious and clean.

"You look like you've been through the wringer," I said, sitting down.

"You don't look so hot yourself."

"I'll be fine. What about you?"

She sat down next to me and put her head in her hands. "It's a bad time for me. My husband and I have separated. I thought ... I thought I would have a future elsewhere."

"With Gil."

She nodded in agreement. "You know about us."

"Yes. What happened the other night was very tragic," I said, and looked at her carefully. "Can I ask you something? I assume Gil told you he'd leave his wife?"

"Yes," she sighed. "That he did. Many times. But this time I thought he was serious. I just didn't realize he wasn't going to leave her for me."

My eyes widened. "Who was he leaving her for?"

"Well that was the problem," she said. "No one in particular. He was just leaving her. There were ... other women besides me. I should have known. Men like that, they cheat on their wives. If they cheat on their wives, what's to stop them from cheating on their mistresses? I'm not young anymore. I can't compete with women who are in their 20s. I thought I could, that maybe Gil might recognize he needed someone more mature, someone close to his own age. I was wrong."

"How did you find out about the other women?"

She kept her head in her hands and moved it back and forth slowly. "Someone at the dealership told me. But of course this was right after the shootings so I never had a chance to confront Gil. Never had a chance to ... to even ... say goodbye," she said haltingly, choking back tears.

I watched and waited. Losing someone suddenly, whether it be a loved one or just a friend or colleague, is a blow to the system. One moment they are there in your life, and the next moment they've mysteriously been pulled away. You never get to see them again, never get to talk with them again. All you have are the memories. The rawness of Gilbert Horne's murder was obviously going to have an effect on Betty Luttinger for a long time. Mourning a loved one is a process that can take months or even years. There is no shortcut. And it's all the harder when knotty issues about your relationship have never been fully resolved.

"Did your husband know about this affair with Gil?" I asked cautiously.

She looked out the window. "He suspected. We've been having problems for a while. I finally told him a few weeks ago and he moved out right away."

"Do you think," I started cautiously, "that your husband might have had anything to do with what happened to Gil and April? Anything at all?"

Betty said no. "I can't imagine. He's not the type. And in a way I think he might have been relieved when he found out. In a way, I think it gave him the excuse to leave. To move on, be on his own again."

I considered this, but also knew that people are capable of anything, especially when they've been handed the proper motivation. I'd seen the most timid people transform into bloodthirsty killers when something near and dear to them has been ruptured. And even those closest to them are shocked when they discover this. People are capable of anything. Especially when it involves someone they love.

"What's your husband's name?"

"Arthur. Arty. Arty Luttinger."

"Where does he work?"

"He's in sales. Telemarketing actually. He works for one of those pay TV companies now. He has a college degree but it's in anthropology, and he never got a chance to use it."

"Do either of you own a handgun?"

"Well yes, but we haven't used it in years. Arty bought it after we were burglarized a long time ago. We took it to a shooting range a few times, but since then it's been kept in a drawer."

"Do you still have the gun?" I asked warily.

"Why, I don't know, I haven't even thought of that thing in so long," she said, rising and walking into the bedroom. She came out a minute later. "It looks like it's gone. Arty must have taken it."

I drew in a breath. "Do you know what type of gun it was?"

She frowned. "No. I'm not into that sort of thing. You don't seriously think ..."

I looked at her and gave her the universal palms up sign which said I had no idea. And I really didn't. Arty Luttinger may have simply taken the gun with him when he moved, maybe because he felt it was his. He may have had nothing at all to do with the murders. But without much else to go on, someone like this could never be ruled out. A cuckolded man with a weapon was not someone to be taken lightly. And it was certainly a motive that could propel someone to commit murder.

"Let's hope not," I said, and I did mean it. Betty Luttinger had been through a lot already, some of it emanating from her own doing, from her own poor choices. But to have this situation spiral even further downward would be a horrendous punishment for anyone to have to endure.

Sixteen

Leaving Betty's apartment, I knew I needed to follow up with someone at the LAPD, but I didn't want to just stroll aimlessly into the Hollywood Division again. My last encounter with the men in blue resulted in my being detained for half a day. This time, I decided to call first.

"Mulligan here."

"Detective Mulligan. This is Burnside. We met earlier in the week."

"Burnside, sure. My Trojan hero. Heard you've had an exciting week."

"Uh, yeah. More than I wanted, really."

"Happens that way, huh?" he responded, breezily. "So what's up?"

"Are you working on the Horne case?" I asked.

"Nah, that's a wrap, Johnson handed it to the City Attorney. The partner did it, Cliff Roper."

"I have my doubts about that."

"Oh yeah?" he asked, getting interested. "Whatcha got?"

"Lots of other avenues to go down here."

"Tough to beat finding the business partner's gun at the scene of the crime."

"Doesn't that strike you as just a little too obvious?"

"You mean, like it was planted?" he asked.

"Maybe."

"Yeah, I did wonder a little about that. But you know. It's hard to ignore the obvious."

"I know. Listen, there's someone I'm looking at, his name's Arty Luttinger, he's married to Horne's assistant. Over at his car dealership. Horne and the assistant were having an affair. The husband learned about it recently and the couple just split up."

"Oh yeah?"

"Arty owns a gun, not sure of the make. But he has a motive, a bigger motive than Cliff Roper ever had. Roper had just ended a business relationship, so he had no good reason to pull the trigger. He already did that, financially speaking anyway."

"Okay, sounds interesting. Let me sniff around a bit."

"Thanks. I didn't want to go through Jim Johnson. We don't have the best relationship."

"You're part of a big club, my friend. That guy's a first rate piece of work. He's got a way-too-high opinion of himself. Lot of people have a hard-on for him. Inside the department and out."

"I remember your warning me," I laughed. "A UCLA guy."

"Yeah, I figured a Trojan might have a problem with him, too."

After hanging up, I realized it was after 11:00 a.m., and I still hadn't eaten yet. Bacon and eggs no longer seemed appealing, but I did have an idea for lunch. I didn't bother to think whether it was a good idea or a not-so-good-idea; my mind did not seem to be functioning at full capacity today. After placing a quick phone call and confirming, I drove up through the Valley and over to Toluca Lake. I stopped at a cozy little nook called Olive & Thyme, a shop which was a combination gourmet grocery, bakery and restaurant, all crammed into one small space. I arrived a little early and took a table in the back. A few minutes later, my lunch companion sashayed through the door. When she did, it felt like a bright spotlight had immediately focused on her.

"Well hello there," cooed Honey Roper, smiling her sweet smile, her long blonde hair flowing freely down her back. There was a twinkle in her mischievous blue eyes. "It's nice to see you again. And so soon."

"It's only been a couple of days. It just feels longer. I guess that happens sometimes."

"Know that feeling," she agreed.

"I appreciate your making time. I know this was short notice."

"No, this works out perfectly. I had an 11:30 that just got cancelled a little while ago. And I have a 1:00 with the head of marketing at Disney Channel, a meeting that I absolutely have to make. I was wondering how I'd fit lunch in."

"Sometimes things are meant to be," I pointed out as we perused the menu.

Honey ordered a Cobb salad, I had a grilled cheese with the sweetest tomato soup I had ever tasted. Our waiter tried to be fawning, possibly because Honey looked so good. But by noon the place was bustling rapidly, and he was racing up and down the aisle to try and fill orders.

"So your call came as a surprise," she said, her face turning serious. I wasn't sure how she was able to compartmentalize and display such different emotions so quickly. But having met people in the entertainment industry, I knew this was sometimes a job requirement.

"I just wanted to talk a bit," I said. "Your dad is back at the office, acting like everything is business as usual. It feels as if he's ignoring what he's up against."

"Oh, he knows. He thinks things will right themselves and he'll get off. He always does. He has a long history of being exonerated."

"You're confident. And I must say, you worked fast in making bail."

"Our attorney is pretty savvy," she said, digging into her salad. "I just got him some documents and Silverstein did the rest. But you're right. Dad isn't worried about all this, and he's barely thinking about the charges. He's focused on the NFL draft next weekend. But that does have *me* a little worried. I don't think he did it and he's beaten serious charges before. But the evidence the police have seems pretty strong."

I took a bite of grilled cheese and savored it for a moment. "When we met the other day, you told me about Gil's assistant, Betty. What more can you share about her?"

"I honestly don't know that much."

"Anything at all would help. No detail's too small."

She pushed her lower lip forward in that adorable way, and I pushed my eyes to look in another direction and just listen to her. I was engaged to Gail, in love with

Gail, and I knew Gail was the right person for me. The logical part of my brain asked why I was having lunch with a beautiful girl who was half my age. The other side of my brain did not bother with such issues. There was something I needed from Honey, I just wasn't sure what that was yet.

"Well, I'm not sure. Betty wasn't exactly Gil's type, if you know what I mean. Gil usually liked them blonde and young. Betty was older. Oh, she had big boobs and all, that seemed to be a requirement for him. Dad once referred to Gil as a sex addict. And Dad wasn't exactly a monk when it came to women."

"Then why Betty?"

"My guess would be Mommy issues. Some guys never quite get over that. I've heard it might have something to do with not being breast fed as a baby. You miss out on something when you're real young, and you spend the rest of your life trying to get it."

I sat back and pondered. "You sound like a therapist. How do you know all this?"

She laughed again, giving me another glimpse of that wonderful smile. "I took a few psych classes at UNLV. And I got to know one of my Psych professors well. Maybe too well. But honestly, I think I picked up that tidbit from reading *Cosmopolitan*."

"It does make sense," I admitted. "Betty's a woman that people my age might refer to as buxom."

"And people my age might say she has a nice rack," she smiled.

"I wonder if there's any other commonality in Gilbert

Horne's choices, other than his liking women that were, uh, a little top-heavy."

"Well, I don't know as Gil was overly picky about sex partners. Given the option, I think he'd go that way, but he was just a horn dog. Some guys just have to have it."

I took another bite of my sandwich and continued to savor it, along with the conversation. Eating good food with a beautiful young woman and talking about sex. Today might not be such an unlucky day after all. "Anything you can tell me about his wife, April?"

"I didn't really know her. But my guess is they were two peas in a pod. I think April had the same sex drive Gil had. That also may be why he usually went for younger women like April. They can keep up with him."

"So it wouldn't surprise you if I suggested April was having a few flings of her own?"

"Nope," she said, shaking her head emphatically. "They didn't live that far from my Dad, so I'd run into them occasionally. And one time I was at the market, and I saw April with one of Gil's clients. A football player probably. That or he just did steroids and liked to work out every day."

I peered at her. "Do you know who that was?"

"Nope," she said. "But he looked, well, Asian maybe. Or Filipino, or something else. It was hard to tell and it was a while ago. That's about all I can remember."

"That's a pretty good memory, regardless," I said, motioning to the waiter for the bill. As he walked over with it, I handed him a credit card.

"Thanks," she said. "This was a nice idea. I feel like

I'm a big part of this case all of a sudden."

"I appreciate your helping me. And helping your father, of course."

"Like I said before. Your dad's your dad. You only get one."

"The one you have," I said, "is quite a character. He's all right once you get past the rude exterior."

"Some of that comes from his growing up in New York."

"Ah, that would explain some things," I said. "A New Yorker's reputation for rudeness is legendary."

"So I've seen. I didn't grow up there, so I don't really know why that is."

"I've met a lot of New Yorkers out here. Mostly when I was on the police force. I finally figured out the rudeness doesn't always stem from anger. In New York you're surrounded by so many people, buildings, signs and distractions, that all the stimuli can be overwhelming. Most people just shut down to keep their sanity. They focus on certain things and tune out the rest. Their behavior comes off as rude to people who haven't experienced that kind of day-to-day existence."

Honey Roper smiled softly and looked at me in an odd way. "I like you," she said, her blue eyes sparkling. "You're easy to be around. You know a lot. And you make me think. Guys my age don't know how to do that. At least not yet."

"I'm a lot older than you," I said tepidly.

"Oh, I know. And I know my Dad might not be too pleased we're getting together again."

"I doubt he'd be happy with any guy you're with. Fathers can be protective," I said. Cliff Roper might indeed be annoyed that Honey and I were having lunch together. And in the back of my mind, I started to think that Gail Pepper might be rather unhappy at what I'd been doing as well.

Seventeen

I left Toluca Lake and drove across the Valley for a while before turning into Beverly Glen. I thought about Gail, about our impending marriage and about my dwindling bachelor days. Mostly though, I thought of the face of an all-too-young Honey Roper. She was mature for her age, but her age couldn't have been more than 23.

Without coming to any finite conclusions about where my life or even my rented Highlander was heading, I found myself approaching Sunset and decided I needed to make a stop in the heart of Beverly Hills. I had some more detective work to do. No sense missing the opportunity to do so in one of the ritziest cities in the world.

Downtown Beverly Hills exudes glamour in a shiny yet sophisticated way. The buildings are exquisitely designed, the shops frequently exhibiting touches of highly polished marble and granite. Even the sidewalks are noticeably clean and neat. Every now and then you see an oddity like a chain drug store, but for the most part, these mundane anomalies were few and far between. And unlike newer hot spots in the city such as L.A. Live downtown, Beverly Hills has no flashing signs, no electronic billboards, no wild bursts of light and color. Beverly Hills grabs your attention in an understated yet glamorous way.

I parked about a block from Harry Kingston Jewelers, removed my .38 and stowed it in the glove compartment. I strolled casually along Rodeo Drive, among the well-to-do and the ones who worked for them. Walking past various upscale shops, I paused to look in the windows and drink in the scene. Reaching the famed jewelry store, I stopped for a moment and admired the exterior facade. The floor-to-ceiling glass doors were framed by a gorgeous slab of brushed bronze that had a wavy texture. It was unlike anything I had ever seen before. I opened the door and was greeted by a very handsome and well-groomed young man. He wore a jacket and tie, and his sandy blond hair was slicked back stylishly.

"Good afternoon, sir," he said. "I'm Alex. And welcome to the salon."

"Thank you," I responded elegantly. I held back from asking why this shop was called a salon. I took in my new environment, dark and alluring. The air was cool and still and hushed. Rows of brightly lit, glass-encased drawers displayed glittering rings, necklaces, bracelets and earrings of various colors. Maybe they just seemed colorful because of that quick burst of light that emanated from the diamonds. I had heard that the best diamonds were ones where you could see a "fire" deep within. Looking into a few of these, I did notice that each seemed to possess this small fire, a bright multi-colored sparkle. None of the items had a price tag, and the message was obvious. If you had to ask, you couldn't afford it.

I glanced around the room. There were a few customers being tended to by employees. A few women were shopping, as well as a young couple in their 20s. Discreetly standing in a corner was a tall, stocky man wearing a dark suit and nondescript tie. There was a lump next to his hip.

"How may we help you today?" asked Alex.

"I'm actually looking for something unusual," I started.

"We can accommodate almost any taste," he smiled confidently.

"I have no doubt."

"Is this for a special occasion?"

I hesitated. When I bought Gail her engagement ring, she decided she really didn't need a large diamond, and given my up-and-down financial straits, it wasn't practical. But a ring is a requirement for a proper engagement, so we purchased one at a less chi-chi jewelry store. The ring was a nice combination of amethyst set next to a series of small diamonds, and it looked good on Gail's hand. Hell, anything would look good on Gail's hand.

"Well, no, sorry. Actually I'm here on a different type of business," I said, flashing my badge and handing Alex my card. "I'm working on a fraud case for the Differential Insurance Company."

"Oh," he said with a start. "Well I'd better let you speak with our manager."

He led me into the back office and knocked on a door. A camera above the office moved slightly. He gave a three-fingered signal and a buzzer buzzed and we entered the spacious office.

"Mr. Shapiro, this is Mr. Burnside. He has something he needs to speak with you about."

Shapiro was on the phone, but motioned for me to sit in the chair across from him. Alex quickly departed. Shapiro was a rotund man in his 40s, impeccably dressed in a conservative blue suit and tie. He had a small bald spot forming at the top of his head, combed over neatly. A minute later, Shapiro ended the call and looked at me.

"Yes, sir. I'm Larry Shapiro. What can I do for you?"

"I'm working with Harold Stevens at the Differential Insurance Company."

"Never heard of him."

"I, uh, didn't think you would have," I smiled, thinking they moved in very different circles. "We're doing an investigation of a woman named Noreen Giles. Does that name ring a bell?"

Shapiro stared at me and slumped back in his chair. "Yes," he sighed. "I'm afraid it does."

"What can you tell me?"

"We do have a certain confidentiality policy," he said.

"Anything you can provide would be very helpful."

He took a deep breath and blew it out slowly. I got the feeling this was a subject which he didn't mind discussing. I was right.

"It's an age old story I guess, for this business. And in this city. Mrs. Giles used to be a frequent shopper here. The problem was, everything she bought was returned within 30 days. We get that sometimes, usually people going to a party or affair, they need something dazzling. And then after the event is over, well, they return it."

"For a full refund?"

"It really depends," he said. "We sometimes charge a restocking fee, but each customer is treated individually. We try and work with all of our customers to give them what they want. Sometimes people can't be pleased. Sometimes their demands are not what we are able to accommodate. And sometimes they're just using us."

"And in the case of Noreen Giles?"

"She made us work. And work. And work. Sometimes she would come in and buy a diamond necklace on a Monday and return it on a Wednesday. After a while, even with the restocking fees, it was not in our best interest to continue the relationship."

"Did you suspect fraud?"

Shapiro looked at me. "After a few of these incidents, we became suspicious. We maintain relationships with other jewelers. And after doing some research, we discovered she was pulling the same routine at some of our competitors. So we had to tell her we weren't able to accommodate her anymore. Was it fraud? Maybe. Probably. Sometimes you just run into very eccentric people here, so we try not to judge too harshly. But there was clearly something unusual going on. And then her husband came in and began doing the same thing."

"Didn't the same name ring a bell?"

"Well, they had different last names. After a few go-rounds, we looked into it, discovered they were married and decided that working with them any further was not in our best interest."

"How did they take that?"

"Surprisingly well. You're always a little concerned when you have to tell a client you can't do business with them anymore. But in their case, they simply accepted our decision. Almost as if they had heard this before and were anticipating it. I have no idea what they were actually doing, but it struck us that they were not going to be buying anything they planned on keeping."

"What else?"

"I think that's about the extent of it. And I've probably talked too much as it is. But I think you have a sense of what's going on with them."

Indeed I did. I thanked Mr. Shapiro for his time and he escorted me back through the showroom. I took a last look at the dazzling diamonds containing the fire within. I saw a very pretty young woman bending sideways to put on a large pair of glistening earrings, and the effect on how they made her look was remarkable. It wasn't just the sparkle of the gems; her whole facial expression changed when she looked at herself in the mirror. While I was normally a practical person who didn't make many frivolous purchases, I could better understand now why some people were enamored with jewelry. It made you look a little different. It made you glow. And mostly, it made you feel special.

*

As I strolled along Rodeo Drive, I admired what seemed like a never-ending row of Mercedes, BMWs, the occasional Maserati, and a few exotic cars that I couldn't even identify. When I reached my Highlander rental, it seemed wholly out of place. I actually found myself feeling just a little disappointed as I climbed inside. Spending time in a palace like Harry Kingston's can do that to a person.

I was born into a middle-class household, and with the exception of my four years at USC, I had always led a middle-class lifestyle. From being a uniformed LAPD officer to becoming a private investigator, money was always a little tight. I had gotten by through leading a frugal lifestyle, maintaining a rent-controlled apartment, and spending lavishly only when a celebration was called for. I didn't envy those with a lot of money; it did make life easier, but it also brought a different set of problems. While I could never excuse or forgive a person engaging in criminal fraud, I at least had a better understanding of why the Noreen Giles of the world did what they did.

I took a detour onto Pico Boulevard. and stopped by Pacific Repairs. The manager had the name "*Jorge*" stitched over his blue shirt pocket. The standard pronunciation was *OR-hay,* although he introduced himself as George. He was speaking with one of the mechanics, instructing him on which cars had priority this afternoon. I didn't hear the word Pathfinder in the conversation.

"Hi there," I began.

"Yes, sir," Jorge said. "What can I do for you?"

"My car was towed here this morning. Some front-end damage. The brakes failed. It's the black Pathfinder."

"Oh yes," he said. "I've put together an estimate for

the body work. But you'll also need to put in new brake lines."

"Do you know how they got damaged?"

"They were cut. You must have really ticked someone off."

I frowned. "Why do you say that?"

"This type of cut doesn't happen through normal wear-and-tear. Whoever did this cut a hole into the line, and the fluid began to leak out. If they had cut the lines just before you started to drive this morning, you might not have noticed it right away; it would have taken a while for all the fluid to leak out. But if it were sometime last night, it could have all leaked out over a period of a few hours. By morning, most of the fluid would be on the ground. Did you notice a puddle underneath your vehicle before you got in?"

"I honestly don't recall. And I don't even think I needed to apply the brakes right away. I live very close to the California Incline. There are only a couple of stoplights and they were both green when I approached them. And it was early in the morning, so we didn't have much traffic."

"You were lucky," he acknowledged.

"So there's no way that gash in the brake line could have happened any other way? Maybe the underside of the vehicle hitting something on the road?"

Jorge shook his head no. "These brake lines are hard to damage. They're made with reinforced rubber, so they can withstand most elements. Like if you go off-roading. Even if someone tries to cut the lines, it can be tough, takes a lot of effort. But they can always find a way. It looks like they used a hacksaw. Or maybe an awl. It's a long, pointed spike. Since they had to crawl under your vehicle, they needed something portable and compact. And something that wouldn't have drawn much attention."

"Sounds like they knew what they were doing."

"Oh, I'm sure they did," Jorge said. "This wasn't the work of some amateur. If it was, they would have just slashed your tires or jammed a rag into your tailpipe. Whoever did this has a very good knowledge of cars. They knew exactly what to do."

Eighteen

Jorge told me it would be at least a week before they could perform all of the body work, as well as send the Pathfinder out to have new brake lines installed. I didn't ask the price; instead I handed him the name of my auto insurance company. Given my chosen profession, I always made sure I had a low deductible on my policy so my out-of-pocket cost would only be $200. Detective work had more than its share of "accidents."

I tried to think who might have done this, but the list was so long I decided to focus on who knew something about cars. One person sprang to mind, although I didn't know quite where Oscar Romeo fit into this puzzle. One way to find out was to ask him.

Friday afternoons were the worst times of the week to be on the streets and freeways of Los Angeles. To save myself a little time, I called Patrick Washington before heading out. Oscar had stayed with him for a few days, but when he came up from San Diego, he frequently moved around from friend to friend. Last night he was down in Palos Verdes, and Patrick said he was expected to be there for the weekend. I checked traffic and grimaced at the red and yellow lines on the Sigalert.com map. It would take well over an hour to get down to P.V. It ended up as a long and grueling drive, stop and go most of the way. When I reached the Wade residence, the sun was beginning to set, but the mood on Rocky Point Drive was quiet and peaceful. And the bright blue Lamborghini was parked in the long driveway.

I rang the bell and Ted Wade answered, dressed in tan shorts, a dark green Oregon t-shirt and flip-flops. He initially had a pleasant enough look on his face. Then he recognized me.

"What the hell do you want here?" he demanded.

"It's so nice to see you too," I responded pleasantly.

"I thought I told you not to bother my parents anymore," he sneered. "I was pretty clear. I'm not joking around."

"Good. I'm not here to joke either. And I'm not here to see your parents. Or you either, for that matter."

His mouth opened for a moment and it took him about five seconds to form some words. "I think you better leave. Now."

"I'm here to see Oscar. Would you mind telling him he has a visitor?"

"I said fuck off!"

"No, you didn't. You didn't say anything of the kind. And you don't even own this house, so you don't get to tell me to leave."

He stared at me. "I think you're going to be one sorry ass dude if you don't get the fuck out of here now."

"And I think you should have taken the scholarship offer from Stanford. You might have learned a few things about proper diction."

Ted Wade took a couple of deep breaths and then came at me, like a bull charging a red cape. I could practically see the steam flying out of his nose. He tried to grab me, but I took two steps backwards and then moved suddenly to my left, taking hold of his right arm. Sticking my right foot out, I guided his racing body past me, as my foot caught Ted's ankles and took his legs out from under him. This was part of jiu-jitsu theory; using the opponent's own energy against him. He stumbled and lost his balance and careened onto the curved brick path leading toward the front door. Grunting as he crashed to the pavement, a trickle of blood formed on his left knee where a raw red spot would soon form.

"I'm gonna get you, you bastard," he said, breathing heavily.

"Aw, you got a skinned knee," I said. "You want to put something on that? It might get infected."

His eyes now blazing with rage, Ted Wade scrambled to his feet and came at me again. He put his hand to his mouth and wiped it, and shook his stocky arms to get ready to start punching. I moved backward onto the front lawn, and he put up his hands in a boxer's stance and began to bob and weave.

Out of the corner of my eye I saw others emerge from the house, two men and a woman. I continued to move backward, turning slightly so I was facing the front door and could see anyone else who might approach. I raised my hands as well, but stayed in a defensive posture with my fists unballed. Ted stepped forward and threw a haymaker with his right hand, which I easily ducked. He stumbled a little, but quickly regained his balance. Then he threw a left, which I sidestepped, and then he tried a roundhouse kick, which I blocked with my arms. I grabbed Ted's right leg, jerked it upwards, and sent him tumbling down onto the lawn.

Ted groaned and got to his knees, his chest heaving. He looked like he was trying to figure out what to do next. All of a sudden, a deep voice boomed out to him, as if to ameliorate that problem.

"Stand up!" the voice screamed. "You can take that guy! You're bigger than he is."

I looked over at a paunchy man who had to be in his early 60s, with graying hair and a snarl on his face. He wore a yellow golf shirt, white pants and white sneakers. He pointed at me in a hostile manner and shouted encouragement. Ted Wade pulled himself back on his feet. Moving forward aggressively, he came at me again.

"You stand still," the old guy yelled, pointing a finger at me. "Fight like a man!"

Ted's breath now came in spurts and the expression on his face had turned from anger to something which more resembled fear. For a brief moment I thought he was going to cry. Instead, he gathered himself together and charged me, not with the intent of throwing a punch, but of tackling me and getting me on the ground. This was the last thing I wanted, to engage in a wrestling match with someone who outweighed me by 50 pounds. I pushed my left forearm in his face to keep his body at a distance. I then punched him solidly in the stomach. He doubled over in pain and I sent a flurry of quick rabbit punches to his right ear and neck. He fell back down onto the grass and stayed there. I stepped back further to give him some space.

"Come on, get on your feet!" the man yelled. "I didn't raise a sissy!"

"Why don't you back off," I told him, my own breathing starting to come in spurts.

The man ignored me and walked toward Ted and bent over. "You don't give up! You never quit. Get up and take care of this clown."

"Marvin, please," came a female voice. "Stop this nonsense."

"You shut up," the man screamed back at his wife. Ellen Wade looked like she had just been slapped and took two steps back. Rising to one knee now, Ted Wade gave his head a shake and looked dizzy.

"Get up!" he excoriated Ted. "I told you to get up and act like a ..."

With that, I took a few calculated steps and uncorked a hard right punch to the mouth of the man in the yellow shirt. He stumbled straight backward, his eyes wide with shock, his mouth suddenly agape. He landed flat on his back, bounced a few inches and remained motionless.

"Oh my God!" cried Ellen, now unsure of whether to run to her husband or her son. The older man began to stir and rose to one elbow, but I doubted he'd be getting up soon. He put a hand up to his mouth and began to moan and check his teeth.

And just then, one more figure began to approach, a large man who had remained in the background this whole time. He approached cautiously, his hands raised in a peacemaker position. Fortunately for me, Oscar Romeo did not want to fight.

"Let's cool things down," he started.

"Works for me," I panted. "You're not someone I want to tangle with."

"You don't look like a pushover yourself," he responded. "I don't need any bumps or bruises going into OTAs. Plus, there's a clause in my contract saying the team can cut me if I'm arrested."

I was vaguely wondering why Oscar hadn't jumped in, at the very least to break things up. But peacemakers sometimes get dragged into the thick of things. It wasn't uncommon for someone to enter a fight with the intent of breaking it up, only to wind up throwing punches themselves.

"Maybe we could take a walk down the block," I suggested, wanting to move away from this scene quickly.

"Sure," he said and we started to walk. "You came to talk to me?"

"I did. I just wanted to talk. Not sure how I wound up in a brawl, but these things seem to happen sometimes."

"Yeah," he smiled. "Sometimes trouble just follows you."

"Uh-huh," I managed, and then turned toward him. "So tell me something, Oscar."

"What's that?"

"Were you having a thing with April Horne?"

Oscar gave me a funny look. "You came down here to ask me that?"

I felt a bit of exasperation starting to come out. "No, I came down here to punch out your friend and his idiot father. What I'm trying to do is piece together who killed Gilbert Horne. I was hired by Cliff Roper, who swears he didn't do it. Someone pulled the trigger, but I don't know who that was yet. There are a bunch of people with motives and unfortunately you're one of them. So excuse me if I'm a little ticked off right now. But someone messed with the brakes of my car and almost got me killed. And if my *fiancée* had been riding with me, she could have been killed too. So I'm in a pretty rotten mood and I'd appreciate some answers."

Oscar let out a low whistle. "Okay. I'll tell you about April. I did her. Once. She was drunk and came on to me and I did her. I'm not proud of it. I had problems with Gil and I didn't need more problems. But when a girl who looks like that offers herself up, well, I don't see how I could say no." He paused a moment. "If Gil was still alive I probably wouldn't be telling you this."

"Did it matter to you that Ted was doing her too?"

He started at me. "How'd you know that?"

"Detective work. I find out things."

"Yeah. Well this was before she and Ted hooked up. He came along later."

"Do you think Ted was involved in this shooting?"

Oscar frowned. "I don't think so. Ted's got problems. Big ones. But I can't see it. No good reason for him to do this to his uncle."

I pondered that thought. There was some logic to it, but logic was starting to take a back seat in this case.

"One last question," I said.

"Yeah?"

"You know a lot about cars. I remember you said your father owned a repair shop."

"Good memory."

"Usually," I said wearily. "How much knowledge about cars does someone need in order to cut the brake line?"

Oscar looked past me and thought. "Quite a bit. But it depends on the car. They have to know where it is on each vehicle. And they have to be pretty strong. Those lines don't cut easily. Even if you were trying hard."

*

The Palos Verdes Police had arrived by the time we walked back. After a brief period of question and answer, the Wades decided not to press charges, which was a smart move for a few reasons. First, they'd be faced with the fact that Ted attacked me first, and I had Oscar as a witness. I did proactively knock his old man on his butt, but once a melee begins, proving who did what is tricky. The second and probably more salient reason was that Ted Wade already had a bad-boy image due to his drug use. And getting punched out by someone 20 years his senior was not something the media would ignore.

I drove home in the dark, and fortunately traffic had eased considerably. I actually felt somewhat relaxed, not surprising perhaps, since I had gotten some of my frustration out by slugging Marvin Wade. Nothing like a physical altercation to put one in a state of peace. But when I reached the apartment, turning the doorknob sent pain shooting through my right hand. Fortunately I had a pair of greeters who were more than happy to make me feel better.

Chewy was the first to reach me, jumping up and tapping her paws against my thighs, her tail wagging and her tongue hanging out. I scratched her behind the ears and that quieted her down for a minute. Gail walked over and kissed me.

"You're home late," she said. "The two of us were getting concerned."

"I had some business to attend to," I responded holding up my right hand, which was by now red and swollen.

"Uh-oh. Hopefully the other guy is okay."

"He'll survive. But he might think twice about saying any old thing that pops into his head."

Gail treated my hand and I told her about my day. Chewy sat next to me on the couch and occasionally licked my face. Gail had ordered a pizza for dinner, which fortunately meant I didn't have to operate a knife and fork.

"I found out something interesting today," she said, as I reached for a second slice.

"I'm all ears."

"It's about Noreen Giles."

"Really."

"This isn't her first stab at insurance fraud. Not by a long shot."

"Okay."

"Yes, apparently she did this quite a number of times in Nebraska, Texas, Arizona. They moved from state to state. But it was under different names. I thought it might have been due to marriage, but it looks like she just formed new identities wherever she went. Same with her husband."

"So their real name isn't Giles."

"Nope, hers is Noreen Schiller, his is Will Cardigan. At least that's how they started out. They're not even from Nebraska. They were born and raised in Massachusetts. They may have even started their life of crime there, although I couldn't find anything beyond Texas."

"So they've been arrested before?"

"Arrested, charged and convicted. Both have done jail time. Then they get out, change their names and do it again."

"It must be comfortable to have a pattern you can just fall back into. Like a warm blanket."

"Yes it's a pattern all right. Lather, rinse, repeat. They've defrauded a dozen insurance companies, and gotten away with hundreds of thousands of dollars. They do time and they're supposed to make reparations, but it's awfully hard to find them when they disappear, leave the state and change their names."

"Wonder why they went into real estate?" I asked. "That's a very public profession."

"Apparently that's related," she told me. "When they hold open houses for clients whose property they've listed, they make sure the owners aren't there. Then they spend time going through the nooks and crannies where people hide their valuables. Before any buyers arrive. There have been numerous complaints of thefts over the years. Always jewelry. They never touch anything else."

"Makes sense. First thing a client will check is to make sure their cash is still there. They often forget about the more valuable stuff. Especially if it's tucked away somewhere."

"Using a very public alias allows them to hide in plain sight," Gail continued. "When they go by another name like Giles, that means nothing, no one would figure out who they were. It's a clever plan."

"A lot of crooks are smart," I said. "But they're often lazy and don't want to do the hard work that comes with being successful. This is the quick route. And the easy route."

At that point, Chewy nudged me with her paw. I told her pizza wasn't an acceptable food for dogs. Gail got up and went into the kitchen.

"Here, give her this," she said, handing me a piece of rawhide, the size of a candy bar. "I went to the pet store today. I don't want my shoes getting torn up as she starts teething. I have a feeling there's a reason they named her Chewy."

"How old do you think she is?"

"A few months. Maybe six."

"A true puppy."

"Oh yes," she smiled. "We get to raise her."

"I'm really glad you're into her," I said, waving the rawhide in front of Chewy and getting her to stand up on her hind legs following it. I finally gave it to her and she grabbed the treat in her mouth and trotted off to a corner to work on it.

"She's too cute to turn away," Gail said. "I don't fall in love easily, but she's hooked me."

"You did the same for me," I smiled. Gail smiled back and we spent the rest of the evening cuddling in each other's arms.

The next morning was Saturday and I slept soundly until 9:00 a.m. Gail was already off to the gym, and after reading the paper online, making breakfast and downing a pot of French roast, I was wondering what I'd do today. The weather was looking warm and sunny and a run by the beach was sounding better and better. Then the phone rang and I found out my new plans.

"Hey it's Roper," the voice yelled. "Come on down."

"What do you mean?"

"I mean we're taking a field trip."

"Where?"

"Where? To the spring game, of course. Down at the Coliseum. I thought you were a Trojan. You're supposed to know about these things."

"Would have helped to have had some notice."

"Geez, I gotta do everything for you? I'm giving you limo service. You decent?"

"Yeah, I'm dressed."

"Then get down here. I'm double parked and there's a freaking cop down the street. Let's motor."

Nineteen

USC's annual spring game at the Los Angeles Coliseum is not exactly a game, it is more of a glorified practice. The coaches are on the field, positioned about 20 yards behind the quarterback. They keep "score" using metrics that allow the defense to score points without actually crossing the goal line, a calculus that perhaps only fantasy football enthusiasts can truly appreciate. The scrimmage resembled something of an NFL pre-season game, where the returning starters get limited playing time to avoid injuries. Most of the ones playing in the spring game are younger guys and reserves, players who finally get their chance to demonstrate their abilities to the coaches. Almost as importantly, they actually get to play on the legendary Coliseum field.

For some of the crowd however, the spring game was a social event, and this was especially so for Cliff Roper. Current and former players, rival agents, and even some coaches made the pilgrimage to our seats to schmooze, gather intel, pay respects, or jam a proverbial finger in Roper's eye. There's nothing like kicking a guy when he's down. Not that Cliff Roper ever believed he was ever down. The double murder charge was nothing more than a bug on his windshield. In terms of self-image, he presented himself as than nothing less than king of the sports agent world.

"There he is!" boomed an overweight man with big hair, waddling up to shake hands with Cliff. "I figured you'd have busted out of the tank by now. Someone send you a cake with a gun in it?"

"If they did, I'd wind up using it on *you*," Roper retorted.

"Hey be careful with what you say," the man warned. "Lot of lawyers nearby. I told you not to keep that Glock lying around your office."

"It was locked in a safe, numb nuts. The media didn't get that part right, they always mess up something. Last time I touched it was six months ago. When we went over for target practice at the range."

"I remember," the fat man smiled. "I thought half the club members were going to wind up in the ER."

Roper elbowed me in the ribs. "Cullen, this is Burnside. Burnside, Cullen."

We shook hands. "You working for him?" he asked me.

"In a manner of speaking," I said, squinting my eyes to avoid the bright sun directly behind him.

"Runner?"

I started to laugh. I didn't think I looked the part. A runner was an agent's rep, a young guy, usually in his 20s, someone who ingratiated himself with players, smoothing the path for the agent to sign them.

"Nope," I said. "More of a consultant."

"Burnside's gonna find out who did this," Roper declared. "And they're gonna pay a mighty steep price. Then we'll hand them over to the authorities."

That wasn't quite how I saw the way things would play out. But contradicting Roper on anything was pointless. There did not appear to be much of a filter between what he thought and what he said.

The man walked away and I asked Roper who he was. "Just another agent," he said. "Been in the business too long. Thinks he can get away with just handing envelopes of cash to guys in college. The world is changing. You gotta connect with the players today, they need more hand holding. Most of them have been groomed to play pro sports since they came out of the womb. Their parents aren't parents, they're more like career managers. Kids need something more. That's part of my job now."

"Pretty insightful," I acknowledged. "You know something about raising kids. And I'm very impressed with Honey. She's an amazing young woman."

"Yeah, no thanks to her crazy mom. Shared custody is a bitch. When I had time with her, I made sure she had a good, grounded idea of what life was all about. The good and the bad. I spoke frankly with her. I think she appreciated it. And I think she listened."

"Honey's terrific," I agreed. "She'll go far. Unlike some guys I've met lately."

"Anyone in particular?"

"Ted Wade is the one I'm thinking of."

"Yeah, yeah, we talked about him the other day. Kid's a washout. Built like a Mack truck but he's got the backbone of a lollipop. Throw in a drug problem and you've got a Halloween bag full of trouble. Why the focus on Ted?"

"What did you know about Ted and April?" I asked.

"What did I know? What didn't I know. Look he's a sick kid. Hot or not, who goes and bones his aunt?"

"Step aunt," I pointed out.

"Same difference."

"You don't think Ted could have had anything to do with Gil and April?"

Roper smirked. "I think you're barking up the wrong tree. Maybe if it were an accident, or Ted happened to be at the wrong place at the wrong time. Still ... nah. Kid wouldn't have pulled the trigger. He's a wacko and an ingrate, but no way he did this. Not after everything Gil did for him. Gil treated him like his own son. Gil tried to teach him right from wrong. But he couldn't undo the mess his father made. Marv's an idiot. The kid's damaged goods. But a murderer? Nope. Not Ted."

"Okay," I said, and as I was about to add something, a wide shadow formed over us. It was as if a cloud was passing overhead and a blanket of shade was thrown across the Coliseum. It was, in fact, just thrown over the two of us.

"Well, look who's here," Roper crowed, glancing up with a sudden smile pasted onto his face. "You looking to come back into the fold, big fella?"

Patrick Washington smiled and shook hands with us. "I just came by to pay my respects."

"As well you should, my friend. It's a small world. I can help you make money in ways you never dreamed of."

"I can just imagine, Mr. Roper," he said and turned to me. "How you doing, my man?"

"Hanging in there."

"Heard you really pack a punch," he smiled.

"Word travels fast," I said, impressed.

"What the hell?" Roper asked, looking bewildered.

Patrick turned back to Roper. "Your boy here slapped around both Ted Wade and his dad last night. Both needed treatment from the paramedics."

"Geez, you don't exactly toot your own horn, do you?" Roper exclaimed. "I'm paying you for info. That's big info. I want to know about that stuff."

I shrugged. "Minor altercation. Ted started something, I finished it."

"Yeah," Patrick laughed, "you also shut his dad up pretty good. Lots of people been wanting to put their fist down Marv's throat. But you're the one who did it."

"Glad I could be of service," I managed. "I imagine you talked to Oscar."

"Yeah. Old Oscar said he'd be here today, but I don't see him. You didn't take him out too, did you?"

"Oscar's not in my league," I explained. "Some people you don't mess with."

"Hey, Patrick," Roper broke in, getting antsy about not being the center of attention. "What brings you down here today? You're not a Trojan."

"No, but I got a cousin who's a redshirt freshman here. Devin Jackson. Looking at being second-string nose tackle this year. Probably be a starter soon. He's a beast, he'll do well. Wanted to support him. I'm still an L.A. guy at heart, you know."

"Yeah, yeah. So who's representing you now?"

Patrick Washington smiled and pointed a few rows up in the stands. "Josh Lieberman. He used to be with you a few years ago. Broke off and started his own agency. We got a good rapport. I just signed with him."

Roper looked at him warily. "Josh is a good kid," he said. "But if you want to make a grown man's income, you and I should talk."

Patrick laughed. "I wanted a Jewish agent. Get me the best deal."

"So why didn't you call me?" Roper asked, acting hurt.

"You're Jewish?" Patrick peered at him.

"Let's not quibble about details," Roper said, giving him a wink.

Patrick laughed again and went back to his seat. Roper stared onto the field and watched the next play unfold and Patrick's cousin helped out on the tackle. "Devin Jackson. Got good bloodlines, but I don't see him making it," he said. "He has Patrick's size but not his athleticism. I don't see him starting. He's two years away from being two years away."

Down on the field, the punter boomed a 60-yarder but he outkicked the coverage. The punt returner caught the ball, moved up the field and found a seam in the coverage. He cut back across the grain and then outran everyone on his way toward the end zone. The crowd came alive and began to cheer as he crossed the goal line.

"Who's that?" I asked.

"Andre Mazin. True freshman, just enrolled this spring. I watched him play high school ball down in Santa Ana last season. Kid's a natural. Best tailback I've seen in years. He'll be starting before the end of this season."

"Tailback's one of the few positions a true freshman can come in and start making plays right away," I acknowledged. "With that position, it's all about talent. Speed and moves. If he can handle the faster pace of the college game, he doesn't need to learn that much. Unlike most other positions."

Roper looked at me curiously. "I sometimes forget you used to play this game."

"Yeah," I said, a little wistfully. "Me too."

Over the years, I had tried to watch as many Trojan games as my free time allowed. But between LAPD shifts and the demands from running my own agency, my work often took me away from the game. I tried to attend at least one or two football games a year. Hopefully, Gail would take a shine to this culture and join me.

"So you got anyone else you're looking at for this case?" Roper asked. "Ted Wade sounds like a dry well."

"I'm still looking at Oscar Romeo. And Horne's assistant has a husband who may hold a grudge. But neither strikes me as the one. Just a hunch. I'm still scratching the surface here. There's more to this, I know there is. I just need to keep digging."

"Dig faster," Roper commanded. "And, oh, yeah, one other thing I need to say. Honey's off limits to you."

I looked at him. "She's a little young. And I'm a little engaged."

"Yeah, yeah, don't give me that engaged stuff. Everyone who meets her wants to get into her pants. You've seen what she looks like. And she's not too young, you're too old. And you don't make enough money."

"I'm glad you've laid out the requirements for her prospective mate. Have you told Honey about these?"

"I'm telling you," he warned, pointing a finger at me. "You got a good thing there with that lawyer girlfriend; she's way hotter than someone at your pay level deserves. Stick with what you got and count your blessings."

I sat back and took a deep breath. Cliff Roper's innate ability to quickly size up a situation was impressive. I assumed Honey told Cliff about our lunch and he snapped the pieces together. Just like I did in my job. But it's a lot harder to look at yourself in the mirror and put things into perspective. I know people often have bachelor parties and some have one last fling before tying the knot. But that didn't seem appealing to me. And whether or not Gail was above my pay grade was inconsequential. We were together because we filled the holes in each other's lives. I just needed to make sure I didn't create any new holes. Staying away from Honey Roper was not bad advice.

Twenty

Cliff dropped me back home in the late afternoon. Gail had learned about a fenced-in dog park near Santa Monica Airport, so the three of us piled into my Highlander to go check it out. Chewy had a blast running around and making some new friends. She seemed to take delight in teasing the other dogs into chasing her, and then using her speed and moves to outrun them. If she were a human, she'd be a natural tailback.

The next day was Sunday, and we slept in. I got up and cruised the Internet for a little while until Gail began to get hungry. During a casual lunch at Izzy's, a local coffee shop, we went over some wedding plans. Or I should say, Gail went over them, and I agreed enthusiastically and complimented her on her excellent taste and keen sense of design. I think I listened to most of what she said, but I couldn't be sure. Then I told Gail I'd need to go off and do some work today.

"You've got a 24-7 business," she remarked.

"It's the nature of what I do. Feast or famine. I had a steady paycheck for years with the LAPD, but then I needed to move on to something else. So I picked a new job, and became the person who did it. Whatever my case is, I dive in fully. This is who I am now."

"And I do love who you are," she said. "And I respect the fact that you care so much about your work, and that you feel it's important. I need to be with someone who has a passion for what they do."

I sensed a "but" coming along, so I provided it for her. "But...?"

"No buts, *amigo*. I do like spending time with you."

"Good thing, because we're getting married soon. And at some point, we'll have more time together. So much so, that I may wind up getting underfoot."

"And that's where some of my concern comes in," she said, eyeing me closely. "If you work every weekend, we'll be getting ourselves into patterns. I'll find other things to do, hobbies of my own, and when you become available, you may not want to share these with me. Or you may, but only because you'll feel obliged. And you might end up resenting it."

I held up my hand. "I think we're getting ahead of ourselves here. Not every weekend is going to be like this. And I think I'm getting closer to cracking this case."

"How so?"

"Gilbert Horne was having affairs. Lots of them. So was his wife April. It's possible one of their playthings found out they weren't the one and only as it were, got mad and did something about it. But there's also some bystanders that may have gotten hurt. Meaning there's at least one woman who had her marriage wrecked over it. Maybe this couple would have broken up anyway. But it's possible one of these spouses could have gone off and taken some action on their own."

"You also mentioned Horne had money problems. Are they related to what happened to him in the end?"

"Maybe," I said. "This one's a little complicated because the Hornes' extra-marital indulgences spilled over into their business interests."

"How does Roper's daughter fit into this?"

I froze. "What do you mean?"

"I mean," she said, her clear gray eyes staring straight at me, "why are you spending some of your valuable time with her?"

"She's part of the case," I said, and this was partially true. And partially not. Honey Roper certainly gave me some insight into the Hornes. But I had gone out of my way to see her for a different, more personal reason, a reason I was still trying to untangle in my mind.

Honey was my last fling, figuratively perhaps, a flirtation that I thought neither of us wanted to let get out of hand. Her father even more so. But there was something else. In an odd way, she reminded me of someone from my past, someone I kept trying to forget but really couldn't. Judy Atkin, the 17 year-old runaway who changed my life. But Honey wasn't Judy. Honey was a young adult and seemingly self-assured. But Honey did strike me as a little damaged inside. Her exterior brimmed with confidence, but maybe not so much within. I had met enough people in the entertainment industry to see the signs, and Honey had them. A part of me would always feel the need to reach out to someone who was wounded. Call it paternal instinct. Or maybe just foolishness.

"Do you like her?" Gail asked softly.

I stared at her. "It's different. She's not you. You're my life, she's not. I can't fully explain it other than to say you have nothing to worry about. We have nothing to worry about."

"That's good," she said quietly.

"How did you come to bring up Honey Roper?" I asked. Gail wasn't the type to read my emails, and I doubted Honey would try to phone me at home.

"Cliff Roper called me."

"Cliff Roper called you?" my eyes widening, and starting to blaze. "Why?"

"He wanted to know when you would be home yesterday. Said he needed to speak with you about Honey. He also said I had nothing to worry about, which suddenly made me start to worry. I guess he wants to look out for his daughter. Said he needed to have a conversation with you. Did he?"

"He did," I replied. My first reaction was to go and throttle Cliff Roper for sticking his nose into my personal business and for saying anything at all to my *fiancée*. But as I thought it through, I began to understand his fatherly concern, as twisted and poorly executed as it might be. Cliff Roper looked at the world of women in the same way athletes did, that they were there to service men and that was the beginning and the end of it. Honey was different however, as daughters often are. Cliff's talking to Gail about this, however, was going beyond what I considered reasonable behavior.

"So Cliff went and talked to you about her," she said. "And?"

"And I assured him nothing was going on. And I'm assuring you the same thing. There's only one woman in the world that I want to be with. That's you."

"Good," she said, her face starting to relax. "That's good. I want our marriage to work. And trust is imperative. You don't have to tell me everything you do. But I want to be able to trust your heart."

"You can," I said, and then smiled and took her hand. "And I know it's especially important because we have another mouth to feed."

Gail gave me a puzzled look.

"Chewy."

"Oh," she laughed. "Of course. And I get to play with her again today. Actually I think I'm going to take her in for a bath. She needs one."

"Every girl deserves a spa day once in a while."

"Well today's going to be hers."

We kissed and I dropped Gail back at the apartment. I had a few to-do items on my agenda for the rest of the day. The first was to go talk to Art Luttinger. I did an Internet search, but it came up empty, he was still listed as living on 11th Street with his wife, Betty. I didn't want to go back to Betty's apartment, so I decided to drive over to Bay City Motor Cars. It was a Sunday, so it was unlikely she'd be around. Maybe those who were there might be in the mood to talk.

I parked down the street from the dealership and walked onto the lot. Betty Luttinger wasn't there, and not many others were either. I saw one other patron walk around a BMW three times before they opened the driver's-side door and peeked tepidly inside. I pretended to be interested in a Porsche Cayenne, a small SUV that had a retail price of $90,000.

"Now that's a good family vehicle," said a voice from behind me. I turned and saw a familiar face. Christy Vale approached, looking like she was wearing some extra rouge on her cheeks. Her eyes were bloodshot, and her eyelids looked heavy. It wasn't hard to tell she had been crying recently.

"Maybe if you're a Kardashian," I commented.

"Well now, you're going to be a married man soon. You have to plan for the future."

"I'm certainly trying to," I said wryly. "And you have a good memory."

"It's an occupational requirement," Christy said. "Know thy customer."

"I'll bet you're a good salesperson," I remarked.

Christy nodded sadly. "I am," she sighed. "When there are people to sell to. But you can't sell when you don't have floor traffic. This is a slow period. And it's tough without Gil. I miss him a lot. We all miss him."

"I'm sure this whole episode has been quite a shock."

"It's been very traumatic," she agreed. "I don't even think I'm able to mourn yet. I keep trying to forget this whole nightmare ever happened. It feels like that's the only way I can get through it."

"Denial only helps for so long," I pointed out.

"Oh, I know. It's bad for me personally, and it doesn't help that our business is bad too right now. Gil was the marketing guy, he knew how to bring customers in the door. It's not the same without him. I'm trying to keep my spirits up. We'll get through this, but it's tough."

"Have you heard anything from Betty?"

"No, she hasn't been in all week. I'm a little worried about her."

"Because of Gil?"

"Sure."

"What about Art?"

She peered at me. "What do you know about Art?"

"Not much. I was hoping you might fill me in."

"Arty," she sighed. "What a lame-o. Betty's had it rough."

"Why do you say that about her husband?"

"He's a failure. A never-do well, I think you call him."

I decided not to tell her it's pronounced ne'er do well. And I didn't want to sidetrack her.

"I heard he was in sales too," I said.

"Sure, I guess you could call Arty a salesperson. He works in telemarketing, which is the lowest of the low. He used to work here. Hard to believe, but he did. In six months I think he sold one car."

I stared at her. "Art Luttinger worked at the dealership?"

"He did. I guess Betty leaned on Gil to hire him. Big mistake. He can't sell toner, much less expensive cars. They finally got him out of here, which was a relief to everyone. Legit buyers were walking out the door because he was a bumbling fool. If a client is going to spend upwards of six figures, they want to be sure their salesperson knows what they're talking about."

"He didn't know much about cars?"

"He knew something about them. He just couldn't communicate it well," she said, her voice starting to rise suddenly and become more animated. "He'd have been better off working for Ike in the service department! Oh hi, baby!"

I turned to see Isaac Vale, dressed in his usual short sleeve shirt that displayed his massive, hairy arms. I guess if I had guns like that, I'd wear short sleeve shirts too. If you've got it, flaunt it.

"Hello again," Isaac boomed.

I stuck up a hand and waved, lest he decided to test his grip on my right hand again. Given its tender status, I didn't need any more damage inflicted.

"You're becoming almost like family," he said. "I keep seeing you here."

"I just can't stay away," I said. "You always work Sundays?"

"Just stopped by to take care of some loose ends. No rest for the weary."

"Know the feeling," I agreed.

Christy slipped her arm inside Isaac's. "I was giving Mr. Burnside the skinny on Arty Luttinger."

Isaac moved a step away from Christy. "Oh yeah. Him. Didn't work out. Why the interest?"

"I'm doing an investigation. About Gil and his wife."

"Oh ... I thought ... well, I had read that the police arrested his partner in that other business. That sports agent."

"I don't think he did it."

"Really? You're thinking Art was involved?"

I turned my palms skyward. "I'm not sure what to make of things. I've never met the guy, but he does have a motive. Gil was sleeping with his wife."

"Yeah," he said, nodding slowly as he pondered this. "That's plenty of motive. I could see where he'd be totally pissed."

They both stopped talking and looked behind me. I turned and saw a very unhappy Duncan Whitestone approaching.

"Mr. Burnside," he started. "May I ask the reason for your visit today?"

I stared at him. "I need a reason?"

"Yes, you're taking up my people's valuable time with your investigation."

"Sounds like you have something to hide."

"I have nothing to hide," Whitestone said angrily. "And you're not the police. I am not going to have my place of business disturbed by some rent-a-cop who is wasting everyone's time."

"I don't care whose time I'm wasting," I said evenly, not liking the rent-a-cop crack one bit. "My job is to make sure a man doesn't go to jail for a crime he may not have committed."

"And you don't know that. And that's why we have a process, a system of justice in this country. To prevent those types of mistakes."

"That process doesn't work so well. Maybe you should stick to selling overpriced cars and not give me a lecture on our criminal justice system."

"Overpriced?!" he snarled. "Maybe to people like you who can't afford them."

"Most of the world can't afford what your peddling," I fired back. "And judging by the number of people on your lot today, I'd say the world agrees with me."

Duncan Whitestone drew in a breath and I half-expected it to come out of his ears in the form of steam. "Ike. Christy. I think you both have work to do," he said to them and then he turned to me. "It's time for you to leave."

I briefly thought about challenging him to see if he could make me leave. But then I remembered the big arms of Isaac Vale, as well as my sore right hand, and decided not to push the envelope any further. At least not right now.

"Sure," I said. "I wouldn't want to interrupt everyone's busy day."

Twenty-one

I walked a few blocks to cool off before stopping at a familiar sign. Growing up decades ago in Los Angeles, we had not yet been blessed with convenience stores such as 7-Eleven or Circle K. The liquor stores effectively served as convenience stores. Besides alcohol, they sold everything from newspapers and magazines to candy bars and milk. Stopping at Jerry's Liquor, I bought a paper copy of the Sunday *L.A. Times*, something I hadn't done in a dozen years. With the advent of the Internet, I got my news electronically. But no matter how hard I searched the *Times* website, I could find nothing on open houses for Giles & Giles today. Perusing through the hard copy provided me with the answer I needed. They had one open house on June Street, tucked inside the exclusive enclave of Hancock Park. I drove there, parked, read the newspaper, and waited for it to end at 4:00 p.m.

At roughly 4:05 p.m., Noreen Giles and her husband walked outside, locked the door and removed the open house signs from the property. It was a beautiful home, older, stately, very dignified, certainly very expensive. It screamed Old Money. The pair drove off and about 30 minutes later another couple arrived and entered the home. I waited 10 minutes and walked to the front door and rang the bell. A small sign with the words "Pelletier" sat above the buzzer. A man and a woman, both in their late 60s, both well dressed, opened the door together.

"Yes?"

"Hello," I said and flashed my P.I. badge. "The name's Burnside. I'm a private investigator. Do you mind if I have a word with you?"

They looked at each other. "My goodness. What's wrong?" the woman said.

I smiled. "It's a little complicated. May I come in?"

"What does this concern?" she asked, suspiciously.

"This concerns theft at open houses," I said. "Have you checked your valuables yet."

"Why no, we just arrived home," said the woman. "What's happening?"

"There have been reports lately regarding theft of jewelry."

She turned to her husband. "Charlie, would you mind checking?"

"I don't know where you keep your diamonds," he protested. "Hell, I barely know where you keep my single malt Scotch."

"Oh good lord, I'll go check," she said. Charlie stood at the door. We looked at each other for a few minutes and said nothing. A yelp from the back of the house told me what I needed to know.

"It's gone!" she cried. "All of it! All of my jewelry! And the diamond necklace, that was priceless! And your Rolex, Charlie. And those diamond earrings you gave me for our silver anniversary."

"Damn!" yelled Charlie. "I knew we shouldn't have had an open house. Laura, I told you so. It makes us sitting ducks for burglars. But those realtors, they insisted."

"Insisted?" I asked.

"Yes," Laura wailed as she returned to the front door. "They told us that was the only way to sell a house these days. Buyers don't get driven around by realtors much anymore. They just come by the Sunday open houses to check them out."

"They make it all sound so reasonable."

"Oh yes," she continued. "They also said we couldn't be here. They said buyers and sellers should never meet. They said we should never be at our own open house."

I closed my eyes for a moment and then blinked them open. "May I come in?"

Charlie threw up his hands. "Why not? Anything valuable we own is now gone. Nothing else left to steal. Come on in! Make yourself at home!"

I walked into their home. It was neat and tidy and elegant. A handwritten note from Noreen Giles was sitting on the large oak kitchen table, which probably could seat a dozen people. The note let them know there had been a number of interested parties, and she thought multiple offers would be coming this week.

"How well do you know your realtors?"

"Know them?" Laura asked.

"Yes. How did you meet?"

"We got some of their flyers," she answered. "Seems like they leave one on our doorstep every week. When we decided to sell our house, we talked to three or four different realtors. Noreen and Will said they lived nearby and said they worked this neighborhood almost exclusively. They seemed liked good salespeople. They said they could get a lot more money for our house than any of the other realtors said they could."

"Say," Charlie broke in. "You don't think ... "

"Oh no." she moaned.

"Oh yes," I said. "They've been involved in a variety of insurance fraud schemes. I can't be positive they're the ones who stole your valuables, but it makes sense at this stage. There are burglars who go through open houses, but in this instance, I think this was an inside job."

"I'm calling the cops!" Laura declared.

"No, I'm gonna find out where they live," Charlie declared. "I'll go get everything back."

"Wait a minute," I broke in and turned to Charlie. "How are you going to do that? They'll just deny everything."

"I'll make 'em understand the situation," he said. "They don't know who they're messing with."

I stared at him. "You don't happen to have a gun, do you?"

"Sure I do. This is L.A. Everybody's got a gun."

I rubbed the bridge of my nose. "Your wife has the right idea, Charlie. Let the police handle this. You're dealing with professional thieves. You don't know what they're capable of."

"Oh, yeah? They don't know what I'm capable of," he insisted.

"Charlie, he's right," Laura told him. "Calm down. It's not worth it. You don't want to wind up in jail yourself. Or worse."

Looking sheepish but feeling outnumbered, Charlie shook his head and muttered something before going over to the couch and sitting down.

"Do you happen to have photos of the stolen jewelry?" I asked.

Laura said yes. "I do. Our insurance agent suggested I take shots of valuables. More in case of a fire, but theft is covered on our policy too. I have photos of everything."

"Great. Do you have a copier here?

"Yes. Do you want a copy of the photos? But why?"

"I have an idea of how we might get these back. And I could actually use two copies."

Laura went and found the photos while I watched Charlie stare at the floor, obviously disappointed he wouldn't be able to threaten anyone with a gun today. She returned a few minutes later with the copies.

"Should I file a police report?" she asked.

I thought for a moment. "Why don't you wait until tomorrow," I said. "I have an idea here." Knowing how under-staffed the LAPD was these days, it was unlikely this would be a priority for them. But it might be for Harold Stevens.

On the drive home, the freeway was wide open. The Dodger game had gone into extra innings and there were relatively few cars on the road. I arrived in Santa Monica feeling good. And then, as I drove up 4th Street, I knew immediately that something was wrong. There was commotion up the road and the police had Montana Avenue sealed off. Barricades were set up and there were about 10 police cars, as well as half a dozen TV news vans. I parked two blocks away and walked the rest of the way back to Montana.

"What happened here?" I asked a bystander, a young man in his late 20s, wearing a t-shirt and shorts.

"Police found a body. In a dumpster behind that building," he said, pointing to my apartment building.

I froze, although my imagination began to go wild. "Man or woman?" I managed.

"Oh it was a man, all right. A very big man. Apparently someone really clobbered him, hit him in the back of the head."

I stared at him. "That's pretty gruesome. And that certainly counts as news. No surprise the media's here. But why so many of these news trucks?"

"Guy's famous. He plays for the Chargers. Or used to, I guess. Linebacker. Name's Oscar Romeo."

Twenty-two

I knew there was no point in calling Detective Mulligan, or anyone else at the Hollywood Division. If they hadn't already figured out I lived in the apartment building next to where Oscar's body was left, they would do so eventually. It was better to be proactive and start the process. I decided to go down first thing the next morning.

"Sweetie, I think you should have a lawyer present when you're being questioned," Gail said.

I considered this. "You know, this is something I've been through before and I know the drill. I've been on both sides of the table. I understand you're just being careful. But this is something I can handle."

"I worry about you," she said, reaching over and squeezing my hand.

"I worry about you too," I said and stroked her long brown hair. "When I saw all those police cars, my mind went to dark places."

The next morning brought more of the usual. Overcast, gloomy and depressing. I opted to stop for a maple scone and a *vente* dark roast at a Starbucks on the way over to the Hollywood Division. I ate the scone at a small table as I combed through my iPad, reading the various articles on Oscar Romeo's murder. In the time it took for me to finish my scone, I learned everything that was publicly available. The coffee was always too hot to drink right away, so I sipped it on the drive over to the LAPD station. The coffee wasn't bad, although I still preferred the taste of my home-brewed French roast.

It was almost 7:00 a.m. when I arrived at the Hollywood Division. This time I dumped both my .38 special and my cell phone in the glove compartment. I walked into the Division and it was as busy as ever. When I reached the homicide unit, the assistant there knew exactly who I was.

"Oh, my," she said. "Mr. Burnside. Detective Johnson was going to call you."

"I figured as much."

"I'll go get him."

A minute later Jim Johnson appeared, and he carried his own cup of Starbucks. His was a smaller, *grande* size. He gave me a long look. I looked back at him and then motioned to my coffee cup.

"Mine's bigger than yours," I said.

Johnson continued to stare at me. "Trouble seems to follow you everywhere, doesn't it, Burnside?"

I smiled. "Trouble is my middle name."

"A real wise guy. Okay, follow me. You know the routine."

We entered the same room we had been in for last week's interrogation. It was still as bare and stark as it was last week. A window on one side, a two-way mirror on the other. The two-tone green paint job still needed some touch up work. I noticed some additional paint chips lining the floor just underneath the baseboards.

"You guys paint these rooms now and then?"

"Sit down. Forget about the paint."

I took a sip of my Starbucks. I wondered what roast they were using. Maybe Ethiopian, the birthplace of coffee. While the flavor would take some getting accustomed to, the caffeine kick I was getting was as good as my French roast. Maybe better.

"This Starbucks is good coffee," I remarked.

"Yeah. Sure. Better than what we serve here."

"I'll bet you ordered the blonde roast."

He looked at me and opened his mouth for a brief moment and then closed it. He continued to stare at me for a long minute. Maybe it was two minutes. Very standard. It was a tactic designed to try and make me feel ill at ease and start to squirm. Unfortunately he forgot I had been a cop for thirteen years.

"Oh, Burnside. You've really gotten your pecker in a wringer, haven't you?"

"Mine feels pretty good right now. How does yours feel?"

"You just don't know what you're looking at, do you?"

"Sure I do. I'm a looking at a lazy detective. I'm looking at a stupid cop who takes the easy way out. I'm looking at someone who wanted a gold shield so he wouldn't have to put on a blue uniform every day and look like everyone else. I'm looking at a vain police officer who gets his manhood from a badge."

Johnson's mouth curled again in that nasty way of his. "You're looking at someone who's going to knock your teeth out in a minute."

"Go ahead and try," I sneered. "But open a window first. That way someone might hear your cries for help."

Johnson's mouth curled even further and his voice growled with anger. "You better start talking about your activities this week," he growled. "Right now. It'll make life a lot easier for you down the road."

"Tell me why I should."

"Why you should? Maybe to avoid having to take your last breath lying on a gurney with a needle sticking out of each arm. If you're lucky you'll get 30-to-life. Keep being a jackass and you'll wind up on death row. Are those good enough reasons?"

"You'll have to do better than that," I said.

Johnson took a breath and pretended to be deep in thought. "We'll put aside your role in the Horne murders for a moment."

"Oh, please do. You've wrapped that one up. Put a bow on it and everything. Cliff Roper's your man there."

"Maybe he did it with your help."

"And maybe you're making this stuff up as you go," I said.

"Oh no, I don't think so. Let's see. You encountered Oscar Romeo a number of times. First at Patrick Washington's house. Then you were snooping around the Horne residence after the murders. Looking to see if there was any evidence lying around that you needed to get rid of. Then you discovered Oscar was there. Oh, yeah. We talked to that neighbor, that famous screenwriter. We know all about your comings and goings. You kept heading back to that dealership where Oscar bought his cars. Then you followed Oscar down to Ted Wade's house in P.V. and picked a fight. Took a walk with Oscar right after that. You threatened him then and there? Pretty interesting how you seemed to know where he was all the time. Just how does that happen?"

"I'm a lucky guy. I carry a four-leaf clover with me."

"Uh-huh. And then Oscar winds up dead, his body tossed in a dumpster next to your apartment. What's the matter? Was he too heavy to move anywhere else?"

"If I had killed him, would I really have left the body right by my home? Is that what you think? Are you that stupid?"

"What I think," Johnson said, in a measured voice, "is that you dumped the body there to make us believe someone else did it. Make it so obvious, we would never be foolish enough to imagine you had done it."

"Wow, you're a genius, Johnson. Another Sigmund Freud. You piece that together yourself, or did you get help from some inpatient at a psych ward?"

"You're a real smartass," he said. "But I think this time you've out-smarted yourself."

"Tell me something. You discovered the body yesterday, right?"

"Wow. You watch the evening news."

"But the body had been there for 24 hours."

"And you've got an alibi for where you were on Saturday."

"Indeed I do."

"So tell me, smart guy, where were you on Saturday?"

"I was at home in the morning and at the USC spring game in the afternoon. Down at the Coliseum."

"Oh that's convenient. Who were you with?"

"Cliff Roper."

Jim Johnson smiled. It was an ugly smile. His teeth were straight and his mouth was big but it was the type of smile formed by a broken person who didn't see humor in anything. It was the smile of a man who looked like he was about to bite something.

"Oh, that's priceless, Burnside! Just priceless! Your alibi is that you were with a guy who's out on bail for committing double murder. And the football player who got whacked this weekend was a client of Cliff Roper's partner. How perfect is that? I can't wait to see the look of the jury when they hear you spin that yarn to them. Better confess now, Burnside. The trial is going to be an afterthought."

"I guess you forgot the other 25,000 people at the Coliseum. Not to mention the dozen or so people who came up to us there."

"We can work our way around that."

I suddenly started getting a little uneasy. I didn't like the sound of that one. Lazy cops sometimes took liberties with evidence. But there was no way this one was going to get pinned on me. The evidence was circumstantial and the police investigation was shoddy and full of holes.

"You can do whatever you want and mishandle whatever evidence you get your grubby paws on. But I keep waiting to hear a motive and I'm not getting one. Why on earth would I want to kill three people?"

"Oh, I don't know. Maybe because you just had 10 grand in cash dumped into your bank account."

I stared at him, but I shouldn't have been surprised. Privacy was a commodity that had disappeared long ago in America. Whatever you do, wherever you go, someone could find out about it. There were cameras on many street corners, devices grabbing every license plate number of every car that drives through an intersection. Mobile phones that tracked your every move, wherever you went. So law enforcement accessing someone's bank records was not all that unusual. Whether it was legal or not was another question.

"That $10,000 was my investigation fee from Cliff Roper," I told him.

Johnson smiled again. "Oh this is getting better and better. You get paid 10 grand to go ask a few questions? I say Roper paid you to knock those people off. Now you can go share a cell with him in San Quentin."

I was getting more and more irritated with this line of questioning. "Have you bothered to track Oscar's cell phone? I know he still had it on him because that's what it said in the *Times* article. Once you analyze the GPS inside Oscar's phone you'll figure out how long he'd been in the dumpster. Then you can work backward and figure out time of death. And then you can track my cell phone and see where I've been the last two days. You'll be mighty disappointed when you find out there's no match."

Johnson took a breath. "That doesn't mean anything," he stammered. "That doesn't exonerate you. That doesn't get you off the hook."

"Oh it will," I countered. "You have nothing on me and you know it. You were hoping I'd come in and start crying and confess this morning, weren't you? Make everything easy, wrap things up in a nice package so you don't have to dirty your hands by doing real police work? I guess you figured lightning would strike twice, the Horne murders and Oscar's murder all neatly solved and wrapped up. Sorry to disappoint. But there's still a killer at large. And someone better get on them. They're covering their tracks now. By the time you get around to them, there'll be nothing to find."

"Okay, wise guy. Let's have your cell phone. We can determine that easy enough."

"I don't have it on me," I said. "You can check. But if that's what you want, go do things the right way and get a court order. And send someone else around to pick it up. I won't surrender it to you. Your credibility is shot. And from what I hear, I'm hardly the only one around here who thinks so."

Johnson's nose wrinkled in anger. I stood up.

"Where are you going?" he asked.

"I came here voluntarily. And unless you're going to charge me with something, I'm leaving. But you're not going to charge me with anything and you know it. You don't have jack on me, other than a stupid hunch and a pathetic amount of circumstantial evidence. You place me under arrest now and I'll make it my life's mission to have your badge on a silver platter. And if you've done your homework on me, you know I can deliver. When I get my teeth into something, I don't let go. I would suggest you start doing some real detective work and stop being a pussy and taking the easy way out."

I walked out of the room and down the hall. No one followed me. I passed what served as a kitchen and took a quick look at the institutional coffee machine and the black swill they offered here. Even someone like Jim Johnson got his coffee elsewhere. I walked downstairs and approached the Highlander. A meter maid had placed a parking ticket under the wiper blade. I looked up at a sign which told me street sweeping was that morning. Getting into the Highlander, I drove quickly down the street. The ticket blew off after about three blocks.

Twenty-three

I decided I could use a friendly face right about now and headed down La Brea to stop in on Harold Stevens. He seemed to welcome my presence, and unlike Jim Johnson, it was not so he could mess up my life. His reaction was a comforting change of pace.

"Come in!" he boomed happily. "Good to see you! I've been wondering about you lately."

"Join the club," I said, and took a seat. "It's been a busy week. But I've got something for you on the Giles couple."

"Do tell."

I related the life of crime the two of them had chosen, the numerous insurance companies they had defrauded, the jewelry stores they manipulated, and clients they had burglarized. They were realtors who didn't sell many houses; Noreen and Will Giles made their living on guile. They lifted whatever valuables they could when their clients were away. They purchased expensive jewelry, returned it, and then filed false claims with their insurance companies. I passed Harold photos of the various diamond rings, necklaces and bracelets that their latest victims were relieved of. He perused them and tossed the photos onto his desk.

"Okay," Harold said. "This is good work. We have enough to deny their claim. But I don't know as we have enough solid evidence to put them away. And even if we did, it would probably only be for a period of time. After that they'd go back to their same old habits. They're career criminals and they do only one thing. Steal."

"Quite true," I said. "Their most recent victims wanted to go after them with a gun. I had to dissuade them."

Harold nodded. "You made a good call. Crooks like this expect retribution from some of the saps they rip off. I'm sure if any of their victims confronted them, they would react pretty swiftly. And probably violently. People like that are quick on the draw. They have to be. They have a lot to lose."

"They could stand to learn a lesson," I said.

Harold tilted his head. "Maybe," he replied. "I'm not a fan of vigilante justice. But I also know that thieves like these are usually not redeemable. They just go back to stealing when they get out of jail. I see it over and over."

"They're XYY," I joked.

"What's that?" Harold frowned.

"XYY is what they used to refer to as the genetic makeup of a criminal."

"You pick that up at USC?"

I smiled. "I think it might have been off some graffiti scrawl."

Harold smiled back. "You're a veritable gold mine of information."

"I get that a lot."

"So it sounds like you might have a plan?"

234

Indeed I did. Harold smiled as I told him about it, and said he'd help arrange for some police backup. Leaving his office, I drove over to the Giles home and parked down the street, close enough so that I could see them coming and going, yet far enough away so that I was not noticeable. It was a quiet neighborhood, and in the 30 minutes I waited, the only activity I saw was a neighbor walking an Irish Setter.

There were two cars in their driveway, a silver Honda Civic and a red Dodge Dart. This posed a problem if both Noreen and Will left at the same time. That is to say, I could only follow one of them. I reached into the glove compartment and retrieved my pistol and slipped it into the holster. And then sat back and waited. Fortunately, Noreen Giles made it easy. She not only departed by herself, but she was carrying a brown satchel, in addition to having a black purse slung over her shoulder. The satchel might contain nothing more valuable than some random papers. But I had a feeling that was not the case.

Wearing slacks and a denim jacket, she drove off in the Dodge Dart. I maintained a short distance behind her. In most tail operations it was not uncommon to be two or three car lengths behind. In L.A., however, that could easily result in losing the tail. So many drivers blasted through yellow and even red lights these days, that it was imperative that no one block my access to her. Since I was driving a different vehicle than last time, I didn't imagine she would notice it was me tailing her. I also didn't imagine she'd be suspecting anyone at all would be following her.

I stayed behind her down La Brea and onto the 10 Freeway going towards downtown. I wondered if she'd head to the jewelry mart, a small area near Pershing Square. But she drove straight through the downtown interchange, past the four-level, and exited at Caesar E. Chavez Avenue in Boyle Heights. I hadn't expected her to end up in East L.A.

During the earlier part of the 20th century, Boyle Heights was a bustling Jewish neighborhood. What is now Caesar E. Chavez Avenue was previously called Brooklyn Avenue. That was not a name given by happenstance, but rather to welcome New Yorkers who were thinking of moving west. The neighborhood eventually gave way to other ethnic groups. The Jewish community moved into the Fairfax district, and eventually on to Beverlywood and up into the Valley enclaves of Encino and Tarzana. Jews were replaced in East L.A. by Mexican immigrants, so the Boyle Heights of today bears little resemblance to the one that existed prior to World War II. Back in the 1990s, the city officially removed Brooklyn Avenue from the map, and Caesar E. Chavez Avenue was born. But as in any transitional community, a few stragglers remained, those who either couldn't afford to move or chose to stay because of familiarity with the area.

Noreen Giles parked in front of a group of aging shops that lined most of the street. One of those was Bernie's Loan & Jewelry Shop. On one side of it was a hair salon, on the other was an adult bookstore. The sidewalks looked as if they hadn't been swept in years. I parked right behind Noreen and quickly hopped out of my Highlander. I ran over to the Dart's passenger door and when she turned off the engine, the automatic door locks immediately opened on all four doors. This was a convenience feature which mostly showcased the ingenuity of an automotive engineer. It also served to put the driver in potential danger if a criminal wanted to quickly enter the vehicle. Or a cagey private investigator.

I drew my .38 and jerked open the door. I had no idea whether Noreen Giles was packing a weapon, but thieves often do. No sense taking chances. Plus, a gun gets the message across so much cleaner and so much faster. Climbing in, I pointed my weapon at her in as menacing a manner as I could. It was probably a good act. She gave a startled scream and jumped back.

"Don't make another sound," I growled. "Drive around the corner."

Noreen Giles fumbled with the keys for a moment and wound up dropping them in her lap. Her breathing was heavy and she looked on the verge of tears.

"Oh, my God!"

"I said don't make a sound. Do what I say and you won't get hurt," I said, with a snarl. Playing the role of a bully was fun when the person you were bullying was a career criminal.

She finally inserted the key and turned over the engine. Putting the car into drive, she accelerated slowly to the corner and jerked to a stop. A man in a janitor's uniform was crossing the street, and I lowered the gun down to a level where he couldn't see it. She waited until they reached the curb and then made the right turn. After driving partway down the block, I told her to pull over. A small, dark car behind us followed and stopped a few car lengths back. Maybe they were following us. Maybe not. But I had other matters to deal with. Noreen Giles stared straight ahead, her lower lip trembling. Finally she spoke.

"Are ... are you going to kill me?"

"Shut up," I said. "Open the satchel. And remove one thing at a time."

She followed my directive and pulled out a diamond necklace. I directed her to lay it on the console between us. Then out came a number of earrings, bracelets and rings. With my left hand I took out the paper copies of the stolen items that the Pelletiers had provided. I examined the pieces and they matched up perfectly. I put the copies back in my pocket and instructed Noreen Giles to put the jewelry back in the satchel. She complied without saying a word. At first anyway.

"Hand it over," I said.

"You're not going to get away with this," she said, her voice uneven, but finally finding some bravado.

"I'm shaking in my shoes," I said. "But really, I'm not getting a bad feeling from it."

"You just wait," she stammered.

I laughed in her face. "Oh, yeah? What are you going to do? Call the cops? Tell them that I stole the jewelry that you stole from your open house yesterday? Is that your story? Get real. You and your husband are professional thieves. Or were. You're out of business. As of right now."

Her face tightened and mine did too. I took the satchel and placed it on my lap. I told her to drive around the block twice before instructing her to turn right into an alley behind the row of stores. The small dark car followed us the first time around, but not the second. They must have known they'd been made. I told her to park in the alley. Getting out of the car, I ordered her to follow me and we walked over to a narrow staircase leading into a cellar. Patting her down, I pulled a can of pepper spray out of one pocket of her jacket and a switchblade knife out of the other.

"You come prepared," I remarked, glad I had brandished my pistol early on. "Get down on your knees and put your hands behind your head," I ordered.

"Oh, God."

"It's not as bad as you think. I'm not going to kill you. But you are going to jail."

"You don't really work for the insurance company, do you?"

I smiled. "In a manner of speaking, I do."

Taking her wrists and pinning them behind her back, I removed a pair of plastic flex handcuffs and tied her hands behind her back. Extra tight. I then pushed her gently so she toppled over on her side.

"Hey wait a minute, you're not going to leave me here like this, are you?!" she said, alarmed.

"No," I replied, and walked over to a trash bin. Reaching inside, I found a rag and walked back and shoved it in her mouth to prevent her from screaming and attracting attention. I then went over and retrieved the satchel, put on some gloves, and pulled out the diamond necklace. I slipped it into the pocket of her denim jacket, the same one that had held the switchblade. I heard her try and say some words, but the rag blocked her speech. And the handcuffs blocked her from removing the rag. I got into her Dodge Dart, drove back around the corner and parked it in back of my Highlander. The car that had been following us was nowhere to be seen. Feeling a little more comfortable, I took her car keys, walked down the block, and threw them into a storm drain.

I called Harold and gave him our location. About 15 minutes later, an LAPD cruiser approached and I flagged them down. Harold Stevens apparently had a lot of juice with the department.

"You Burnside?"

"I am."

"Hear you have a pickup for us."

"Around the block in the alley. Follow me."

I led them to Noreen Giles, who by now had twisted herself onto her back and was fruitlessly struggling with the plastic cuffs. The two uniforms emerged from their patrol car and walked over to look at her. Then they looked back at me.

"The name Burnside sounds familiar," one of them said. "You ever on the job?"

"I certainly was. Thirteen years with the department," I told them.

"Bound and gagged," he said. "A little over the top, don't you think?"

"She's a career criminal. I don't have much sympathy. You'll find the stolen item in her pocket, probably worth six figures. She lifted it yesterday at an open house in

Hancock Park. Owners are filing a complaint. Their name's Pelletier."

One of the uniforms removed the rag from Noreen Giles mouth. She immediately went into her act and began talking rapidly.

"Officer, arrest this man. He kidnapped me and he planted evidence. He pulled a gun on me, and said he was going to kill me. He's a menace to society. He needs to be locked up. He impersonated a police officer. He ... "

At that point the uniform sighed and put the rag back into her mouth. I handed him my gloves. "Use these to pull the stolen item out of her pocket. No sense getting your prints on them."

"Thanks," he said. "We'll take it from here. How do we get in touch with you if we need a statement?"

I gave him my card, and then flashed my P.I. license, not the fake shield I used as a prop. He looked at it and motioned to his partner. They lifted Noreen Giles up, replaced my plastic cuffs with official police handcuffs, and put her into the squad car. They didn't give me back my plastic cuffs and I didn't ask for them.

The drive back to June Street took about 20 minutes. Laura Pelletier answered the door and I gave her back her jewelry, minus one piece. I instructed her to call the police with the instructions that a priceless diamond necklace was missing following her open house yesterday, and she suspected her realtor, Noreen Giles. She seemed a bit shocked at getting most of her valuables back and asked what she could do to thank me. I smiled and said to forget she ever met me and not to tell the police about anything I had said or done. Seriously. My actions today could easily cost me my P.I. license. But I didn't become a private investigator just to mindlessly follow a set of bureaucratic rules. If I wanted to do that I'd have remained a cop.

Twenty-four

With one case almost closed, I was now free to focus entirely on the murders of the Hornes and of Oscar Romeo. Which was important, because it was increasingly looking like my own fate might rest in the balance. Being able to apprehend who did it was probably the only thing that would fully remove me as a suspect.

At this stage, the two people who could best tell me more about Oscar Romeo were Ted Wade and Patrick Washington. Ted Wade was unlikely to give me anything more than a rematch from the other night, so I decided to stop in on Patrick. He answered the door and nodded, as if he were expecting me. We walked into the living room.

"I'm sorry," I said, sitting down on a couch across from him. "I know you and Oscar were good friends."

"More like brothers," he said sadly. "You don't know how hard this is for me."

"I can't even imagine," I said, although with 20 years of law enforcement experience behind me, I had seen this scenario play out many times. In some parts of Los Angeles, death was a regular part of everyday existence. Robberies, gang wars, drive-by shootings, all were part of the fabric woven into inner city life. And never more so than in the South Los Angeles neighborhood that Patrick Washington grew up in.

"I had this happen once before to someone close to me. My cousin. Devin's little brother. Got caught up in crossfire. It was the middle of the afternoon and he was just walking home from school. Good kid. Minding his own business, never did nothing to no one. He was only 12 years old."

"This one looks different," I said gently. "Oscar was targeted. Your cousin sounds like he was just an innocent bystander."

"Dead is dead," Patrick muttered. "Neither one deserved it. Both were good people. Now they're gone."

"You're right," I said, wanting to be sensitive to his pain, but also needing Patrick's help. "If this isn't a good time, I can come back another day. But I'm really hoping to try and figure out who did this. Because whoever killed Oscar, had to be involved in killing Gilbert Horne and his wife too. This is no coincidence. It has to be connected."

Patrick looked at me with moist, bloodshot eyes. "I get it. Whatever I can do to help. I just don't know what that is. Oscar didn't have any enemies. He was a fun-loving guy. Everyone liked Oscar. Even guys he played against. He'd knock them down hard on a play and then go over and help them up afterwards. Slap 'em on the butt and even give them some encouragement. His coaches hated that. They told Oscar to treat the other team as the enemy. Oscar didn't buy that. He said they were the opponent, not the enemy."

"He was right," I said. "Especially in the world of the NFL. The guy you hit today could be your teammate next season."

"True," Patrick said. "The NFL's a business. We learn that early on. You know what play Oscar liked the best?"

"What's that?"

"He liked it when the QB had to use a safety valve. Oscar could blow that play up like nobody else."

A safety valve play is pretty much what it sounds like. Whether on a boiler or on a football field, it's designed to relieve pressure and keep a catastrophe from happening. When the quarterback drops back to pass and his receivers are all covered, he only has a few choices. He can throw the ball away, tuck it under his arm and run, or invoke the safety valve. This is where one of his pass-eligible blockers, usually a running back, stops blocking and becomes a pass receiver. The quarterback tosses him the ball and it's then up to the running back to make things happen with his speed and moves.

"That's a play that drives defenses crazy," I said. "The secondary blankets the receivers so they can't get open. The goal is to have the quarterback hold the ball long enough for the blocking to break down and the pass rush get to him. When the quarterback can use the safety valve, the play starts all over again."

Patrick gave a sad smile. "Spoken like a defensive back," he said. "You do your job, shut down your receivers and good things will happen. But sometimes they don't, especially if the quarterback is smart and knows the tools he has at his disposal. And that means he has to go through all his progressions. The last one is the safety valve. Without it, the quarterback becomes a sitting duck, just waiting to get clobbered."

"And Oscar did a good job of reading that."

"Partly reading it, but mostly he was so damn quick for a linebacker, he could get to the running back right after he caught the pass. He could usually blow the play up and tackle him for a loss. I saw it firsthand, playing with him for years, and then on the field against him. Just when the quarterback thinks he's out of the woods, Oscar takes the safety valve and turns it upside down."

Patrick wanted to talk more about Oscar, and he wanted to pay homage to his friend. All very natural and all very human. When someone dies, we push aside the negative memories and focus on the glorious ones. We want to remember the people we cared about in a positive way that celebrates their achievements. It makes us feel reassured they had led a life filled with meaning. I didn't want to push Patrick away from this, but recalling Oscar's exploits on the gridiron wasn't going to help me find the person who killed him.

"I appreciate what a great player he was," I said softly. "And the fact that you two had been friends for most of your lives. But I need a little direction here. And maybe you can help guide me. Could you possibly tell me about the last few days. What do you know about what Oscar was doing? Anything at all would help."

"Oscar was mostly just seeing friends," Patrick said. "Off season, you know. That and he was planning to get a new ride. He was over at Bay City looking at new Lamborghinis. Man, he loved those machines."

I thought of something. "Since Gil's not there, who was he working with?"

"Some blonde girl. He was talking about her the other day."

My antenna went up all of a sudden. "He mention a name?"

"No. He usually didn't. In Oscar's mind women were pretty much all the same. Just the hair color and body shapes were different."

I thought a moment. "You know if there was anything going on between them? Anything that actually transpired?"

"Hard to tell. With Oscar, any girl who looked at him was someone he thought he could do. He would say it's a question of when, not if."

"I'm sure being a pro athlete attracts a lot of women," I mused.

"Sometimes more than you want," said Patrick. "I have more women coming on to me than I can handle. And I'm just big and rich. Oscar was good looking too. He didn't have to work very hard to get them."

"Anything else you can think of here? Anyone else he saw? Ted Wade? His family?"

Patrick shook his head. "No, Ted and Oscar were friends. They didn't have any problems."

I tried something. "If I told you that both Ted and Oscar were having a thing with Gil Horne's wife, would that surprise you?"

Patrick shrugged. "The only thing that would surprise me would be if someone *wasn't* having a thing with April Horne. Oscar and Ted, they looked at women as just toys to be used and then discarded."

I sat back for a moment and took this in. When I was at USC, there was no shortage of women who came on to me because I was a starter on the Trojan football team. I went out with some of them for no better reason than because I could. But I was still in my teens and early 20s, not a fully formed adult, and didn't have an appreciation of just what I was doing. I like to think I've evolved since then, and I like to think that Gail Pepper could only be attracted to the person I am today, not the person I was two decades ago.

I thanked Patrick for his time and once again expressed my condolences. Walking outside, I thought about where to head next. Nothing seemed like a sure thing right now. I felt as if I still had a number of paths to go down on this case, but none seemed obvious. I leaned on my car for a while and looked out at the street. This part of Beverly Hills always seemed so quiet and peaceful. And then something happened. Seemingly out of nowhere, a dark blue sedan entered the long driveway and pulled up next to my Highlander. Out stepped Detective Sean Mulligan, who stopped and stared at me. We both seemed surprised to see one another.

"Burnside."

"Detective."

"What are you doing here?" he asked.

"Probably the same thing as you," I said.

"I'm working the Oscar Romeo case."

"What a coincidence," I said. "Me too."

"Uh-huh."

"I'm a little surprised. I thought that Jim Johnson had

me lined up as the person of interest here. Johnson all but wrote out a confession for me to sign this morning."

"Uh, yeah," Sean smiled. "I think he may be having second thoughts about that. What you said apparently hit a nerve and got him thinking. And that's certainly a nice change of pace."

"So he's keeping the investigation open."

"He is. And Patrick Washington was Oscar's best friend. Looks like you're one step ahead of us," Sean said.

I didn't bother to agree. "Patrick's in a lot of pain. I don't know how much information he can provide."

"Can't hurt to ask a few questions."

"Maybe you guys should just follow me around and I'll lead you to the killer," I said, only half-joking.

"Jesus. You think we can't run our own investigation? We know a little about detective work too. Long as Johnson doesn't join me in the field, I can work better. Rely on hunches rather than use some by-the-numbers manual."

"Hunches always worked for me," I told him, and climbed into my Highlander.

Leaving Patrick's estate, I thought about driving back to the dealership once more. Oscar and a saleswoman sounded like a subject which needed some looking into. I began thinking how I would approach this. Duncan Whitestone had already told me I was *persona non grata* at his place of business, and if I kept returning, I was sure to get a security escort out of there. Calling in the police would be pointless, they were hardly on my side. I also thought about returning to Betty Luttinger's apartment to try and get a lead on her husband. His potential role in the Horne murders made him a serious person of interest. How he fit in with Oscar's murder was another matter entirely. While attractive for a middle-aged woman, Betty Luttinger didn't seem to fit Oscar's profile. I also thought about stopping for lunch, but at that point my cell phone buzzed. I punched the Talk button on my dashboard and a voice came over the speaker.

"Mr. Burnside?" asked a high pitched male voice.

"That's right. Who is this?"

"It's Warren Tell down at the Seaside. I'm the desk clerk, remember?"

"Sure. The guy who doesn't make enough money. What can I do for you?"

"Uh ... yeah. Well I have something I wanted to share with you. I'd actually prefer to show you. Thought you might find it interesting."

"Anything you can tell me over the phone?"

"I kinda need to show you in person."

I said okay and that I'd be right over. Bay City Motor Cars would still be there later today. I made it to the Marina in 25 minutes, drove into the self-park lot, and entered the hotel. At one point it looked as if there had been automatic door openers installed, but I guess once the national chain pulled out, patrons had to make do on their own. I approached the front desk. Warren saw me and motioned to follow him into an empty hallway.

"I wanted to know if there's anything I can do to help you," he said.

"Help me?"

"Yeah, in the investigation," he said. "I heard about Oscar Romeo. And his agent was Gilbert Horne. And Horne used to spend a lot of time here."

"Did Oscar spend time here?"

He gave me a blank look. "Yeah. He was here a few nights ago. With a woman. And the two have to be linked right? This is where Gilbert Horne spent a lot of time."

"Go on."

"That's about it."

I sighed and wondered why this conversation needed to be in person. Or take place at all.

"Look. What you say may be correct. And the part about Oscar being here with a woman is a good lead. But I need more than this. You said you had something to show me."

"Uh, yeah. Well actually Gretchen has something. Over at the bar. I think it'd be, uh, worth your time going over there," he said.

I looked across the lobby and saw that there were already a few customers getting primed. Warren cleared his throat in a too-obvious way, and I reached into my pocket and slipped the thin young man a twenty. Not because he deserved it or earned but, well, because I had a weird feeling there was something more going on, and I wanted to have the option of going back to him at some point. Twenty dollars wasn't a lot, but it did buy lunch.

I walked over to the bar and approached Gretchen, the aspiring actress I had met last week. She was wearing a pink top and white shorts, with a cute green apron draped over both.

"How's the budding starlet?" I asked.

"Oh, I'm good," she smiled. "So good. I just got my first gig. A commercial."

"For who?'

"One of the Indian casinos out in the desert. Which is pretty weird, considering my family doesn't drink, smoke or gamble."

"Do *you*?"

"Ha! Maybe a little. Anyway, it's a start and it's a speaking role and well, I'm just absolutely thrilled about it. A one-day shoot pays more than a month hustling drinks here."

I smiled paternally. "Good for you. I'm glad things are going well."

"So did Warren send you over?"

"Yes. He was a bit surreptitious about the whole thing."

"Surrep ... huh?"

"A little secretive."

"Oh. Yeah. He's weird. But we've been having fun with that car brochure you left behind."

I gave her a puzzled look. "The one for Bay City Motor Cars?"

"That's the one," she smiled.

"I guess I forgot it here."

"I guess you did. Anyway, we've been leaving that brochure out on the little tables where customers sit. Well, talk about an ice breaker! People are gabbing about what they'd buy if they won the lottery, how many they'd buy, in what color. You name it. It's been great."

"Glad I could improve their afternoons," I said. It came out a little more sarcastically then I intended. "But how does that help me?"

"Well there was this big guy in here the other day and he had a really pretty girl with him. They were all over each other. You know, kissing, hugging. People started to tell them to get a room. I mean, that's funny you know? In a hotel?"

"Sure," I managed. "Funny. Who was the big guy?"

"It was Oscar Romeo," she said. "That football player who was killed. But he found a picture of the girl he was with. In that brochure. They got a big kick out of that."

I stared at her. "Who was it?"

"I don't know. They took the brochure with them. Sucks, doesn't it?"

"Maybe yes, maybe no," I said. "What did the girl look like?"

"You know. Blonde and pretty. Like every other girl in L.A."

"Anything more you can tell me? What cars they were driving?"

She thought for a brief moment. "Nope. Everyone in L.A. drives nice cars. That about covers it. Do you think you might know who she is?"

"Maybe," I said, and got up to leave. I tossed a fifty on her tray. Sexist perhaps, but I liked Gretchen better than Warren.

"Why thank you, such a gentleman," she smiled. "Hey, if you can bring another brochure next time, that would be fantastic."

I told her I'd see what I could do. I walked out of the Seaside and into the parking lot. I had some ideas, not all fully formed, but I was getting convinced this little tidbit was going to lead me down the slanted path toward cracking this case. I felt an excitement and a determination.

I opened the Highlander and climbed inside, but just when I did, the passenger door swung open quickly and someone joined me. His massive forearms bulged out of his short sleeve shirt. He used the exact same maneuver I had pulled this morning on Noreen Giles. Maybe lightening does strike twice. But even though I had threatened her, I had mostly wanted to teach Noreen Giles a lesson, one that would likely come with a prison term. The person pointing a pistol at me didn't look like he had any lesson plan on his mind. Isaac Vale looked very much like he wanted to kill me. Reaching over, he yanked my .38 from its holster.

"Drive," he ordered. "Now."

Twenty-five

We headed up Lincoln Boulevard for a few minutes and then I was directed to turn onto the westbound 10 Freeway. Within a minute we were cruising through the curvy McClure Tunnel, then past the California Incline and heading north on Pacific Coast Highway. The blue ocean sparkled to my left. The sun was out and it was growing warm. It was turning into a glorious California day.

I drove up PCH at a moderate speed and stayed in the right lane. A number of impatient drivers went around us and gave dirty looks. A few car lengths behind, however, was another dark vehicle, albeit not the same one that was following me earlier into Boyle Heights. I slowed, but they did not make any motion to pass me. I tried to see who it was, but didn't want to alert Isaac Vale or give him any reason for concern. It did occur to me that Vale might have a partner in the other car, and that thought was unsettling, to say the least. I could often handle one person, even someone who was big and who was armed. Handling two was a much taller task.

"You know, I'm going to get a ticket if you don't put on your seat belt," I finally said.

"You got bigger things to worry about, wise guy."

"If you wanted an appointment, you could have just called."

"Uh-huh. I tried following you today. Learned a few things. That was a nifty move, carjacking a woman by waiting until her doors unlocked. I figured I'd borrow a page from a pro."

"I didn't carjack anyone," I said.

"Sure," Vale laughed. "What do you call entering someone's vehicle and pointing a gun at them?"

"Law enforcement."

Vale laughed again. "Oh you're a funny guy. I'm gonna hate not having you around. And just what law were you enforcing?"

"Law of the street," I answered. "When someone steals, the quickest course of action is to steal the merchandise back."

"An eye for an eye?"

"Not exactly."

"How come you didn't just go and call the cops?" he asked.

"They take too long," I said. "I can mete out justice more efficiently."

"Uh-huh," he agreed. "Me too."

I took a deep breath and drove slower. The blue Pacific never looked more beautiful than it did right now. I was certainly feeling very alive, in the moment, drinking in every aspect of the world around me. I wondered if this was the last time I would ever see this picturesque vista. I thought of the active life I had lived and the people I had helped. I thought of my vow to never take a case just because of the money. I thought of Gail Pepper's beautiful smile and how I might never see it again. I thought of the possibility of not even having the chance to say goodbye to her. And I thought about the ongoing pain she would feel if she never heard from me again. Or if she never even found out what happened to me.

"So that was you following me this morning," I said. "In that little car."

"It wasn't that little. A BMW 320i. It's about the cheapest thing we have on the lot."

"Sorry you had to go lowbrow."

"Well," he said, "I thought if I was in something fancy, it would draw attention. Guess you made me anyhow. Driving around the block twice."

"But you didn't follow me after that."

"My cover was blown. I needed to get to you another way. I figured you might swing by the dealership, but I certainly couldn't grab you there. Too many people know you there. And everyone knows me."

"How'd you know I'd be at the Seaside?" I asked, knowing it would be one of two answers, Warren or Gretchen. My money was on Warren.

"I made an arrangement to get you there. Cost me two hundred but it was worth it. That little desk twerp. Couldn't keep a secret about anything. Blabbed more about who was screwing who than TMZ. When he mentioned a private eye who was sniffing around last week, I figured I'd hit pay dirt. I'll go back to the hotel later and take care of him. I have to make sure no trail leads back to me."

I nodded cautiously. "Sounds like you've thought this out thoroughly."

"I have."

"So why are you doing this then?" I pressed him. "A lot of people have had an unhappy marriage and can't trust their spouse to be faithful. They solve that problem with a divorce."

Isaac Vale looked at me as if I were stark raving mad. "A divorce?!" he asked incredulously. "Divorce just frees my wife up to play around some more. I'm still the one who got cockled."

"Cockled?" I glanced at him.

"Uh-huh. When another man screws your wife. Or in this case other men. As in plural."

I blew out a breath of disgust. It was better than laughing in his face. "I think you mean cuckolded."

"Whatever you want to call it. That's not something I'm going to live with. That's not something any real man is going to live with. Let some fucker do your wife and then see him strut around like a peacock. Uh-uh. Not me."

We had passed Chautauqua and Sunset Boulevards, both of which led into Pacific Palisades. We were now approaching Topanga Canyon. Vale told me to make a right. I did so and picked up a little speed. Green grass and rolling hills framed both sides of the narrow highway. Glancing quickly into the side view mirror, I saw our tail make a right turn as well. I slowed down a little, in part to navigate some of the hairpin turns this stretch of road presented. But I also didn't want to get too far ahead of my tail. I didn't know who they were, but they might be my only road to salvation. I had a funny feeling they weren't working with Vale. But I knew for sure they weren't working for me.

Topanga Canyon was another area that was uniquely L.A. Starting at the beach, it twisted its way up through the Santa Monica Mountains, and driving through it made you feel as if you were hundreds of miles away from any urban area. It provided a getaway for people to hike and camp, and leave the worries and pressures of the big city behind them. But Topanga has had something of a foreboding history. A century ago it was a place where outlaws were known to have gravitated, often to hide out from the law. It was a difficult stretch to navigate, with many small dirt roads branching off from the main drag. For a while during the 1960s, even the Manson family called it home. But by then it had started to become more of a bohemian enclave, and managed to stay that way over the decades, despite steadily escalating real estate prices.

We drove through a tiny area which seemed to serve as a central meeting place, but didn't hold much more than a general store, post office and a couple of funky restaurants. A few people sold arts and crafts from folding tables on the side of the road. Topanga Canyon was only about 20 minutes from bustling Santa Monica, but it felt like it was a world apart. The people who moved here usually did so because they wanted a semi-rural environment. This was an area where everything from jackrabbits and snakes to coyotes and even mountain lions roamed free. It was apparently also a place where criminals still drifted.

"Left turn," he ordered.

"Are you going to tell me what we're doing here?" I asked, making the turn and slowing down considerably as the asphalt road narrowed and became less well paved. I also slowed to keep pace with our tail. But the car that had seemingly been following us was nowhere to be found. Maybe it was just around the bend. Or two bends.

Vale laughed. "Uh-huh. But you can't figure it out? Aren't you a little scared?"

"Yeah," I said. "I'm shaking in my shoes. And I'm starting to get a bad feeling from it."

"Can't say as I blame you."

"What's going on here? I didn't have anything to do with Christy. I never laid a hand on her."

"No, but others did. And I took care of 'em."

I thought back to my last visit to the dealership. "Christy was wearing a lot of makeup yesterday. I thought she was trying to hide the fact that she had been crying. But maybe it was to also hide some bruises."

Isaac gave a small, evil smile. "You're good at figuring things out. I sensed that about you. And you were getting too close for comfort. I got the feeling you'd unravel this thing sooner or later. So I knew I had to deal with you too."

"I appreciate your faith in me," I said sardonically.

"You're smart, " he said. "But I'm smarter."

"I don't doubt that," I said, knowing enough to flatter a hairy ape who had a gun pointed at my rib cage. "Maybe you could give another smart guy a break and let me go."

"Ha! Like I said before. You're funny. But I tried to

warn you, didn't I?"

"Did you?"

"Tell me you don't remember what happened to your Pathfinder."

I thought back to the other day, when my brakes failed going down the California Incline. It all made sense now. Isaac was the service manager at Bay City, and he had the tools and the arm strength to pop a hole in my brake lining. The slow leak would take all night to drain, but when I drove out in the morning, the brake fluid would be gone.

"So you were the one who tampered with my vehicle."

"You got that right. Pretty easy job really. You just need to know where to cut."

"And your message was back off the case."

"It took you a while to get that, huh? I was a little disappointed when you kept going."

"And dumping Oscar Romeo's body in the dumpster next to my building. That was another message you were sending me?"

"A stronger one perhaps. But yes. Oscar was messing with my lady and like I said, I'm not going to get cock ... what was that word?"

"Cuckolded," I said evenly, doing my best to keep from rolling my eyes.

"Yeah, that one. Wasn't going to let that one slide."

"So you killed Oscar out of revenge and then dumped his body near my building ... as a warning to me."

"There you go. I knew you'd get it. Again, it just seems to take you a while. I thought you were smarter than that."

I ignored the crack. Only a lunatic would be able to decipher Isaac Vale's cryptic messages. "And the Hornes? Why did you kill both of them?"

Isaac Vale's eyes darkened and his face scrunched. He drew his lips in and took a couple of breaths. The mere name seemed to get his motor running in a way nothing else had. I pushed a little more.

"Gilbert Horne," I continued. "He was your boss at the dealership, right? And he paid for your wedding too, if I recall."

Isaac's breathing started coming in spurts now and his hands started trembling. I thought of whether there was an opportunity to grab the gun from him at the right moment. I steadied the wheel with my left hand, but when I measured the distance between us, I knew I'd have to lunge and that was a split second longer than I could give him. And considering his deranged mental state, Isaac Vale was not a man to trifle with. I also looked down at those massive forearms and wondered if I could even wrestle the gun away from him.

"That prick," he said. "That double-talking snake. Horne was a goddamned son of a bitch."

"So you didn't care for him, I take it."

"Didn't care for him?! He was fucking my wife the whole time she was going out with me! The guy was married and he couldn't afford a divorce, so he decided to just stay on in his marriage and screw everything around him."

"So you fired a shot at his house to warn him?" I asked.

"Warn him, my ass!" he yelled. "I was shooting to kill, it was just too dark out. That gun his partner had was all show. A Glock's an impressive firearm, but the accuracy is shit from a distance."

"You used Cliff Roper's gun."

"Yeah. That felt like just desserts. Getting whacked with your partner's gun. I certainly wasn't going to use mine. After I finished him off, I left the Glock in the bushes so the police would find it. Figured they would pin it on Roper once it got traced. If I left it inside the house, they might have thought it was a murder-suicide. Boy, the police are easy to manipulate. Bunch of coffee-sipping government sponges. They really are a pack of goldbricks."

One thought puzzled me. "How'd you get a hold of Roper's gun in the first place?"

"Horne took it out of Roper's safe. He told Christy he thought someone was after him and he needed it for self-protection. The cheap bastard wouldn't even buy his own weapon. Christy saw it and convinced Horne to give it to her. She was concerned he was going to hurt himself. Can you imagine? Pricks like Horne don't commit suicide."

"So he gave Christy the gun. And then ... "

"And then I took it from Christy. For safekeeping, I told her. But I had a plan, I was going to use it on Horne. When things didn't go right the first time, that first night, I had to go back there. Back to that house on Lookout Mountain."

"But you killed both Horne and his wife. Why the wife?"

Vale slumped a little in his seat. "Collateral damage," he said. "Couldn't be helped. Horne was alone when I got there. I told him I needed to talk to him about some stuff at the dealership. He was such a two-faced prick. Made me a drink, talked to me like I was an old pal even though he was screwing my wife behind my back. Then just as I was about to plug him, April walks in. She sees me, she sees the gun. I had to finish her. No turning back at that point. When you have a head of steam, you just gotta keep rolling. He who hesitates, and all that."

I looked out at the rolling green hills in the distance, and the ancient trees and jagged shrubbery we were passing along the side of the narrow road. So that was how multiple murders got committed. Someone has a fling with your wife, and murder becomes the obvious solution. Someone else has a fling, someone else gets murdered. Someone sees your face, they get murdered too. Be at the wrong place at the wrong time, and your number is up as well. Isaac had been like a boiler about to explode. He had an enormous amount of pent-up rage and he had no ability to allow some of that steam to get out. Finally he just blew up. If only he had an outlet. If only he had a safety valve.

"And Christy didn't suspect anything?" I asked incredulously. "Two of her lovers killed within a week. She had to have known this wasn't a coincidence."

Vale shook his head. "You don't understand, do you? I caught her and that football player together at the hotel on Saturday morning. Followed 'em. They were supposed to be test driving a car, turns out he was test driving her."

"You didn't use a gun on him."

"Hell, no. The police are dopes, so I figured I'd break the pattern. Used a tire iron instead. Popped him over the head a few times when he wasn't looking."

"Did Christy see you do it?"

Vale smiled. "No. But I took care of her later. Her days of cheating on me are over. Her days of cheating on anyone are over. For good."

I stared at him and then a question popped into my head. "So if you're planning on killing me also," I said slowly, "then just who are you going to lead the police to? They're not going to believe I did all this."

"No, they won't. And you're the one who gave me the idea of who to pin this on."

"Who's that," I asked, shaking my head.

"Art Luttinger. He's my next stop."

I took a breath and didn't say anything. The murder tally had now grown to four and was rising quickly. I didn't bother to ask what he had done with Christy's body, maybe he had another obtuse message he was planning to send. Isaac was one sick guy. I needed to figure a way out of this situation and none jumped out at me. Isaac Vale had size, strength, and two handguns, one of which had been pointed right at me for half an hour. Overcoming him inside of the car did not look possible.

At some point we would stop. But by then, the distance between us was sure to grow and my chances of disarming him were sure to diminish. I had no access to anyone outside of this vehicle, and we were now in such a remote part of Topanga Canyon, that it was unlikely there was another person within miles. But as my hands tightened around the steering wheel, I suddenly realized I did have one weapon in my arsenal. A weapon that was far bigger and even more powerful than anything Isaac had at his disposal. And the trick would be to dispense it quickly and suddenly.

I saw that the road ahead began to straighten and ease downhill. I pressed down slightly on the accelerator and tried to build some speed. The Highlander responded and began to surge. Isaac didn't realize it at first. He was lost in thought, most likely marveling at his own genius, his ability to get away with murdering four people, with a fifth about to get notched on his belt. But as the Highlander built up speed, he began to take notice. The speedometer was now passing 40 and rising quickly.

"Hey, what's your hurry? This is a country road. You're going to die today anyway."

I ignored him and pressed the accelerator harder. The vehicle responded and surged forward quickly.

"Hey! I said slow down! I mean it!" he yelled, waving the gun near my head.

And with that, I tightened my grip on the steering wheel and jerked it hard to the left. The Highlander swerved sharply off the road and Vale fell back against the door. He wasn't wearing a seat belt, but I was. The passenger side of the vehicle did not have air bags but the driver's side did. I floored the accelerator enough so that he was unable to react well. And when we smashed suddenly and violently into an oak tree that must have been over one hundred years old, it was the Highlander that took the brunt of the damage, not the tree. Because I had buckled my seat belt and forced the driver-side air bag to engage, I was spared from the brutal consequences that ravaged Isaac Vale.

His face went straight into the windshield, causing a massive, light green spider web of cracked glass. From there, his body was thrown violently backward, breaking the passenger seat. He then flew up into the top of the car where his skull smashed into the ceiling. He came back down, and after ping-ponging one or two more times, including bouncing painfully off of my right shoulder, his body finally came to rest. The last I saw of him, his body was sprawled awkwardly out of the passenger door, which had become unhinged during the collision.

I breathed in and out, slowly and repetitively. A wall of silence permeated the car. Blood was splattered everywhere. I moved my arms and they worked. I moved my legs and they worked too. So did my fingers and toes. After a few minutes, I managed to pull myself out of the vehicle and stumbled a few feet away, landing on a patch of dirt. I didn't know whether Isaac Vale was dead or alive, and at this point I didn't really care much. I only knew that I was alive, barely, and I was very much grateful for that.

I pulled out my cell phone and somehow managed to get a signal and called Sean Mulligan. I'd let him contact 9-1-1. Cell phones had a history of being notoriously poor at accessing emergency services. Getting a call from an LAPD officer would bring a quicker response. That, and the fact that I really had no idea where we were. I stumbled over to where Isaac Vale was hanging out of the car. I reached into his pocket and removed my .38. I noticed his pistol was nowhere to be found, but I was sure it would turn up. These things always did.

I couldn't believe it when I saw Sean Mulligan pull up five minutes later. He went around the side of the car, checked Isaac Vale's pulse and then pulled out his own phone and called it in. A few minutes after that, the paramedics were on the scene. I crawled under a nearby tree and watched them work on Isaac Vale. Sean Mulligan came over and sat down next to me.

"You been drinking?" he asked.

"Nope."

"That tree just jump out into the road and hit you?"

"Yup."

Mulligan smiled. "Feel like telling me about it? I'm a better listener than Johnson."

"I'll bet you are," I said, and told him about my outing with Isaac Vale, beginning with my arrival at the Seaside and omitting the morning's escapade of carjacking and robbing a jewelry thief. Telling the story took about the same amount of time as the Paramedics took to pull Isaac Vale out of the Highlander, load him onto a stretcher and grunt as they lifted him into the back of their unit. As they drove off, two LAPD cruisers arrived.

"I guess this long day is going to get even longer," I said, resigning myself to the inevitable.

"It will," Mulligan said. "But I think it's going to have a happy ending, even if it's a late one. Besides, I owe you."

"How's that?"

"You really tore Johnson a new one this morning. Lots of guys have wanted to tell him where to go and how to get there. But you're the one who did it."

"Were you watching me behind that two-way mirror?" I asked.

"Nah. Someone recorded it. Within five minutes, everyone at the Division had a copy of that clip sent to them."

"Glad I could help the cause."

"Hey, you made everyone's day. Look, I'll even try and keep your name out of the media. Unless you want the publicity."

"Not this kind of publicity," I said. "Hey, Sean, I need to ask you something."

"What's that?"

"Were you the one following me all the way from Santa Monica?"

"Uh-huh. All the way from Patrick Washington's, actually. I saw what was happening. Didn't jump in right away because I figured Vale might lead us to an interesting place. But then you made a quick left turn and I lost you. Good thing you called. I was ready to go back to the Division. You can only trust your hunches so much."

Twenty-six

Sean Mulligan was correct, the day was indeed a long one. Isaac Vale was still alive when they got him to Saint John's Hospital in Santa Monica, although he was in critical condition for almost a week. After he stabilized, the City Attorney charged him with four counts of murder. He pleaded not guilty due to insanity. Gail and I both agreed that he might very well have a good argument there.

The media excluded me from their coverage, and I felt feel very grateful to Sean for whatever role he played in that. I was simply mentioned as an unidentified carjacking victim who survived an auto accident. Since the Highlander was rented, there was no direct link back to me, and none of the reporters bothered to investigate why Oscar Romeo's body was left in a dumpster next to my building. Sean had a hunch about Topanga, and organized a search in the area of the crash, complete with a canine team in tow. It took a few hours, but the dogs led investigators to the body of Christy Vale, buried in a shallow grave about two miles away.

The media lauded Detective Mulligan for cracking the case of a quadruple murder and quoted him extensively in numerous articles. I called him and said this would likely get him promoted. He told me he owed me one, and I put him on alert that I would one day collect on the debt. Jim Johnson wasn't mentioned in any press coverage, one more pleasant footnote to an otherwise arduous journey.

Cliff Roper was exonerated and he had a few choice words for the LAPD's ability to think and chew gum at the same time. He told the media that this whole episode had cost him millions and he would be filing a civil suit for false arrest and a handful of other issues that could only be salved with financial remedy. I had doubts he would successfully collect one dime, but I think Cliff Roper may have been more interested in the publicity this would generate, and the chance to keep his name on the front page. When I called him after the accident and Vale's subsequent arrest, he told me to stop by after the weekend for a chat, the NFL draft would be taking up most of his time during the next few days. He didn't bother to thank me and I didn't really expect him to.

The morning after the accident, my downstairs neighbor Ms. Linzmeier slept in and so did I. Gail had long since gone off to work when I rolled out of bed just before 11:00 a.m. We had spoken ever-so-briefly when I crawled under the covers with her at about 2:00 in the morning. She was more than willing to talk, but I was not, and we settled by cuddling for a long time until we both fell softly asleep. Gail departed quietly for work, being extra careful not to wake me, even though I vaguely remember her leaving. Our bed became just a little less warm and secure than it had been with her in it.

The first thing I did when I got up was to limp into the kitchen and make a pot of French roast, but this time taking steps to make it extra strong. I downed some Advil and sipped my coffee in the living room, listening to nothing more than the cars driving by and the birds chirping. Chewy climbed onto the sofa and sat down next to me. I scratched behind her ears and she responded by lovingly putting her chin down on my lap.

Having a calm morning was a welcome relief from the past few days. My ribs ached from the impact of the air bag, my hand was still sore from belting Ted Wade's father, and I was nursing a headache as well. Gail had liked the scones from La Brea Bakery so much that she had stopped by there the previous day. I helped myself to a ginger scone and ate it slowly, savoring every bite. I was still a little tired, hurting on a number of levels and probably suffering through a bout of post-traumatic stress disorder. But I also knew how good it felt to be alive, and shuddered at how close I had come to death. Had I waited another minute or two before driving the Highlander into the tree, Isaac might well have ordered me to stop the car so I could get out and begin digging my own grave. When Isaac Vale told me I was going to die, it was obvious that it was no veiled threat.

By 12:30 p.m. I was feeling a little better. I showered, dressed and thought about what I would do today. The phone buzzed at that point, and it was Jorge from Pacific Repairs, telling me my Pathfinder was ready for pickup. When I asked about getting a ride, he said he'd send someone by to fetch me. That sounded just fine.

The Pathfinder looked as good as new. They had even done me the courtesy of washing it and applying a layer of wax. The black vehicle gleamed in the sunlight, and even though it was 8 years old and had rolled up a lot of mileage, it still looked good. I cautiously moved behind the wheel and drove off slowly, testing the brakes a few times as I drove down Pico Boulevard. Everything seemed functional, although the driver was probably not at his best. I drove east on Pico for a while, aimlessly passing the Westside Pavilion and the Rancho Park Golf Course before I decided on a destination for this afternoon. I continued to drive east until I arrived at the offices of the Differential Insurance Company's claims investigation unit. Harold Stevens was finishing lunch at his desk when I walked in.

"Well," he exclaimed. "Long time no see! It's been over 24 hours since our last meeting. A lot's happened!"

"You're telling me," I commented, and pulled a chair up to his desk.

"You do look the worse for wear," he said. "I hope Noreen Giles didn't do this to you."

"No, she was the fun part of my day yesterday."

I took Harold through my investigation of the Horne murders, Cliff Roper's alleged involvement, and the cast of characters I became engaged with over the past week. The culmination, of course, was the E-ticket ride I had with Isaac Vale yesterday, and my all-too-close brush with death in one of the rural nooks hidden inside Topanga Canyon. Topped off by the many hours fielding questions from the LAPD. That finally ended when the police found Isaac Vale's gun lodged underneath one of the seats in the Highlander, and my story took on some weight. Christy

Vale's body was found shortly thereafter, and the police finally decided I might actually have been telling them the truth all along.

"That is a remarkable tale," Harold acknowledged. "But it's funny how I didn't catch your name anywhere on the news. The story just focused on how Isaac Vale carjacked someone, there was an accident, and the police found his wife's body nearby."

"I don't think the police wanted me speaking with the media and telling them how badly they mishandled this case. Arresting Cliff Roper and then suspecting that I had something to do with any of this was ludicrous. It was lazy police work. At some point, some reporter is going to figure it out and find me. But I can't imagine how being neck deep in a quadruple murder case is going to be good for my business."

"Even though you were about to crack the case when Isaac jumped in your car."

"I was this close," I said, holding my thumb and index finger a quarter of an inch apart. "I sensed this was related to love and not money. But I was just focused on the wrong couple, the Luttingers. When the cocktail waitress told me that Oscar had been carrying on there with one of the Bay City saleswomen, I was sure it was Christy. I couldn't imagine Christy being the one who pulled the trigger, but people can fool you. I just knew that the trail for all of this led right to the dealership. Only someone who was connected there would have had the wherewithal and the motive to take that step. The person had to know about cars, and especially how to mess up someone's brakes. It was just a matter of time before I got to him. Isaac Vale got to me first."

"Indeed. And I'm happy to hear this all turned out well and you got out unscathed."

"That makes two of us. So tell me what happened to Noreen Giles."

Harold smiled a big smile. "The police booked her for grand theft. She was screaming your name, saying she wanted to press charges for carjacking, kidnapping and even attempted murder."

"Sounds like she's familiar with criminal charges."

"Oh yes, she's quite the pro. But the police had the diamond necklace and the Pelletiers identified it. Quite a beautiful piece apparently. I wouldn't be surprised if the retail value of that didn't run well into six figures. If that were the case she might have gotten a good $30,000 or so from the pawn shop. That is, if they carried that kind of cash. Why she chose a pawn shop in the *barrio* is strange. I guess she figured that would be a shop the Pelletiers wouldn't think to visit."

"Smart," I said. "In a twisted sort of way."

"True. Anyway, the Pelletiers filed their police report, and once the cops told Noreen that the victims identified the item and had a photo of it, she crumbled and admitted guilt. Well, sort of. She actually said her husband Will stole it."

"So much for honor among thieves."

"Yes, and Will Giles himself took a powder right after his wife was picked up. They found out he bought a plane ticket to Buenos Aires and fled the country yesterday."

"I guess that's the official end of Giles & Giles, a real estate partnership."

"And we in L.A. are all the better for their breakup," Harold said. "Which reminds me, I owe you something."

"You do."

Harold opened a desk drawer and pulled out a large white envelope with my name on it and handed it to me. "There's a little something extra in there. For service above and beyond the call of duty."

"Aw, thanks. You didn't have to do that."

"Well, you made our community a little safer yesterday. In more ways than one. And with Noreen Giles in jail and Will out of the country, you've made everyone a little less susceptible to fraud. Especially the Differential Insurance Company."

I pocketed the check. "I'll call this an advance on my wedding present."

"Sure. How is that going?"

I shrugged. "You were right. I'm leaving most of that to Gail. I'm just agreeing to whatever she wants, showing up and saying I do. And oh yeah, paying for most of it."

"Smart man," Harold said, standing up and shaking my hand. "Happy wife, happy life."

*

By the time I meandered back to the Westside it was after 4:00 p.m. I decided to swing by my office and take care of some paperwork. As I walked up to my office however, I noticed my door wide open and I heard some voices inside. My last few days had been a whirlwind of activity and I knew I was skittish about things. I had two cases that were seemingly put to bed, but a few odds and ends had slipped through the cracks. One of which was Will Giles, who had supposedly skipped town. And I never got to speak with Art Luttinger. And Duncan Whitestone was pretty angry over our last encounter. Drawing my .38 from its holster. I kept it in my right hand, my arm hanging loosely at my side. My gun was ready if I needed it, but it turned out a firearm wouldn't be necessary. One peek inside told me things might actually be far more dangerous.

They were sitting in my office, chatting and laughing and even eating together. The two of them were getting to know each other and seemed to like what they saw. I probably shouldn't have been surprised. There were reasons I was drawn to both women; they had traits I found marvelous. They were savvy and smart and direct. They were also both insanely beautiful. But the picture of Gail Pepper and Honey Roper sitting on a couch together, smiling and giggling, was something my stress-addled brain was having some trouble comprehending.

I secured my .38 safely back in its holster where it couldn't do any accidental damage. Walking casually into my office, I pasted a smile onto my face and wondered what fate had in store for me now.

"Well, you finally got here," Gail smiled.

I said hello and went right over to give her a kiss on the cheek. I turned and looked at Honey. "Hello to you too." I said. I made no motion to kiss her.

"I think I better settle for a handshake," she said, an impish grin on her face.

I shook her hand and was surprised at the firm, professional grip. I looked at the two of them, and they were not only enjoying themselves, but they both had plates filled with dessert sitting on their laps. On my desk sat four small cakes, each one different, but each looking rather exquisite.

"So what brings you both to my humble office," I asked with great hesitancy. "Bake sale at the local PTA?"

"You know something, sweetie," Gail said, "you and I have been talking about doing a cake tasting. And I know how busy you've gotten. So I thought I'd bring the tasting to you. Grab a plate."

I walked behind my desk and took samples of all of four. Thankfully I had had a light lunch. There was a classic white cake, a chocolate cake with buttercream frosting, a strawberry shortcake and a carrot cake. All four looked good and all four tasted good.

"They're fantastic," I said after sampling the fourth one. "Where are they from?"

"Sweet Lady Jane," said Gail. "On Montana. Best cakes in town."

"Now, my favorite is the carrot cake," Honey said, taking a small bite of one that seemed to have toasted coconut embedded in the frosting wall. "But you can't go wrong with any of them. And you can't go wrong with Sweet Lady Jane."

"I am finding," Gail said, "that Honey and I agree on quite a bit."

This could be good or bad. I took another bite of the carrot cake. It was good, but not my favorite. I'm not so keen on sweets and I tend to default to chocolate. But I decided that my own humble opinion mattered less in situations such as these. This was not one in which I needed to draw a line in the sand.

"I agree," I said. "The carrot cake is sensational. It's not traditional for a wedding cake, but I like to think we're something of a non-traditional couple."

"Indeed we are," Gail smiled. "And I'm glad you agree. Carrot cake it is."

I turned to Honey. "It's nice to see you once again. Did you just happen to be in the neighborhood?"

Honey smiled. "No, not exactly. I'm actually here as an emissary of sorts."

"Oh?"

"My dad is very busy right now. But he wanted to send a special thank you for your work over the past week. He feels very grateful."

"That's nice," I said, pondering all this. "But I'm sure your Dad could have worked in a meeting with me. Especially for the guy who got him off the hook for double murder. Not that he doesn't have more pressing issues, what with the NFL draft this weekend and all."

Honey smiled and looked at Gail. "He is so cute. You are so lucky to have nabbed him."

"I know," Gail smiled in return.

Honey looked at me and then back at Gail. "Under the right circumstances, I'd try to steal him away from you," she said, a twinkle in her eye. "But something tells me I'm in over my head here. I don't think I could pry him away."

Gail continued to smile. It seemed she was enjoying Honey almost as much as I was. "No, Honey. I don't think you could manage to pull that one off."

Turning back to me, Honey's face all of a sudden turned serious in that odd way of hers. "Dad has something of a more tangible thank you which he wanted me to deliver."

I looked at her and kept my mouth shut.

Honey reached into her bag and pulled out a large, white envelope. She leaned over and handed it to me. "Dad said he always takes care of people that do a good job. It's good karma and it's good business."

I opened the envelope. It was a check for $10,000, made out to me. I looked up at Honey. "I'm not sure quite what to say. Thank you springs to mind. But your father already paid me. And he paid me for 10 days, which I didn't quite fully put in. Although there might have been some overtime in there."

"Dad mentioned that; he figured you would remember the details."

"So what is this for?"

"Well, Dad said to tell you it's kind of a bonus."

I frowned and remembered I was dealing with Cliff Roper. "That sounds like kind of pregnant. Either it is or it isn't."

"What Dad told me," Honey said as she stood up, her lithe body catching my eye almost as much as the large check. I quickly turned to Gail. Fortunately, she was captivated by Honey as well. "Was that this is for future considerations."

"Future considerations," I laughed. "Dare I ask just what that means?"

"You know Dad," she said, as she moved toward the door. "It means whatever he wants it to mean."

Twenty-seven

Gail and I went home and spent some quality time with Chewy. We took her to a dog-friendly park we found in Mar Vista and played fetch with a tennis ball. I brought along a Frisbee, but every time I tossed it to her, she just watched it slowly sail by. Gail and I sat and cuddled underneath a silver maple tree and watched Chewy play and run and make friends with every dog and person who came near her. After about 20 minutes of sprinting around the park, Chewy's tongue was hanging out and she came over and curled up between us. When I started to stroke Gail's hair, her snout jutted up in the air and we could hear a low level of growling. I wasn't sure if she was jealous of Gail or me. Clearly, a substantial amount of training was going to have to be done.

Having eaten more than our share of cake, neither of us were in the mood for dinner that night. With a $10,000 check in my wallet, I felt comfortable enough to take Gail to Spago a few nights later. An L.A. institution for over three decades, Spago had maintained the contemporary quality of everything from the decor to the food. It had almost graduated to the level of old-school. Maybe not quite as much as The Apple Pan, but it was on its way. We had a wonderfully expensive dinner, and were even visited by Wolfgang himself. As we were finishing dessert, the famous owner stopped by our table to ask how everything was, and then gave us a talk on the subtle differences between a blackberry and an olallieberry. Everyone should be an expert on something.

I picked up a few more cases from Harold Stevens over the next month, simple investigations that required neither the brandishing of weapons nor the raising of fists. Thankfully, my life gravitated back to being peaceful and routine for a while. Our wedding plans were finalized over the next month, and Gail and I were married on the first Saturday in June. Our wedding was held at the Miramar Hotel in Santa Monica, only a few blocks from our home and just across the street from the famous California Incline.

It was a warm evening and as we walked slowly down the aisle, I glanced around at our group of guests. Gail's side included her family, her friends from college and law school, and some new colleagues at the City Attorney's office. On my side of the aisle sat mostly friends I had from either USC or from law enforcement. Johnny Cleary stood up for me as best man, and some of our old teammates from 20 years ago were able to make it as well. Juan Saavedra and a number of past and present LAPD officers were in attendance. Harold Stevens was there, as was a pair of special guests whom Gail and I had a long discussion about whether to invite. Cliff and Honey Roper were finally green-lighted, but only because Gail insisted. I glanced at them and saw Honey beaming at us. Cliff's eyes were downcast; he was texting someone on his iPhone.

We exchanged our vows and after slipping rings on each other's fingers, we kissed and smiled at each other and began walking back up the aisle. As we did, Gail, her left arm interlocked with my right, leaned over and whispered something in my ear.

"I guess it's time to tell you this," she said.

I looked at her with more than a measured amount of curiosity. "You've been keeping something from me?"

"I'm afraid I have."

"Now's a heck of a time to tell me, you know."

"There's never a perfect time," she sighed.

"Were you afraid I wouldn't show up if you told me beforehand?" I asked.

"No. But I didn't want you to be pre-occupied during the ceremony."

I look hard into Gail soft gray eyes, the eyes that always made me think of spring raindrops. They were clear and warm and added immeasurably to an extraordinarily beautiful face. We continued walking past the point where the flower girl, Juan Saavedra's daughter, had been tossing lavender rose petals. We continued over to a fountain, not far from where the cocktail reception would begin.

"I think I can handle doing two things at once," I pointed out. "But now I can focus on this. Just what is it you want to tell me?"

Gail stopped and put her arms around my neck. I drew her closer so that we only needed to whisper to one another. I held her so that it felt like we were the only two people in the world. We formed our own little cocoon.

"I want to tell you that Chewy is going to have a sibling soon," she smiled. "I'm pregnant. We're going to have a baby."

My breath started coming in spurts and I held her a little tighter. "Well, now," I said, smiling nervously back at her. "That's the best wedding present you could have ever given me."

"Are you a little scared?" she asked. "They say a lot of men are at first."

"I'm shaking in my shoes," I said. "But it's quite a wonderful feeling."

The End

David Chill

About The Author

David Chill was born and raised in New York City and educated in the public schools. After receiving his undergraduate degree from SUNY-Oswego, he moved to Los Angeles where he earned a Masters degree from the University of Southern California. David Chill is the author of five novels: Post Pattern, Fade Route, Bubble Screen, Safety Valve and Corner Blitz, all featuring Burnside, a private investigator and former LAPD officer and college football star.

Post Pattern was a finalist in the St. Martin's Press contest for New Private Eye Mystery Writers. The Burnside series has received much critical acclaim, and all five novels have spent time on the Amazon.com best seller lists. David Chill currently lives in Los Angeles with his wife and son. If you wish to contact David Chill directly, please email him at: davidchill3214@gmail.com

If you enjoyed Safety Valve, then don't miss David Chill's fifth Burnside novel....

Corner Blitz

Here is a sample of this terrific new mystery...

David Chill

CORNER BLITZ PREVIEW

The governor of California does not typically meet with people like me. But the governor of California does not typically have his teenage daughter go missing.

Governor Rex Palmer was a handsome man, tall and slim, with a square jaw and a distinguished face. He had a head full of black hair that was graying at the temples. His voice was a deep baritone, normally dynamic and upbeat, but now somber and subdued. The agonizing thought that he might not see his only child again was apparent. We were sitting around a conference room table; the governor, myself, and two members of his staff, one flanked on either side of him.

"She was supposed to appear at a campaign event on Saturday night," he said, gripping the armrests of his chair tightly. "But she was a no-show. And my wife told me she didn't come home that night. Or last night either."

"Has there been any communication from her at all?" I asked.

A few long seconds went by. "No," he finally managed. "I don't know who to turn to, Mr. Burnside."

"The police would normally be a good start," I suggested. "Or the FBI."

"Not with an election coming up," said the professional-looking woman to his right. "There's too much at stake here."

"And the last thing we need to do is involve the Federal Bureau of Incompetence," growled the tough looking man on his left.

The tough looking aide was Bill Thorn, the person in charge of the governor's security detail. The professional looking woman was Shelly Busch, who was managing the governor's campaign. The election was two weeks away and it had turned into a nasty race. Politics could be an ugly business, but never more so than at the end of a campaign. In this race, Governor Palmer, a moderate Republican, was running against State Assemblyman Justin Woo, a moderate Democrat. They were both centrists, which meant they agreed on more things than they disagreed. And when two candidates' political stances are similar, the campaign is bound to get personal. There's not much else to quibble about.

"Well, I'm impressed someone would rank my talents above an entire federal agency," I said to Thorn and then turned back to Palmer. "But I understand your concern."

In fact, I did not understand this at all. When children go missing, the natural reaction for most parents would be to hunt tirelessly for them. Most parents would look to any and every law enforcement arm at their disposal. But most parents did not have a high-profile career that now stood at a critical juncture.

"This is a sensitive issue, Burnside," said Thorn, eyeing me carefully.

"That's good," I answered. "You know, I'm a sensitive guy."

He didn't reply and was now eyeing me even more carefully. I responded by pretending not to notice.

"You come highly recommended," the governor finally said. "Jeremy Hoffman was very lavish in his praise. He said you were the best."

I nodded appreciatively. My USC connections were coming into play once again. Jeremy Hoffman served on the Coliseum Commission, as well as on various committees at the university. He had been a fixture at USC long before I played football there. And that was a few decades ago.

"I'll thank him for the referral. His offices are just down the street."

"Yes," Palmer continued, "Jeremy is an old friend of the family. And as much as I respect Bill here, we need an outsider looking into this. I don't want this to be part of the campaign. It has to be a stealth investigation. This can't go public."

"Why not?" I asked.

An uneasy silence hung over the room like a cloud. The three of them looked down at the table. The governor finally spoke. "There are elements of my family life that just need to be kept private."

"All right," I said, not liking that a piece of information was being withheld. "Maybe you can provide some background on your daughter."

He sighed, stole a glance at his watch, and turned to his left. "Bill, could you share the particulars? The debate's tomorrow and I need to prepare and focus. This is the most important event of the campaign. The election may hang in the balance."

"Of course," he said.

Rex Palmer rose and turned to me before he left. "Mr. Burnside, my staff is at your complete disposal. Bill Thorn is a consummate law enforcement professional, please work with him. And keep us informed. But above all else, be discreet."

I stood up also and shook his hand. It was big and soft and warm. A politician's handshake. As he walked out, I looked over at his two associates and sat back down. Without the governor, it felt as if the molecules around us had changed. Another awkward moment of silence filled the room.

"So. How did you two come to know the governor?" I asked, more because I didn't know where else to begin.

Bill Thorn spoke first. "I was a captain in the Sacramento PD. Got to know the governor when he was the state treasurer. Sacramento's a small place. But Shelly's been with him a lot longer."

"Oh, yes," Shelly said in a knowing voice. "Rex and I go way back, college at Stanford. In fact, my husband, Land, ran against him for class president our senior year. Of course, Land wasn't my husband back then."

"Land?"

"Landon Busch. He's a state senator now."

"Ah."

Shelly continued. "I was actually a math major at Stanford and got interested in political polling when I graduated. That led me into managing campaigns. I directed Rex's campaign four years ago," she said, adding with a hint of pride, "I helped put Rex in the governor's mansion."

"Why aren't you managing your husband's campaign?"

"He was just elected two years ago, and his term in office is four years. So he's not up for re-election this year. If he was," she said with a sly smile, "I'd have a tough time choosing which campaign to work on."

"So who won class president?" I asked.

"Rex did," she laughed. "And Land resented him a little. Rex had advantages that Land didn't. When your father's a former governor, it paves the way. Politics was the family business for him, and Buster Palmer provided Rex with name recognition. My husband had to practically claw his way into elective office."

"That's not such a bad way to go," I commented. "You have to work harder, but you learn more. And you know you've made it because of your own efforts. Not someone else's."

Shelly considered this. "I suppose."

"So tell me about the daughter," I said. "What's her name?"

Bill Thorn spoke, clearing his throat first. "Her name's Molly."

"All right. And when was Molly last seen? And where?"

"Two days ago. At the Coliseum. The USC-Oregon State game. I suppose part of the reason the governor chose you was because of your USC background."

"Mmm. Who was Molly with?" I asked.

"A few kids from her school. Stone Canyon. It's a private school over in Bel-Air."

"Got any names?"

"Riley Joyner, Molly's best friend, is one. Connor Pierce and Alex Gateley were with them. Molly and Riley play together on the school volleyball team. I think Molly used to go out with Connor. But there's another kid who's involved here. Name's Diego Garcia."

"Was he at the game?"

"Yes," Thorn said. "But not as a spectator."

I frowned. The name didn't ring a bell. "Is he a football player?"

"No, he's a vendor. You know. Walks around selling peanuts and ice cream, stuff like that."

"Yeah, I know what a vendor does," I said, starting to frown. In fact, I knew all about that type of job. For a couple of summers during high school, I had worked as a vendor at Dodger Stadium. It was physically demanding, but it paid a lot more money than working for minimum wage at a Burger King. Another big plus was I would sometimes stop in the 7th inning and watch the end of the ballgame. Usually in a box seat someone had vacated early to get a jump on post-game traffic.

"You look a little puzzled," Shelly said.

"What I don't get is how a stadium vendor would come to know the daughter of a sitting governor."

"They go to school together," she responded.

I frowned harder. "Private school tuition can be very high. Staggering. If a kid works part-time as a vendor, how does he wind up at a school like Stone Canyon?"

"Diego's on scholarship. But the reason his name comes up is that Molly and Diego have been spending a lot of time together lately."

"Rich girl, poor boy," I mused. "Opposites attract."

"Yes," Shelly said. "Classic tale."

"So do you think foul play's involved?"

"I don't want to think that," she replied. "But I also know that neither Molly nor Diego showed up at school today. We can't ignore the possibility Molly may have been taken against her will. We just don't know."

Something didn't add up here. The USC-Oregon State game ended less than 48 hours ago. When a person goes missing, time is crucial. If they're not found within a day, the odds they could have met with tragic circumstances increase exponentially. That a parent would wait this long to start looking into a disappearance was unusual to say the least. Even if they had more important things on their plate. Like running for governor.

"Has anyone had any contact with Molly since the game?" I asked. "Have you checked the kids' Facebook and Instagram accounts?"

"Of course," Thorn said, "and there's been no activity. We've checked with airports, bus and train stations, hotels. We got nada. I've spoken to the kids who went with her to the game. They say Molly went to use the rest room in the 4th quarter and never came back."

"Okay."

"The only one we haven't talked with is Diego. We can't get a hold of him. Or his family. No one picks up the phone and no one answers the door."

"And that's where I come in."

"Uh-huh. At this point we need an outsider to step in."

I allowed for a pregnant pause. "You're aware of my fee."

"Yes, a thousand dollars a day."

"Plus expenses," I said. "And I'll need a week's retainer before I leave." No sense pussyfooting around this subject. I was keenly aware that it didn't matter how wealthy a candidate was. Political campaigns usually operated in the red, and it could take years before they retired their debt. And that's if the candidate won.

"I don't know if we can pay for a week up front," Shelly said.

"I don't work for free," I answered and started to get up.

"Wait," she said. "Look. Rex wants you. I'll make the arrangements."

"Okay," I said and sat back down. "Now I need to get a few things straight here. The daughter of a major public figure is missing. She's savvy enough to know if her disappearance was intentional it might adversely affect her father's political career. If she was taken against her will, however, that's another issue entirely. But the idea that a teenage girl could somehow be abducted in a crowd of 90,000 people at a major sporting event is a little unlikely."

Bill and Shelly looked at each other, turned back to me, and shrugged in agreement.

"Okay," I said. "I'll need a way to get in touch with the kids she went with, and I'll need Diego's contact info, too. If you have photos of them, even better."

"We have a copy of the Stone Canyon School yearbook around here somewhere. it has pictures of every kid. You can have it."

"There's something else," I pointed out. "It's curious you haven't mentioned her mother. I'll need to speak with her, too."

Thorn nodded slowly. "We've spoken with Molly's mother. Her name's Nicole. She doesn't know any more than we do. You don't need to speak with her."

"Really?" I asked, my eyebrows shooting up. "A mother typically knows more about her kids than anyone else. Primary caregiver and all."

Shelly looked at me oddly. "This is not a typical case, I can assure you. And Molly's relationship with her mother is, oh, complicated."

"She's a teenager. It's supposed to be complicated. This is the time they separate and start forming their own selves."

"Are you a psychologist?" she said sarcastically.

"No. I'm just a student of human nature."

"Any children yourself, Mr. Burnside?" she asked.

"Not yet," I said, deciding not to push on speaking with the mother right now. "But my wife's expecting. She's due right around Christmas. Should make for a great present."

"Congratulations. But you know, first babies are usually late. I have three sisters, same thing happened with all of them."

"Good to know. Do you have kids?"

"No children myself," she added hastily. "Haven't had the time."

I knew the feeling. Shelly appeared to be about my age, and I was over 40. I always assumed I would have children, but it took a long time to meet the right girl. And my demanding career never relented. Then Gail Pepper entered my life, and things changed quickly. We hadn't spoken about having kids until she informed me she was pregnant on the day of our wedding. But since then, we shared so much excitement about our impending addition that it seemed as if we didn't talk about much else.

"They say kids change your life," I remarked.

"They do," Thorn broke in. "I've got three grown ones. Trying to kick the last one out of the house now."

"Sounds like he's not going willingly."

"Oh, he'll go. I may have to invoke the sink-or-swim method. Worked for me when my old man tossed me into the street."

I looked hard at Thorn. He was in his mid-50s, solidly built, with graying hair, a graying mustache and a sour expression. He reminded me of some of the older cops I knew when I was on the police force. The ones who punched the clock, waiting for their 20 years to kick in so they could collect a pension and go find another job they didn't like. They took their ire out on suspects, and sometimes on their own families.

"My guess is your kid won't go to bed thinking kind thoughts about you."

"He'll understand one day," Thorn declared. "Life is tough and you have to deal with it. Just like in politics."

"Not something I recall my political science professors saying."

Shelly gave me a bored look. "You know something about politics, do you?"

"Just enough to be dangerous," I said.

"Well, politics is a full-contact sport these days."

I laughed out loud. "Try watching a football game from the sidelines. You won't use that metaphor again."

"Oh, that's right. You played football at SC. I'd invite you to the debate tomorrow but it's at Royce Hall. Your rival's campus."

"I don't mind going to UCLA," I said slowly. "It's a nice enough place to visit. In fact, a debate might be a good event for me to attend. You never know who you'll meet or what they'll say. Might learn something pertinent to this case."

"I doubt that," she said, and then hesitated. "You mean you'd really like to go?"

"Sure. Would love to."

"Hmmm. All right. I'm sure I can wrangle you a seat."

"Can you make it two?" I asked. "My wife's a lawyer with the city attorney's office. She's interested in these things."

Shelly leaned back in her chair and sighed. There were dark circles under her eyes. She lit a cigarette and blew the smoke straight up toward the ceiling. "Fine. Why not."

"Thanks. I don't mean to make extra work for you. I'm sure you're swamped."

She reached over and absently tapped the cigarette near a round golden ash tray. She missed by two inches and didn't seem to notice. "This has been a tough campaign. Justin Woo has been hammering us continuously."

"Is it working?"

She waved her hand as if to feign ignorance, but unfortunately this time it pushed a plume of smoke with it. I tilted my head to avoid the trajectory. "We're still leading in the polls, but it's close. What we really want to do now is draw a clear distinction between the governor and his opponent. Rex spent his whole life in California. He has California's best interests at heart. Justin Woo is smart, but he came from somewhere else and can't even speak proper English."

"Let me ask you something. Would Rex Palmer have gotten elected if his name were John Smith?"

She glared at me and spoke in an annoyed voice. "His last name carries some weight around here. But it hasn't been as easy as people think. The reality of politics is Rex inherited half his father's friends and all of his enemies. Boy, you sure were right about one thing, though."

"What's that?" I asked.

"You do know enough to be dangerous. Or at least to be a royal pain in the ass."

I smiled my best smile. She had no idea.

Safety Valve

Made in the USA
Charleston, SC
21 May 2015